The Horse, The Gun and The Piece of Property:

Changing Images of the TV Western

The Horse, The Gun and

The Piece of Property:

Changing Images of the

TV Western

by

Ralph Brauer
with
Donna Brauer

Bowling Green University Popular Press
Bowling Green, Ohio 43403

Library of Congress Catalog Number: 75-15289

ISBN: 0-87972-110-3 Paperback
ISBN: 0-87972-111-1 Cloth

Printed in the United States of America

PHOTOGRAPH CREDITS:
Photographs courtesy of the National Broadcasting Company, Inc.

TO OUR PARENTS

ACKNOWLEDGMENTS

For a young writer seeing a first book through publication is a harrowing and exasperating experience. Most of all, though, it is an experience which alternately inflates and deflates an ego already perilously out of balance with the whole experience of publishing. In this experience you are fortunate if you have the help of people who can give you and the book guidance needed.

First of all I would like to thank Pat Browne, my editor, Without her this book would not have been published or at best would have been published in inferior form. She put up with my sometimes exasperating problems, while always somehow finding ways of solving them. A writer of a first book, above all, needs a good editor and I was fortunate to have one in Pat Browne.

Dorothy Betts of the Popular Press was also extremely helpful. Her help and guidance extended beyond what any writer has reason to expect. She not only worked setting type, correcting spelling, etc., but also took the time to give some much needed guidance at one critical moment.

Patrick Sheehan, Joe Balian and Michael Godwin of the Library of Congress Motion Picture Section were unbelievably helpful in providing me with material which they have in their collection.

Joe Riccuiti of NBC helped me find pictures to illustrate the book.

It is to David Noble of the University of Minnesota that I owe the most thanks. He has helped see this project through from its beginnings as a paper for his doctoral seminar. In that process he has influenced me and hopefully this book with his own unique and vitally alive spirit of interdisciplinary thinking.

Mary Turpie, also of Minnesota, has served as an

advisor and teacher to not only me but to coutless others at Minnesota. As one student put it, "If Mary would have published more we all would have perished."

Joe Roberts, Roy Glover, John Johnson, Dick Ferguson, Jim Dale made helpful suggestions about the project. Nights spent "spewing" with Tom Galt, Tom and Judy Jackson and my brothers Carl and Larry also developed and refined many ideas.

Finally I will add that rather than the usual "and thanks to my wife who put up with me through all this," at the end, I have chosen to include her name on the title page since the book is as much hers as it is mine.

CONTENTS

I'm afraid of what is happening to us . . . these past weeks we've seen our neighbors bullied, our laws defied, we've even seen a man murdered.

After all he was guilty.

Perhaps, but it was not for us to decide. A few weeks ago we would not have let it happen. . . . Don't you see, we've been so anxious to save ourselves that we've given up everything we ever believed in. . . . I'd rather face the enemy out there than the one here inside us.

—THE BIG VALLEY, "Image of Yesterday" (1967)

The main point stems from the fact that I've always acted alone. American's admire that enormously. Americans admire the cowboy leading the caravan alone astride his horse, the cowboy entering a village or city alone on his horse. Without even a pistol, maybe, because he doesn't go in for shooting. He acts, that's all: aiming at the right spot at the right time. A wild West tale, if you like.

—Henry Kissinger, "An Interview with Oriana Fallaci," THE NEW REPUBLIC, December 16, 1972, p. 21.

PREFACE

RECENTLY I HAVE BEEN READING *365 DAYS*, RONALD GLASSER'S brilliant series of sketches and images of American soldiers caught up in the pain and irrationality of Vietnam. That book and that war and the crazy hell of the world of assassinations, Kent States, and Chicagos that has been reality for my generation for the last decade seems strangely removed from the world of television Westerns, and what scholars now term popular culture. In fact there are many who have claimed that the world of one is an escape from the world of the other; that for a decade and perhaps longer we Americans have lived a schizophrenic existence in two worlds.

This book comes to some understanding of that schizophrenia. It is not merely about television Westerns —in fact there is much about the TV Western that is not

1

in this book. Instead it tries to see the evolution of the
television Western in terms of the larger society, the world
"out there." This study of TV Westerns then is also
about movie Westerns, and Nixon's Manson Speech and
Dylan's *John Wesley Harding*. It is also about the period
of my growing up, beginning with watching *The Lone
Ranger* and the Army-McCarthy hearings on the tube,
through watching *Bonanza* and John Kennedy's funeral,
to watching *Gunsmoke* and "The Selling of the Penta-
gon."

  If there can be said to be a controlling assumption
in this study it is that changes in the TV Western do not
happen in a vacuum and that to write about the changes
without some understanding of their context is a waste of
time. It is a waste of time because my generation has an
aching need to come to terms with the world "out there"
and it is a waste of your time because unless you happen
to be interested in such things as television Westerns the
book would be useless. It is in this regard that Nixon's
Manson Speech, television, the Western, Bob Dylan and
certain cultural trends all become a part of the context
of the TV Western. When viewed in this type of context
there is for me a sense of the Western as a fable of our
identity. To some it may not have the meanings of the
Vietnam War, or the deaths of Malcolm X, Martin Luther
King, Robert and John Kennedy or even in a personal
sense as important as the murder of my mother-in-law in
Philadelphia. Yet the TV Western is a part of these con-
texts in some subtle and some not so subtle ways. The
ripples keep widening, as they should, but also in the TV
Western they have a unifying center that should help cast
some perspectives on them. Ultimately Nixon, Manson,
television, the Western and a great deal more in our culture are all interrelated. Perhaps through using the West-

ern as a focus for understanding we can begin to understand these relationships.

There are patterns of imagery, philosophy and
values that are common in television Westerns, in the cultural changes of the last twenty years and in my own experiences growing up in the midst of these changes. If
the TV Western is the focus for understanding relationships between these areas, then it is these patterns which
form the structure for that understanding.

A special problem for this study is that it deals with
a difficult medium to find patterns in—television. The
difficulty lies in the fact that there is such a voluminous
amount of programing to cover. I cannot claim to have
watched all the episodes of all the programs that can be
called TV Westerns, nor do I claim to be an expert on all
those programs. That could take years—and besides it
would probably drive me out of my mind. Even the sheer
exercise of finding patterns has its pitfalls. One wonders
whether he isn't seeing mirages—interpreting something
falsely or even interpreting something that isn't even
there. I would be surprised as hell if I haven't done that
—the whole book may be a mirage. That thought has
given me a few sleepless nights and a lot of caution. I
still wonder. The only answer would be to plug it all
into a computer, which someone probably will try to do.
If so, I wish him luck. He still has to watch all those
shows and after several hundred your eyes and ears can
play tricks on you. As a matter of procedure I started
using a tape recorder to get the dialogue because it
allowed me to be accurate and to concentrate on visual
effects. Yet still it is a human being pushing the buttons,
whether it be a tape recorder or a computer, and that is
as it should be. Let's hope it stays that way.

The problem of avoiding mirages is often lessened if

one has others to check his observations. In this I was fortunate to have the help of teachers, advisors, friends. Sometimes the mirages led me off on wild goose chases and yet always these friends tolerated my wildness, while at the same time quietly and gently turning my head back towards reality. There are many acknowledgment pages where people say, "This book is as much theirs as it is mine," but many times I'm not sure they mean it. Being young and "green," I have found you can't help but say something like that and really mean it, because without these people this book would in no way be what it is now —as anyone who has seen my "working" copy with its voluminous marginal notes, added and subtracted pages, and the countless wording and grammar errors can testify.

Without the help of David Noble this book never would have been published. It began as an idea in Dr. Noble's doctoral seminar, was nursed through several revisions to reach its final form. Through all this process Dr. Noble's criticisms and suggestions served to crystallize vague ideas and to eliminate foggy thinking.

Mary Turpie, Director of the American Studies Program at Minnesota, was also of great help. Besides reading this book and making suggestions she served through four years of Ph.D. work as an advisor and counselor—helping a rather free-spirited graduate student who several times almost dropped out—to come to a better understanding of his own personality and potential.

Donald Browne of the Television Department at Minnesota made many helpful suggestions as did Harvey Sarles of Anthropology and Bernard Bowron of English.

Friends like Jim Dale, Joe Roberts, Roy Glover, Dick Ferguson, John Johnson and others were a lot of help in this study. Nights spent "spewing" with Tom Galt, Tom and Judy Jackson and my brothers Carl and

Larry also developed and refined many ideas.

One final note about the authors and style of the book. The book was originally Ralph's Ph.D. thesis, but we had done so much of it together that it was hard to not place both our names on the title page, rather than the usual "and thanks to my wife who put up with me through all this" at the end. We decided to retain the first person singular style throughout the book because to our ears the "we" sounded strange. Yet always the "I" is a "we."

Tales of Wells Fargo   "Royal Maroon"   Harold J. Stone (left)
and Dale Robertson

PART ONE

Television and the Western

7

Who are they kidding? This is the West? No beards? No moustaches? Just clean cut boys from Warner Brothers. This isn't the West, 1895; this is 77 WYOMING STRIP.

—An Actor

CHAPTER I

F-TROOP in the WILD, WILD WEST
or
Just What Is a Western Anyway?

WHEN I FIRST STARTED THIS STUDY I THOUGHT I KNEW WHAT I was doing—at least in a general sort of way. I was watching TV Westerns. Every week I would scan the local tube program and duly mark down the time and station of each Western. Then I would tune in and watch, noting the title of each episode, the director and writer and making notes about whatever struck me as important. I had not been doing this for too long, when people who had heard about what I was doing, would ask me how I decided which programs to watch. This was usually followed by a dialogue similar to:

"What do you mean? I just watch Westerns."

"Well, like how do you decide what's a Western?"

SILENCE . . . which I learned to cut short with a reply like, "I have my criteria."

"Like what? Is Wild, Wild West *a Western?"*

"I guess so. It takes place in the wild, wild West, has stars dressed like cowboys, has lots of action—gunfights, etc."

"O.K. What about Sky King?*"*

"Who?" followed by a brief description of the

9

show.
    "Well if it's got airplanes and all that I'm not sure it's a Western."
    "What about Roy Rogers? Pat Brady drove a jeep on his show."
    "Well . . ."

Then the scholars deluged me with questions: What do you think of Cawelti's essays? Warshow's definition? Fenin and Everson's? Kitses'?

So I went and read all the scholars, who were just as confusing as my questioners. There were some who thought the Western needed a very precise, neat definition and who proceded to concoct one which held its coherence just long enough for someone to blow the coherence apart with a few well-directed shots. Then there were vague, nebulous definitions that had ample room not only for *Sky King*, but for *F-Troop*, *Fury*, *Frontier Doctor*, *McCloud* and anything else that had either 1) a cowboy star or a star who looked like a cowboy or 2) a "Western" setting. After reading a sheaf of these scholarly articles I became convinced that the whole thing was another irrelevant scholarly argument best left to the scholars. It seemed to me that all anybody could say was a Western is a Western is a Western. So back I went to where I had started, getting out the tube program, marking down Westerns, until I came to *F-Troop*. At which point I realized I still had not answered my original questioner and that this definition thing was not just another scholarly argument. It was everybody's argument and had been ever since there were Westerns. It was not an irrelevant argument either, for in this attempt to define the Western lay our attempt to define ourselves.

As foreigners like to point out, the Western *is* Amer-

ica and pressed on the point few Americans would disagree. The Western is a part of our sense of ourselves—of
our sense of the experience of America as our unique experience, our unique identity. It is our history in mythic
and symbolic form. Its themes are among the deepest in
our literature from Huck Finn's desire to light out for the
territories to Norman Mailer's White Negro, "the frontiersman of American night life." As Henry Nash Smith demonstrated in his classic *Virgin Land*, the West as myth and
symbol has affected our culture in areas as diverse as dime
novels and Congressional legislation.

Strangely enough—or perhaps not so strangely—it is
the scholars, especially the ones with the rigid definitions,
who forget that the Western is America, while it is the
people who say a Western is a Western who are closer to
an understanding. Scholars try to plug the Western into
literary categories like genre, or speak of it in historical
terms as being "about a certain area at a certain time."
The trouble with these categories is that they do not fit
the Western. In fact the whole exercise reminds me of
those old comedy sketches where a comedian would try
to stuff a pile of clothes into a small suitcase. He would
first fold them neatly and then scientifically try to put
everything in its proper place, sit on the top, just manage
to get the latches engaged only to have the suitcase spring
open. Then he'd get mad and just start throwing things
into the suitcase, wadding them up, crumpling them, eventually even snipping them into little pieces, only to have
the suitcase again spring open and little pieces fly all over
the room. Take the idea of genre for example. *Genre* is
a slippery term. It has been ever since Aristotle set out to
define comedy and tragedy. But even if we give genre the
widest possible definition—snip up the clothes so to speak
—it does not really fit the Western. Genre is an abstract

term, tied to neither time nor space. The Western is not. It is intimately tied to time and space in a multiplicity of ways. Most importantly it is tied to a nation, a national self-consciousness in a way no genre can be. In his book *Horizons West* Jim Kitses shows how Northrop Frye's five basic modes of fiction *all* apply to the Western. We can all name comic, tragic, epic, tragi-comic, and ad infinitum Westerns. The point is, like the suitcase, none of these categories fit. *F-Troop* may be a comedy, but is it a Western?

Strangely enough it was Kitses' mention of Northrop Frye that led me to begin to get it all together. Frye published *Fables of Identity*—and that phrase "fables of identity" seems to describe the Western. Fable, like Aesop, only without animals; an untrue-in-the-historical-sense story, a story with moral or meaning. Fables also have other characteristics, too. Sometimes they deal with legendary happenings; sometimes they take on connotations of a tall tale. The other part of the definition "of identity" is even more important for it cuts to the heart of the problem of giving the Western a once-and-for-all, suitcase definition. The Western is America. It is a fable of *our* identity, our image of ourselves, it changes. One generation's Western—its idea of what is a Western and what is America—may be the next generation's idea of Camp. Even within generations there may be differing conceptions of the Western just as there are differing conceptions of what America is. John Ford, for example, remarked that the Westerns he made with Harry Carey kidded the Mix and Hart Westerns of the time. (He is quick to point out that he did not kid *"the* Western"—but again is Ford's *the* Western Peckinpah's?) On a generational level there are similar examples of differing ideas of the Western. In her study *Villains Galore* Mary Noel points

out that the Prentice Ingraham, Ned Buntline Westerns
followed the conventions of the sentimentalist fiction of
the late nineteenth century. Later Bronco Billy and William S. Hart gave another definition. In the "New Wave,"
adult Westerns of the forties and fifties—Westerns like *High
Noon*, *The Gunfighter*, and *The Left-Handed Gun*—new
battle lines were drawn over the definition and meaning of
the Western.

Now given this sense of the Western as a fable of our
identity it would seem obvious that today's cultural re-
assessment and confusion would be reflected in our Westerns and our definitions. This makes understanding even
more difficult. Where fifties' Western fans might cite
several ideas of the Western, today's fans would probably
come up with twice as many—and many of them might
even offer to say that the Western is dead, irrelevant or
capable of several definitions. Fifties' fans and critics, for
the most part, thought they knew what they were talking
about; many today are not as certain. An article like John
Cawelti's "Prolegomena to the Western," which admits
that defining the Western is a problem, probably would
not have been written in the fifties. Yet it seems to me
that for my generation—on one side of a media-created
gap—a definition is evolving which draws its deepest insights from the Westerns being produced by a newer wave
of Western directors. Whereas fifties' Western fans might
mention *The Left-Handed Gun*, with its similarities to
Rebel Without a Cause, many of my generation prefer
Westerns like Monte Hellman's *The Shooting* and *Ride in
the Whirlwind* or Sam Peckinpah's *The Wild Bunch*, *Cable
Hogue*, and *Ride the High Country*. In fact for me Peckinpah's films are *the* Western in the sense that John Ford's
or Hart's or a novel like *The Virginian* were for an earlier
generation. The films of Peckinpah, Hellman and others

like Robert Altman are bringing new insights to the Western which express for me and many who have lived through the America of the sixties, a new definition of the Western, a fable for our identity. This, then, is how the Western is defined—by evolvement, with each new Western commenting on those that have come before, with the best suggesting a new definition which includes not only past Westerns but those meanings which another generation or group wishes to incorporate into this fable of identity. As we all know identity is at once a very strong and a very fragile thing, changing with time and circumstance. Once again time and circumstance force us into a new period of redefining the Western.

Besides seeing the Westerns of Peckinpah, Hellman and Altman, one of the best places to begin this redefinition is the introductory chapter of Jim Kitses' book *Horizons West*. In the course of advancing innumerable insights about the Western, Kitses mentions one aspect of the Western which to me is the key to this new definition. Kitses says that "what gives the form a particular thrust and centrality is its historical setting; its being placed at *exactly that moment when options are still open* (my italics), the dream of primitivistic individualism, the ambivalence of at once beneficient and threatening horizons, still tenable."[1]

With those words "at exactly that moment when options are still open" Kitses sums up for me the definition of the Western, of the fable of our identity, which I find to be the central theme in the films of Peckinpah, Hellman, and Altman—and ultimately in all Westerns.

The beauty of the Kitses definition is that it is neither an attempt to neatly fold everything into the suitcase nor a collection of snippings.

In their now out-of-print book, *The Western*, George

Fenin and William K. Everson attempted to say that William S. Hart's films were not only *the* Western but the most realistic portrayal of the West and the Western we have ever had. According to Fenin and Everson all Westerns are judged by how they measure up to the Hart standard. The problem with this approach is that while a lot of Hart's costuming and settings were realistic, his dialogue, plot, and characterizations—what *today's* directors would see as the meat of the Western—were not "realistic." They were simplistic, sentimental and at times a bit silly. Kitses' definition avoids this trap because it enables us to see Hart, Ford and Peckinpah all as Western directors. Understanding the Western as a fable of our identity enables us to see how the particular twist each director gave to the definition is a reflection of ourselves.

Much more valuable than the Fenin-Everson approach and perhaps next to Kitses' definition the most valuable attempts to understand the Western have been John Cawelti's articles and especially his book *The Six Gun Mystique*.

In his article, "Cowboys, Indians and Outlaws,"[2] Cawelti observes that what seems to give the Western its tension and power is the conflict between the individualistic, code-following frontiersman or cowboy and the law and order, organization-man society of the Easterner. As we shall see there is a lot to be said for Cawelti's conception, yet it seems to me to be another variation of the Kitses open-options idea in that the conflict between code and law is encompassed in Kitses' phrase "the dream of primitivistic individualism, the ambivalence of at once beneficent and threatening horizons is still tenable." Cawelti's definition seems to place emphasis on a dialectic in the Western, while Kitses' seems more to emphasize an attempt to find unity, to balance what seem to be opposing elements—to be at once both and neither; to have law

and order for the townspeople and freedom for the
roaming cowboy, yet allow for the possibility of both to
change roles.

In his book *The Six Gun Mystique*, Cawelti ad-
vances further in his attempt to understand the power of
the Western to attract audiences regardless of the age or
the medium. The book ranges over plots, characterizations, themes, social and psychological factors in trying
to explain the popularity of the Western. The Western
and "popular culture" are viewed as conventionalized
forms—closely akin to games like football or baseball, with
all their rules. Perhaps Cawelti (who does not mention
Kitses) and Kitses are not really so far apart. For Kitses'
open options idea is a convention of a sort. If one views
Westerns and, say, baseball or football as a conventionalized fable of our identity one can even begin to advance
explanations for the changes in uniforms, strategy (for example the T, the Split T, Hank Stram's I, and now the
Wishbone T) and popularity. Yet for all the sparks he
shoots off, Cawelti's book is a lot like the snipping definition. One constantly finds him grabbing at pieces, sometimes finding one that is especially stimulating, eventually
going on to another one and finally at the end wondering
what it was all about. It is one of those exercises in personal searching that is good to read, but no substitute for
a theory like Kitses.

The importance of the Kitses definition can perhaps
best be suggested by viewing a few of the areas in our cultural mythology which reflect our faith in the idea.

Several years ago Leslie Fiedler wrote an essay,
"Come Back To The Raft Ag'in, Huck Honey," and then
a book, *Love and Death In The American Novel*, which
purported to find an essential theme in American literature in the relationship, bordering on out and out homo-

sexuality, between a white and a non-white man. In
Hawkeye and Chingachgook, Huck and Jim, Ishmael and
Queequeg, and in the casual cameraderie of the locker
room, Fiedler found the man-man relationship to be
stronger than the man-woman relationship. Nowhere in
our literature could Fiedler find a mature description of
adult heterosexual love. Need we add that the importance
of this theme in the Western is obvious, starting with the
Lone Ranger and Tonto (and Lenny Bruce's immortal mon-
ologue). In another volume of essays, *An End to Innocence,*
Fiedler related this theme to an even more basic theme,
the theme of innocence. R. W. B. Lewis, Leo Marx, and
David Noble have also related it to an American conception of time and space.[3]

    Through all these writings the common theme is one
of open options. Innocence, virginity, and endless time
and space are different expressions of this one basic idea.
In this world of open options the ideal American becomes
a New World Adam living in an eternal garden of endless
space.

    What the Western does is to place these thematic
elements within a certain framework. It is this framework
which has caused most scholars their problems. There has
been much talk about the Western as *a* form. This talk is
as much bunk as talk about *the* Western. There is not *a*
form. The form evolves with the definition, the definition
defining the form. Many nineteenth-century Westerns
operating within the conventions of sentimental romance
adopted the melodramatic form of that convention—the
old villain, pure hero, and virgin Little Nell routine trans-
ferred to the definition of open options.

    The usual critical ploy is to define the form within
a structural and historical framework. Generally the critics see the Western as taking place in the past, west of the

Mississippi—in a setting of time and space that all of us know as the West. In addition, say the critics, the Western takes place within a dialectical, Manichean framework. Kitses draws up a whole chart of these opposites, then several pages later speaks of "the complex moral and metaphysical rhetoric of *Johnny Guitar*"[4] and the work of the three directors he discusses in *Horizons West. The Wild Bunch* certainly does not follow a dialectical, Manichean framework nor do the Hellman Westerns. Yet nobody would deny that they are Westerns. As to the historical element Larry McMurty in an essay entitled "Cowboys, Movies, Myths and Cadillacs: Realism in the Western"[5] makes a convincing case for *Hud* (based on his novel *Horseman, Pass By*) which is about a twentieth-century cowboy.

Yet for all this debunking of form and structure the Western does have a framework; it is more than the idea of open options. There are certain pictures which at a glance everyone knows are Westerns. In all these pictures there are certain conventionalized elements of dress, location, etc., which serve to let the viewer know he is watching a Western. There was an episode of *Star Trek* which, for me, symbolized this sense of the Western. What the show did was to evoke the Western by an effective use of a few symbols. In the episode Capt. Kirk and some of the crew of the spaceship Enterprise mysteriously found themselves involved in the Gunfight at the O. K. Corral. The setting was minimal, seeming to place the West in some abstract world outside the "time warp." Only a few props, plus the evocation of the Gunfight, were used to suggest the West and the Western. There were a few tumbleweeds, hitching posts, a few flat painted buildings and, of course, the Earps and a few others in cowboy clothes, the necessary saloon, barkeep, and bargirl. Even though

Kirk and his crew, who were mistaken for the Clantons, escaped through the un-Western device of a Vulcan mind-meld, I would still consider the episode a Western.

This *Star Trek* episode led me to rethink the whole idea of conventions and its relationship to open options. The definition which each generation gives the Western does define the form and there is not *a* form, but there do seem to be certain elements which make a Western a Western. When we think of a Western we think of cowboy clothes, horses, guns, a "Western" setting, etc. Now the trouble is that in certain Westerns some of these elements are prominent, while in others they are not. Many Westerns like the *Star Trek* episode incorporate un-Western elements, or elements we feel are un-Western. Tom Mix made some Westerns during the thirties that had science fiction touches reminiscent of the *Star Trek* show. The point of all this talk about conventions seems to be that certain symbolic elements are needed to help evoke the atmosphere of the Western. These may involve clothing, location, or other props. In the case of a cowboy hero like Mix, the mere presence of such a figure playing his role with all he brought to it (a certain style of dress, way of acting, and, of course, Tony) may be all that is required. What happens in the case of someone who is not Mix? What happens with *Star Trek* or *F-Troop*? What is this atmosphere and how is it related to theme and the idea of open options?

In essence the atmosphere is created by open options. The idea and its relationship to American history suggest what elements can and cannot create this atmosphere. First and foremost the Western is definitely anti-technology. All Westerns explicitly affirm this. Where the trappings of technology are found in the Western they are always portrayed negatively. In the Mix Westerns, he and Tony always triumphed over technology. In the *Star Trek* episode Capt. Kirk and his crew were deprived of all their technological resources, and had to rely on their own and ultimately Mr. Spock's innate resources. When Pekinpah uses the automobile as his symbol of closing options, he is merely following this convention. But wait a minute, what about Pat Brady's jeep and Hud's car? Perhaps with the automobile there is an exception, as McMurty points out in his essay.

Being anti-technological the Western also is against the complex social order which created technology. The Westerner may be seen as a harbinger of civilization but characteristically he does not choose to live in civilization. Henry Nash Smith wrote that Daniel Boone and his eventual sire, the Westerner, was subject to this schizophrenic division of being seen on the one hand as an isolated individual living out where he could find some elbow room and also as the pathfinder who showed the way for settlers and civilization. Perhaps this schizophrenia can be explained by the idea of open options: the Westerner cannot be seen as either a reclusive hermit or as the representative of coming civilization. Each is a closed rather than an open option. Rather the Westerner must be on that razor's edge of advancing civilization, not too far and not too near. He can be neither savage nor civilization.

The Westener's position vis-a-vis civilization and technology puts him in an ambiguous relationship to the social order, its laws, courts and morality. While the Western may defend law and order it is always against the complicated trappings of ordinances, civil suits, legal maneuvering, etc. Politics, politicians, intellectuals also are anti-Western. Again the idea of open options seems to indicate that the Westerner must be on a razor's edge between these "civilized" elements and out and out barbarism. The

Westerner may not be an intellectual, he may even at times be anti-intellectual, but he is not a barbarian.

The Western and the Westerner, then, sit on that razor's edge that is open options: between civilization and barbarism, between technology and primitivism, between legalism and amoralism.

So is *F-Troop* a Western? I think the obvious answer is no. *F-Troop* is merely a TV situation comedy in a pseudo-Western setting. It has more similarities with *Sgt. Bilko*, *McHale's Navy* and other TV military comedies than it does with the Western. Why isn't *F-Troop* a Western? Thematically it does not attempt to treat or examine the Western myth and its components. Unlike other comic Westerns such as *Maverick* or *Little Big Man* it does not even treat various elements of the Western. Its one half-hearted attempt at debunking the West is a busty girl who plays a gun-toting scout; yet even this image owes as much to Tugboat Annie as it does to Calamity Jane—even though our scout may not look like Tugboat Annie. Rather than do a comic Western like *Maverick*, it seems as though TV executives desired to switch the successful *McHale*, *Bilko* format to the West.

Wild, Wild West is also not a Western for similar reasons. Its gadgetry is more suggestive of James Bond or *The Man From U.N.C.L.E.* than the Western. The use of the jeep in Roy Rogers' TV show, however, does not mean that it is not a Western, any more than Hud's Cadillac or Peckinpah's automobile disqualify them from being Westerns.

No doubt in the future, Westerns will be made which will continue to challenge our ideas of the Western and of ourselves. In one respect, however, they will resemble the Westerns of the past and that will be that they will be neither a form nor a genre, but rather will continue to re-

flect the ever changing fable of our identity. In this respect the television Western is no different from the movie
or dime novel Western. The fable it has to tell may reflect
differing attitudes towards our identity, but it is still our
fable and our identity.

PART TWO

The Horse, the Gun, and the Piece of Property

Back in the saddle again
Out where a friend is a friend . . .
    *   *   *   *
Where we sleep out every night
And the only law is right.
           —Gene Autry

CHAPTER II

The Horse:
Robin Hood and His Sidekick Defend the Code

IT IS FITTING THAT A QUOTATION FROM GENE AUTRY BEGIN THIS chapter on the early TV Westerns, for above all, it was Autry who recognized the importance and possibilities of the television Western. Autry's own entry into TV was met with a great deal of resistance by theater owners and movie magnates who felt that an Autry TV series would cut down on attendance at Autry movies. Autry advanced the argument that his TV series would attract more people to his movies. Whether this argument fully convinced his detractors or whether the financial possibilities already suggested by the success of old movie serials and programs like *The Lone Ranger* moved them, Autry managed to get his series on the air. Operating under the banner of Flying A Productions, Autry capitalized on the success of his own series by producing several other Westerns—*Annie Oakley, Range Rider, Buffalo Bill Jr.,* and *The Adventures of Champion. Range Rider* was especially notable in that it starred Jock Mahoney, a superb stuntman who made that series one of the most action packed.

All of these series followed a similar formula outlined by Autry in an article written for the October 1952 issue of *Television Magazine.* In the article (entitled "Producing

25

a Television Western") Autry lays down several ground-
rules for making good Westerns in television as opposed
to movies. He boils it down to the maxim, "Keep it
simple, keep it moving, keep it close and make it fast."
It is debatable whether Autry's rules define good TV; certainly we can think of many exceptions to them. Yet the
Autry formula produced shows that were enormously
successful.

Autry's success encouraged other Western movie
starts like William Boyd (Hopalong Cassidy) and Roy
Rogers to start their own TV series. Boyd began by buying up the rights to his old movies and showing them on
TV. Their success convinced him to start shooting his
own episodes. For awhile Hoppy was the most popular
star—Western and otherwise—on the tube, and Boyd ex-
ploited his fame, as Walt Disney would later do with Davy
Crockett, by selling all kinds of Cassidy paraphernalia.
Autry, Rogers and other stars also turned out thousands
of school lunchboxes, holster sets and cowboy clothes.

Other early Western shows followed the Autry-
Rogers route from the movies and other media to the
tube as producers sensed that they could attract audiences to the new TV shows by using characters who were
already well known. The Lone Ranger had been both a
highly popular movie and radio serial. Although the movie
Ranger wore a bandanna type mask over his face rather
than the now famous black eye mask of his TV counterpart, the TV Ranger kept most of the other ingredients
of that successful serial. A Kit Carson TV series also was
made for TV, but having never seen the movie serial based
on Carson, it is hard to say whether it was a direct de-
scendant of those serials. ZIV Productions took the basic
premise of the Cisco Kid movie serials and began filming
the first Western shot in color for TV. ZIV decided to

shoot in color because they anticipated a breakthrough during TV's early experiments with color. The gamble seemed to have fizzled when color development reached a roadblock, but the increasing use of color in recent years has made *Cisco* reruns the most popular of the early Westerns which are still shown on television.

The early TV Westerns—when I speak of TV Westerns I mean programs that were made exclusively for TV, not the old "B" Westerns that showed up on many a Saturday afternoon *Western Theater*—were a very sparse group of shows. By sparse I mean they had few actors, simple sets, and sometimes used stock shots of chases, stunts and cattle stampedes—in short all the elements of the Autry Formula. No doubt many of these features were the result of small budgets, shooting schedules as short as three days and the need to cram all of this into the half hour time slot, complete with commercials, that the networks of the time considered standard. Many people who have looked at the old shows are put off by the sparseness and simplicity. Watching the *Cisco Kid* and others of these early shows on TV or tape is quite an experience. Autry's criteria of keep it simple seems to be followed with a vengeance. The acting is terrible, the plots are silly or mere excuses for action, and even the action sequences seem contrived and overdone, with actors obviously pulling punches and stunts that go awry. Yet the sparse simplicity of these early shows has a disarming quality about it. We laughed when we watched some of them, but the laughter was not a cruel laughter. It was the kind of laughter people use when they see kids playing. Perhaps this kind of reaction is inevitable since these TV Westerns were so much a part of growing up, not only for us but for our whole generation and it is difficult to be a dispassionate adult critic of our child-

The Chevy Show (left to right) Audie Murphy, Roy Rogers and Eddy Arnold
September 27, 1959

The Chevy Show Roy Rogers and The Sons of the Pioneers
September 27, 1959

hood heroes.

Probably more than any generation in this country we have a whole set of universal bonds that form a complex of common experiences no matter where we grew up. There is television, for one, and rock music for another. Today I can start rapping with someone my age or younger and we share this common set of experiences, from watching *The Lone Ranger* to playing at Hopalong Cassidy to listening to Elvis, Chuck Berry, The Beatles, The Stones. Of course, there's a lot of difference as to which of these people one person or even one area will like, but basically we have all heard or watched or experienced these things and no one looks at you like some weirdo if you mention one of them. Until I was twelve years old I lived in Long Island suburbia, yet I can mention Elvis or Roy Rogers to some stranger who is my age and he'll know what I'm talking about. He may say, "Well I didn't dig Elvis or Roy Rogers, what I dug was Chuck Berry and the Lone Ranger," but still the common bond is there.

Not only will he know about Roy Rogers and the Lone Ranger, he'll also eventually start talking about a whole set of experiences that go with these shows and, though these experiences may vary somewhat, they are fairly universal among people of my generation. Take the ritual of watching these shows, for example. For us watching Westerns was a community, group thing not unlike an earlier generation's ritual of attending the Saturday Matinee at the local rundown Bijou. In the earliest days of TV there was probably only one television set on the block, so we'd all get in good with that kid so we could go watch *The Lone Ranger* or *Western Theater* or *Hopalong Cassidy.* Even after the rest of us got sets and they came to be the one essential feature of every living room, we would still

do a lot of group watching, and when we didn't watch together we would still watch the same shows so that when
we'd see each other, we could talk about them as though
we had been in the same room.

Then there was the place of Westerns in the games
we played. In those days before everybody got uptight
about guns or other violent toys, almost every kid had a
set of cowboy guns and/or a bow and arrow. I remember
that as a kid one of my most mystically important possessions was a Hopalong Cassidy suit. When we played
Western games we identified with Roy as Jesse James, or
the Lone Ranger, or Cisco Kid or with old movies with
Johnny Mack Brown, Ken Maynard, Lash LaRue, and
Bob Steele. After awhile we'd dream up new roles, basing
them on something we'd seen. In most of these games it
was more fun to play a star like Jesse James who was
being chased by "the law," because then you could hide
and outwit whoever played "the law." After all who likes
to be "it" in hide and seek or Red Rover or whatever?

The kid-centeredness does seem to be intentional.
First the programs themselves made no bones about the
fact that they were produced for kids, and stars like Roy
Rogers and Dale Evans spoke of teaching the kids basic
American and Christian values. Even the sponsors aimed
at the kid market. The child was exhorted to eat the right
foods and drink the right things so he might grow up to be
strong and healthy like his hero. Many of the sponsors
were cereal companies who pushed their product by including all kinds of neat little goodies in the cereal box.
It was a good time to be a kid. In those days when something came in the box it came free. Besides the TV Westerns there were a host of kid-oriented shows that used
Western motifs. Dayton, Ohio, had *Lucky 13 Ranch
House*, Salt Lake City had *Sheriff Jim's Sagebrush Play-*

house, and Louisville had *The Old Sheriff.* Howdy
Doody and Buffalo Bob were cowboys, and Mr. Phineas
T. Bluster, the show's resident baddie, dressed in a business suit not unlike the baddies of the TV Western. Sponsors who didn't use cowboy stars to sell their products—
remember Gabby Hayes selling Puffed Wheat and Puffed
Rice, "the cereal shot from guns"?—used Western motifs
like the Cheerios Kid. If you were a kid you could not
help but get caught up in Westerns. They tried to sell you
food, toys, and a way of life.

    In a way you could say that these early Westerns
were our fairy tales. Many parents who were hip to this
tried all sorts of devious devices using these Westerns in
order to get us to do something, saying, "Roy wouldn't
do that" or "If you don't do this you can't watch Hopalong Cassidy today." Of course parents didn't understand this game could be played two ways. Some store-
owner might hassle us for reading comic books by saying,
"You kids, get the hell out of there," but we would remember the Kid—as in Billy the and Sundance and Two
Gun, etc.—was always having trouble with storeowners
and businessmen who wore slicked down hair and fancy
clothes, so we would apply one of the Kid's ingenious
plans to our problem.

    To some these thoughts on early TV watching may
seem a nostalgic digression but actually they are an important part of a puzzling cultural riddle which is bound
up in the way of life sold by these fairy tales. In songs
like Bob Dylan's "John Wesley Harding" our generation
seems to be calling up images that are quite like those
found in these early Westerns, yet our elders, who sought
to teach us values through these early Westerns, find the
images very disquieting. What's more, early Western stars
like Roy Rogers and Gene Autry have expressed deep dis-

approval with the "youth revolution" and have become
prominent in right wing causes. In John Wayne, whose
early movie roles resemble those of the TV cowboys, we
find the same situation, with the "Big Duke" criticizing
long hair, permissiveness, and the songs of people like Bob
Dylan. Wayne, Rogers and Autry seem to be marching to
a different drummer than the kids who were the ardent
fans they sought to teach, and much of the tune they
march to can be found in the rhetoric of Nixon's Manson
speech. In this situation we have a classic example of what
seems to be a major cultural shift occurring across generations, yet the riddle is how this change came about when
one generation sought to inculcate certain ideas and values
in another only to find that when their sons and daughters
had grown up the two generations were warring across
what the media has called "the generation gap," with the
younger generation drawing some of its most potent am-
munition from those early fairy tales. The answer can be
found in part in the journeys travelled by our two generations over the last twenty years, and in the TV Western we
have some unique footprints left by that journey which
culminates in *John Wesley Harding* and the Manson Speech.
The beginning lies in the elements of the first TV Westerns,
those early fairy tales which sold a way of life.

In the fairy-tale simplicity of these Westerns there
were four essential elements—the star, his horse, his sidekick, and the baddie. Each week the show dealt with the
attempt of the star, aided by his horse and his sidekick, to
defeat the evil personified in the baddie. One or two minor
characters were added each week to give some variation to
the plots. Even the plots followed old Western plots we've
seen a hundred times before, without adding subplots or
other complexities. Now all Westerns seem to have horses,
a goodie, a baddie, and usually a sidekick of some sort, but

what made these early TV Westerns unique was that they
emphasized the horse to such an extent that in some
shows he became a co-star: Gene Autry, America's Favorite Cowboy, with Champion, America's Wonder Horse;
Roy Rogers, King of the Cowboys, with Trigger, Smartest
Horse in the West. Trigger and Champ were probably the
most prominent of these horses, but the Lone Ranger's
Silver, Hopalong Cassidy's Topper, and the Cisco Kid's
Diablo also had featured roles. Even Dale Evans had a
horse, Buttermilk. In none of the other TV Westerns
does the horse assume this degree of importance. Not
only do the later horses not receive co-star billing, they
don't receive any billing at all. How many people can
name Matt Dillon's horse, or Ben Cartwright's or Wyatt
Earp's? The horses of these later stars are so nondescript
that it's difficult to describe what they look like.

To a large extent this prominence of the horse follows the tradition established by movie cowboys like Tom
Mix and Ken Maynard and, of course, by Roy Rogers and
Gene Autry, who converted their movie drawing power
into TV success. In both movie and TV Western the featured horses of these stars assumed anthropomorphic
qualities. The horse comes at a whistle, can untie knots,
in fact he is sometimes capable of reading the hero's mind.
Champion and Trigger can count, add and subtract and
occasionally whisper secrets to Gene and Roy. In almost
every episode of the Roy Rogers and Gene Autry shows
Trigger and Champ are featured in some such scene. In
an Autry episode, "Million Dollar Fiddle" (1955), Autry
asks a visiting whiz kid if he'd like to see Champ, as
though he were arranging an audience with some high
official. Champ, like all of the horses, has elaborate trappings such as fancy saddles and bits, which adds to this
status.

Roy Rogers, his horse Trigger, and his dog Bullet

The prominence of the hero's horse is further enhanced by his relationship to the other horses in the program. Everybody else rides nondescript horses, usually blacks and browns. Even the most evil baddie is unable to find a horse to match that of the star, since in color, features, "intelligence" no horse is the match of Trigger, Silver, and company. In "The Lone Ranger's Triumph" (1949) Silver warns the Ranger and Tonto of an approaching baddie, a feat which Trigger, Champ, Diablo, and Topper could match but which no baddie's horse was ever able to do. It almost seems as though the horse enhances the star's qualities as much as the star enhances the horse. Nobody but Roy Rogers is capable of riding and commanding the respect of Trigger, since Trigger does what he does for Roy not because he has been trained to do it but because he has an understanding, a respect for him. Other horses who are capable of doing tricks like Trigger may appear in various episodes, but they do tricks because they have been trained to do them. In some cases they have even been forced to do them by cruel masters. But Trigger is invincible. He cannot be trained or broken like an ordinary horse, he must be wooed and won.

In fact this comparison with women is interesting, for all the women are inferior to the star's horse. They are weak, capable of being tricked, and when the star is in trouble, they aren't much help at all—most of the time they bungle the job by falling right into some devious trap laid by the villains. Women are so capable of being fooled that they sometimes are tricked into helping trap the hero. The baddie may bait the trap with a pretty girl, but he is unable to bait it with the horse, because the horse is incapable of being caught or tricked by the baddie. When the star is caught in the trap baited with the girl, it is his horse who gets him out. Once in awhile the horse may be caught, but always he works his escape by unlatching the gate to the corral, or untying the knot on his rope or sometimes even tricking the baddie.

The wooing process by which the star may win the horse is much more complex than the one used to win the girl. Characteristically the star sets out purposely to win the horse, but he avoids the girl. The girl usually falls head over heels for the star, although he does nothing to bring this on, except to be himself—standing as a man above men and mice. Girls—and that is what they are, not women—have all the losing features of a teeny-bopper cuddled up next to the picture of her favorite star. The star knows they are irresistibly drawn towards him and tries his best to play it cool, hoping to ease the heartbreak he knows must come at the end when he rides off into the sunset with the horse, leaving the girl behind goggle-eyed, sometimes in tears, "Who was that masked man?" "That's the Lone Ranger." "Hi ho Silver, Away!" Because the horse is independent, with a "mind of his own," he is won only after much effort. In the beginning the horse may be in a corral—the wild one nobody can break—or may be running free as the leader of a wild herd. In his first attempt to capture and ride the horse the star may fail, but respect is established since the horse can see that the skill of the hero makes him the best man who has tried. After several tries the horse and hero reach an understanding and a relationship begins which is based on trust and mutual admiration.

Compared to the horse the female is weak and submissive. She is a little girl who in many ways resembles the well-scrubbed, girl-next-door, high-school-cheerleader stereotype—a virginal, almost neutral figure who chases after the star, captain of the football team. She giggles a lot and generally makes a fool of herself over the hero.

Dale Evans and Annie Oakley are exceptions to the rule, developed "for the distaff cowboy in the family," as Gene Autry's Flying A Productions put it. Annie and Dale are saved for a later chapter on cowgirls and other types of cowboys, but suffice it to say that their roles were no more feminine than those of their cheer-leader counterparts, with Annie shooting cards while standing on a galloping horse and Dale riding and roping with the best of them. Like a great many women in our art the women in the early Westerns are either the weak or the strong, the submissive or the independent.

This is where the sidekick comes in. All the early TV Westerns had sidekicks, Sancho Panza figures who added humor to the show. Roy Rogers and Dale Evans had Pat Brady, who drove an anthropomorphic jeep named "Nellybelle." Unlike Trigger, who could always be depended on, Nellybelle was quite balky, refusing to start or stop when she was supposed to. Wild Bill Hickock had Jingles, Gene Autry had Pat Buttram, and Cisco had Pancho. The only exception to the humorous sidekick was Tonto, who provided another sort of contrast to the star.

All the sidekicks were outsiders. The humorous sidekicks were outsiders who constantly needed to be shown even the simplest things. As outsiders they were victimized by the baddie, and by society, mostly because of their ignorance or stupidity. Tonto, of course, was also a victimized outsider, although he was never intentionally humorous.

The horses (and vehicles) of the sidekicks were in marked contrast to those of the star. In many ways they reflected the characteristics of the sidekick. Pancho's horse was named Loco; Brady's jeep was unpredictable and temperamental; Jingles was always following behind

Wild Bill shouting "wait for me."

The Sidekicks's unconventionality constantly led to incidents in which the star was having to explain what he was doing. Pancho always asks Cisco about his plans and almost always does not understand them. In one episode[1] Pancho says in exasperation, "Cisco, I'm all mixed-up in the head," and Cisco answers, "Then you're perfectly normal."

Pancho and Tonto are the two most interesting sidekicks because they fit the stereotypes many of us use in speaking of Mexicans and Indians. Pancho is the happy-go-lucky Mexican—what I call the Speedy Gonzales stereotype, after the cartoon character. He is always joking, some of it at his own expense. Frequently he utters some pseudo-Mexican phrase like "Hole Frijoles," and he is fond of pseudo-Mexican comparatives like, "they disappear quicker than the frijoles from the frying pan." Tonto, on the other hand, fits into what I call the Cigar Store Indian stereotype. There used to be a comedy routine in which a comedian would walk up to what looked like a wooden Indian and start taunting him. After several minutes of this, the Indian, who is usually standing with his arms folded and his eyes focused on some faraway view, walks away or grunts. Of course everybody laughs at the comedian for being so stupid, yet they are also laughing at the Indian because the whole effectiveness of the joke depends on the audience's belief that Indians many times *do* stand still like cigar store Indians. Tonto, like the cigar store Indian, is taciturn. His face rarely changes expression, and he speaks in the clipped phrases that quite a few Americans regard as Indian talk: "We go now. See sun. It hot." etc. Like Pancho now and then he throws in a few Indian-sounding phrases like "Kemo Sabe." (Kemo Sabe may well be a real Indian phrase just as frijoles is Mexican, but it is the context in which it is used that makes it racist.)

Tonto's relationship to the Lone Ranger is most dramatically outlined in a 1957 episode entitled "The Courage of Tonto." In this episode Tonto and the Ranger prevent an Indian war which threatens to erupt when several baddies start causing trouble. The Indians threaten to go on the warpath in twenty-four hours if the baddies are not brought to justice. Tonto offers to put himself up as a hostage so the Ranger can bring the baddies in. There are two dimensions to the episode: one is Tonto's willingness to put his life on the line, the other is the episode's constant stressing of the fact that good Indians are those taking up the white man's ways. In fact the episode begins with the line, "The Apaches fought long and hard to stem the tide of civilization." Tonto having adopted the white man's ways is now civilized.

The relationship between star and sidekick, like that of star and horse, is not without its sexual overtones. In his essay, "Come Back To The Raft Ag'in, Huck Honey," Leslie Fiedler discusses the archetypal relationship of white man and colored, which he sees as a major theme in our literature. Huck and Jim, Ishmael and Queequeg and Hawkeye and Chingachgook are all examples of this archetype. The archetype is one in which homosexual overtones are clearly present, especially in the famous bed scene of Ishmael and Queequeg. This observation leads Fiedler to speak about the presence of a homosexual or asexual current in American culture—a culture that revels in the camaraderie of the locker room and that has produced no mature description of adult heterosexual love. As Fiedler puts it, "All our books are boys' books." Certainly on the surface the early Westerns seem to fit right into this pattern. Although only *The Lone Ranger*

The Lone Ranger   Clayton Moore (left) and Jay Silverheels (Tonto)

directly involves a relationship between white and colored, the other shows do involve a white and outsider relationship which is not unlike that of the white and colored. Yet the relationships in the Westerns do differ from the Fiedler archetype in one aspect: in the Fiedler archetype it is usually the colored man, the outsider, who inducts the white youth into manhood, while in the TV Western it is the opposite. What one sees is the white hero educating the outsider, inducting him into manhood.

For the sidekick as well as for the kid the education —the selling of values—was wrapped up in a nice, neat little package—the hero. During the commercials he might sell Sugar Crisp and Sugar Pops, but his message here seemed low key or a part of the larger message as opposed to kids' (and adults') shows today, in which the show seems a commercial for the commercial rather than vice versa. What the hero was really selling was values, an image that was only peripherally related to cereal and certainly, at times, opposed to the corporate giants who owned the cereal companies. The values were personified by the star, not the product, and each week their essential goodness was demonstrated by the downfall of the villain, who was, in every way, the antithesis of the hero.

The hero himself was portrayed as superhuman. In one *Cisco Kid* episode Cisco with a perfectly straight face tells the outlaw leader that he was able to capture him because "I read your mind to find out just what you were going to do." Perhaps what one person says of Gene Autry in "Million Dollar Fiddle" applies to all these early heroes: "From what I've heard Gene Autry's no common cowboy."

The values the hero personified are those values which Americans believe are typically theirs and theirs alone. The hero was clean living and clean thinking—a scout is clean in thought, word and deed. He never drank, never smoked and never uttered even a "heck." William Boyd, speaking of his *Hopalong Cassidy* TV series, put it well, "I have played down violence, tried to make Hoppy an admirable character and insisted on grammatical English."[2] In his fights with the villain he never fought dirty and never, never shot to kill. Roy Rogers or Gene Autry may have fired ten or twelve shots out of a gun that had only six, but they usually captured the villain by roping him or tackling him or at worst knocking him out. When he did fire his gun the hero always fired in self-defense, using the "wing shot" or shooting the gun out of the baddie's hand.

Even more importantly the hero had a sense of mercy. The possibility of redemption was always emphasized. In some episodes a young man who ran with the baddies might aid the hero, perhaps even save his life and the hero would let him go, rather than bring him to trial, while in other episodes the baddie might decide to "go straight" and after testing him, the hero would again let him go. Behind all this was the belief that good men—that good itself—would always win out over bad, in a man's soul as well as on the range, for if a man had a speck of good in him, no matter what his role, it would eventually come out, and he would be forgiven. Of course the star could always be counted on to recognize this spark of virtue in a person others had tagged as bad. In one episode of the *Cisco Kid*, Cisco and Pancho aid a girl who has been accused of murdering her uncle, even though they barely know the girl and all the evidence seems to indicate she was the culprit. In another *Cisco Kid* they aid a bank teller who has been jailed for stealing from his employer. In both episodes Cisco and Pancho seem to instinctively know who is good and who is bad, even though the townspeople might think otherwise.

The values the hero personified were abstract in the sense that they were not written down. Justice was a value and not a set of procedural guarantees. The values might be seen as a code, in the same way that literary critics speak of a code by which Hemingway's heroes live. In fact the whole idea of a code—in the Western and in Hemingway and others—is something we associate with American culture. The myth of the Code of the West has been used not only by Hemingway and Western writers like Zane Grey, but by politicians, preachers, business-men, etc. Heroes and good people naturally adhere to the code as though it were an innate rather than a learned be-havior, while villains, on the other hand, have no code. Perhaps this whole idea stems from Puritan-Protestant sources in which God naturally confers upon the good, the saved, the code which enables them to be good, for good-ness is a gift, not something we must learn. Americans also like to think of goodness in terms of proper upbringing, which also may have an antecedent in the old medieval idea that young boys must be taught proper etiquette. In the early Westerns, however, this idea of upbringing is played down, and it is the innateness of goodness that is stressed.

The hero's personification of these values is import-ant, because, as we shall see, the picture has changed. It is important because the values were identified with the hero and not with his role or his position in society. I think it is significant that this personification is reflected in the fact that the shows were named after the stars—*The Roy Rogers Show, The Lone Ranger, The Cisco Kid*—as opposed to later shows named after roles—*Lawman, Track-down, Wanted: Dead or Alive*—or places—*Bonanza, The Big Valley, The High Chaparral.*

Nowhere is this aspect of the hero as the personification of abstract values better portrayed than in *The Lone Ranger*. The Lone Ranger with his mask, his white costume, his white horse, his silver bullets is abstract morality personified. He has no name like Roy Rogers or Wild Bill Hickock, only an identity. He is "that masked man" (how often have we talked of justice as masked?).   "Kemo Sabe," "The Lone Ranger." He is lone and he is a ranger. What the hell does that mean? Ranger: Texas Ranger, yes, but maybe also ranger, one who ranges around, like one of the heroes in Tolkien's *Lord of the Rings* who is called The Ranger. When the Lone Ranger does a good deed the people speak of him as a sort of *deus ex machina* who appears out of nowhere to right wrongs and then disappears. The man with no name, no history comes from nowhere, everywhere. All he has and all he leaves behind is the personification of the code.

There are times when the hero's personification of abstract values puts him outside the codified laws and against its elected upholders. Roy Rogers made several movies in which he played Jesse James, and the Cisco Kid is referred to as "the Robin Hood of the Old West." In many episodes of these shows the sheriffs and other lawmen are incompetent or else in the pay of the villain. Cisco and Pancho, especially, seem to have a reputation of being outside the law. People speak of them as "notorious" and at times the two have had wanted posters on them. This reputation gets around and many a sheriff captures Cisco and Pancho under the mistaken assumption they are outlaws, only to have them escape. Cisco and Pancho have little respect for sheriffs, since so many of them are incompetent, timid, or inhibited by the fact they are sheriffs. Once when the baddies talk the sheriff into putting them in jail, Pancho remarks, "If you believe these hombres, you are dumber than the sheriff in Ponca City and he don't have no brains at all."

All of this extralegal activity leads to a moral dilemma that is not easily resolved. The anti-social, individualistic, outside-the-law activity of the hero seems unbelievably naive. The line in the old Gene Autry song "where the only law is right" is quite suggestive of this problem. One might read the line as being another statement of the idea that the wild, wild West is an area where there is no law, except right. In Cisco and Pancho's case as well as the other heroes of the early TV Western, this isn't true—at least strictly speaking. There is a law, only it is corrupt or impotent. It is not "right" and must be made right. Of course, the baddie sees it the same way. That the hero is uneasy about this is suggested in a *Lone Ranger* episode entitled "Six Gun Sanctuary." (1954) Here a group of baddies (who have plans of turning the entire area into an "outlaw kingdom") take over a town. The Lone Ranger and Tonto come into the town to break up the gang. The problem is that the gang is holding the sheriff's son as a hostage, so he is unable to enforce the law. The sheriff faces a moral dilemma—break up the baddies and perhaps hurt his son or break the law. In one dialogue father and son confront this dilemma. "Is it a fool notion to believe in the law? Yet you taught me that the ordinary *rules* (my italics) must always apply. That no one had the right to change the meaning of the law just to fit their own personal needs." (Notice how even here there is confusion between the code—rules—and written law.) In the end the sheriff enlists the Lone Ranger and Tonto to help round up the baddies. The Lone Ranger has the last word, "Tampering with the law is like throwing a stone in a brook. You never know where the ripples will reach." Hi ho Silver, Away! In the

next episode our hero is forced to escape from jail in order to track down a gang of rustlers. . . .

The Western hero may live at a time when options
are still open. He may live on a razor's edge between sav-
agism or anarchism and civilization, but it seems as though
many of the early Westerns cut this edge pretty fine.

As a hero the early TV Western star falls right into
the tradition of the free, atomic individual which Henry
Nash Smith described in *Virgin Land.* He has no ties, and
he roams a territory of endless space. As a sort of ideal
kid, with his faithful sidekick and his horse he is certainly
timeless. Usually he is a wandering cowboy—with no
parents, no family, no job to hassle him—a sort of Western knight errant, or if he is a lawman, he is one whose
duties force him to wander through the "wide open
spaces" in search of his quarry. If he stays in town he
stays only long enough to "clean-up" the town or end the
range war. He resembles Daniel Boone, who, Henry Nash
Smith states, "would have pined and died as a nabob in
the midst of civilization. He wanted a frontier, and the
perils and pleasures of a frontier, not wealth; and he was
happier in his log cabin . . . than he would have been
amid the great profusion of modern luxuries."[3]

The Rogers and Autry shows were exceptions to this
image of the free roaming cowboy. Gene Autry lived on
his ranch near a town called Autryville and Roy and Dale
operated out of the Double R Bar Ranch. Yet these ties
were rather tenuous, as the Roy Rogers' theme song
"Happy Trails to You" emphasizes. Autryville and the
Double R Bar are more like whole worlds than ranches
or places within a larger world. Unlike the property Westerns such as *Bonanza,* the Rogers and Autry ranches were
not used as the dominant images of the shows. When
people refer to Roy and Gene they do not refer to them

as the owner of the Ponderosa but as Roy and Gene—
whose reputations do not need to be enhanced by owning ranches.

Individual though he is, the early TV Western hero
has a mission to perform—to right whatever wrongs he
may come across. *The Lone Ranger* is perhaps the most
explicit about this vision. The Ranger is not only a
knight errant, he is the cutting edge of civilization, for by
setting things right he encourages the conditions that
bring more settlers and towns. One of the early shows
contains the description of the Ranger as "a man whose
presence brought fear to the lawless and hope to those
who wanted to make this frontier land their home." In
a 1953 episode entitled "Hidden Fortune" the Ranger
says, "Unsolved crimes are a double threat to order and
progress in the West. It encourages other men to break
the law."

The men who did break the law, the baddies, are
evil personified. Everybody knew the villain the moment
he came on camera. (Like the wicked witches of the fairy
tales he is easy to spot.) In quite a few shows he wears a
black hat, rides a black horse and tends to have a dark
bushy moustache, but no beard. In other shows he wears
a hat and business suit with a fancy vest. In these episodes
he may be a big rancher trying to force some old man and
his daughter to sell their little farm or the mayor of a
town which reeks with corruption. I was overwhelmed by
the fact that in a great many episodes of the early TV
Westerns the baddie was associated with either the town
or a big ranch.

In contrast to the hero's code of values the baddie
has none. As a baddie in a *Cisco Kid* episode puts it,
"What I promise and what I do are two different things."
He just doesn't play by the rules. In another *Cisco Kid*

episode the baddie, who is in a business suit, and Cisco
are fighting. The baddie pulls a gun and there is a look
of surprise on Cisco's face when he realizes that his op-
ponent isn't playing by the rules.

Behind all this gruff exterior, though, the baddie is
basically a coward. He's like the stereotyped bully on the
block who buffaloes everyone until the true blue hero
comes along and whips him into shape. Perhaps in some
way this can be seen to lessen the anarchistic possibilities
of the early Western. In this world might is right, and
wrong is weak. Might sort of comes with the territory if
you are also right. Perhaps you are an innocent victim of
the baddie, unable to fight him on his own terms: never
fear, Cisco, Pancho, the Lone Ranger, Tonto and Company are never far away. The West may be endless space,
but somehow the hero finds the baddie and in the end the
just are rewarded while the bad guys go to jail.

The TV Western heroes' strong emphasis on a code
of moral principles which he will stand for against corrupt or evil forces is a belief which occurs quite prominently in some of the political rhetoric of the time. In
his first inaugural address Harry Truman proclaimed that
"it is fitting that we should take this occasion to pro-
claim to the world the essential principles of faith by
which we live," then went on to speak of the communist
threat to these principles and how the United States
would protect the peace and freedom of the world from
this threat. With the words "from this faith we shall not
be moved," he summed up these beliefs in one ringing
phrase which might have been uttered by the Lone Ranger.
Like the Ranger Truman couches his beliefs with the word
faith, a word with moral and religious overtones. Now
many politicians before and since Truman have used the
image of the just protecting the weak against the unjust,

but very few drew this image in terms of a faith, a code which leads the just to protect the weak. It is significant that over twenty years after Truman's speech, with the ex-President lingering near death, Ralph Gleason should write a *Perspectives* column entitled "Harry Truman—Our Last Human President" in *Rolling Stone*, the paper read by so many who grew up with Truman and the early TV Western. The qualities that Gleason praises in Truman are those which occur in the speech and in the early Westerns —his honesty and his faith. As Gleason puts it, "he was honest and true to both his conscience and his responsibilities," and "he had guts."[4]

This image of the baddie catching his in the end and of the lone hero riding out of nowhere to do what he feels is right—sometimes against a town which is either apathetic or fearful of the baddies who control it—also has a great deal of similarity with a film that several writers have seen as an allegory for the whole era of the late forties and early fifties—*High Noon*.[5] The plot of *High Noon* needs no repeating here since the movie has become a late night movie classic, but the main theme of the film does relate directly to those McCarthy years and to the early TV Westerns. In both *High Noon* and the early Westerns we have lone heroes who out of a sense of rightness or duty or morality stand up against corrupt forces which the townspeople are unable or unwilling to fight.

The tensions of the film and of the early TV shows are emblematic of the tensions of a time when most Americans—pro- or anti-McCarthy felt that there was something seriously wrong with their government and with their society, yet felt themselves powerless to stop it. For the McCarthyites our society was riddled with Reds who wanted to undermine our country and in order to defeat these Reds a strong man was needed to ride in and clean

up the town. To the anti-McCarthy people the powers of
the government were being used to harass and intimidate
innocent citizens whose only crime was that they held
"unorthodox beliefs" or associated with those who held
"unorthodox beliefs." What the times demanded were
men who would stand up against a society out of control,
men who had a basic belief in inalienable rights like free
speech and free association. Gary Cooper's lawman and
the roles played by Gene Autry, the Lone Ranger and the
Cisco Kid all filled these conflicting, yet similar hopes. In
High Noon and in the early TV shows the baddie was easy
to identify but in real life the choice of good and evil was
confusing.

As one who started school during those years, who
can still vaguely remember watching the Army-McCarthy
hearings on TV, and whose parents had strong feelings
about what was happening, I can remember that through
those years I emerged—as no doubt many of my generation—with a belief that one had to follow a code of right
and wrong no matter what the government or someone
who presumed to be the government said. In the early
Westerns the hero was constantly faced with corrupt town
officials, fearful or apathetic townspeople and lawmen who
tried to jail the hero out of the belief that he was the outlaw.

In a larger respect this is a theme that emerges from
some of the deepest literature of the period. I am thinking especially of Joseph Heller's *Catch-22*, with its vision
of sane men trying to cope with a mad society. Ultimately
Yossarian, like Orr, follows his own head and heads off
for Sweden like Roy Rogers or Hopalong Cassidy riding
off into the sunset.

Restless Gun "Crink" Denver Pile (sheriff left), and John Payne

There was a gun that won the West
There was a man among the rest
Faster than any gun or man alive
A lightnin' bolt when he drew his Colt .45

–COLT .45 themesong

CHAPTER III

The Gun:
The Lawman and Associates Defend the Organization Man

IN SEPTEMBER, 1955 A NEW WESTERN MADE ITS DEBUT AND WITH
the appearance of *Wyatt Earp* we enter into the second
phase of the TV Western, the phase of the gun. As its producers conceived it *Wyatt Earp* was to be an "adult" Western. In a statement that must surely rank with the full
blown political rhetoric which is always in season, these
producers claimed to be following in the footsteps of the
"serious" Westerns of the forties and fifties. The producers outlined their ideals:

> *In the past few years a few Westerns have been*
> *realized which deal with their subjects in an*
> *adult fashion. The characters portrayed are be-*
> *lievable men and women, some good, some bad,*
> *but most displaying a mixture of strength and*
> *weakness in varying proportions. The other ele-*
> *ments of Westerns may be present—Indians,*
> *buffaloes, cowboys, etc.—but life is not por-*
> *trayed as an eternal succession of these elements,*
> *one in perpetual pursuit of another. The names*
> *of these movies, significantly, are well known*
> *and have escaped the usual fate of the typical*
> *grade-B Western—the fate of lost identity.*[1]

53

Imitators were quick to follow, many of them eager to capitalize on *Earp*'s success in the ratings race. These shows continued to speak of themselves with the same rhetoric used by *Earp*'s producers. For example, Norman MacDonnell, the original producer of *Gunsmoke*, spoke of his show's premises:

> *We never do action for action's sake. For instance we've never had a chase on* Gunsmoke. *We made a list of things that annoyed us in the regular Westerns. For instance the devotion of the cowboy to his horse. That's a lot of nonsense. The two things a cowboy loves best are his saddle and his hat. And cowboy speech isn't full of things like "shucks" and "side winding varmint." What's more the frontier marshals made mistakes sometimes, and they weren't always pure. The other week's show is a typical example. Matt Dillon kills four guys and then is ashamed of himself.*[2]

New Westerns continued to be churned out. In 1959, during the peak of the "adult" Western, there were 28 Westerns on the air whose 570 hours of new footage was equal to 400 Western movies—far more than Hollywood produced at the peak of the B Western craze.[3] The phrase "oater" became synonymous with TV programing.

For all their talk about being adult, though, for all their pretentious comparisons of their shows with Western movies, these Westerns were no more adult than their predecessors, although as we shall see they were different. Take *Wyatt Earp* for example. When we went to see *Earp* at the Library of Congress, I at least expected to find some fairly good material. We certainly didn't expect to laugh at the show as we did at some of the horse Westerns. On the very first tape we screened we ended up laughing

louder than ever at a scene in which Earp walks into a
bar and orders a glass of milk! In other shows like *Have
Gun, Will Travel* the adultness was couched in another
kind of pretentiousness that won a few plaudits from
critics and academic types, but which seems jaded today.
Have Gun used allusions to Shakespeare and episodes
with famous figures like Alfred Nobel and Oscar Wilde
to give itself an aura of adultness. This attempt to win
the highbrows won the show a few fans, but to me it
seems largely unsuccessful because it was so stilted and
artificial. Paladin and Alfred Nobel running around looking for stolen nitroglycerin, all the while punctuating the
search with remarks about an awesome power that will
end war (catch the allusion to the bomb?) seems to be a
bit heavy-handed. As we shall see there are other factors
in these shows which make their claims to adultness
seem strange. In fact I wonder why they used the term.
Part of it, no doubt, was to set themselves off from the
kid centeredness of the horse Westerns. Young teenage
viewers who had outgrown the kiddie shows could be
attracted by telling them they were watching adult shows.
Most of these so-called adult Westerns were aired early
in the evening during what network executives speak of
as the family time.

After several attempts to discover what was meant
by this idea of adultness, I came to have the nagging
thought that what the network executives meant was
that the shows had more violence. This is not an uncom-
mon maneuver in the movie business, which equates sex
and violence with adultness and frankness. Since sex was
out on the tube, the TV business could only use violence
(which is in itself a weird state of affairs). The mixture
of goodness and badness in the main characters was portrayed in terms of violence. Roy Rogers—the super, un-

believable cowboy—might use ten shots from one re-
volver to shoot the baddie's gun out of his hand, while
the "believable" adult hero merely kills him. Hopalong
Cassidy might hogtie his villain captive with an assortment of knots, but the adult hero beats him senseless. To
show emotion, especially hate, the hero turns to violence.
As for love, well there are some things you can't show on
the tube.

During the period of the adult Western there is an
interesting pattern to the violence ratio. The early shows,
Earp included, de-emphasized killing much in the fashion
of the horse Westerns. During testimony before a Congressional Committee investigating TV violence, Hugh
O'Brien, who played Wyatt Earp, was proud of the fact
that his show had de-emphasized killing. Other shows
had less to be proud of. As more shows hit the air and
the ratings race between the oaters became more vicious,
so did the violence. It was almost as though the networks
figured the best way to be "adult" and to attract more
viewers was to increase the violence. In one episode of
Colt .45 we counted three vicious killings and several
beatings—all this in a half-hour show, including commercials.

Now as I said in the introduction violence figures
are well and good, but it is the context of violence which
makes it either artistically valid or merely pornographic.
For instance in Peckinpah's film *The Wild Bunch* there is
a great deal of violence, but it is related thematically to
the movie, beginning with the opening shot of the scor-
pion and the ants and following through to the concluding donnybrook. Other "B" copies of *The Wild Bunch*
use violence solely for violence's sake, and the same goes
for the TV Western. In the *Colt .45* episode referred to
most of the violence is done by the bad guys. It might

be argued that this helps establish their character. Perhaps, but one can carry this too far. The violence becomes violence for its own sake when it is the *only* characterization used, and it becomes pornographic violence when the camera lingers on dying victims and smoking guns. The horse Westerns and the movie Westerns which the so-called adult Western claimed to imitate got along without this degree of violence, so those who claim violence is "natural" to the Western just haven't done their homework.

That the shows could get along without violence or de-emphasize it became obvious when the heat of investigations and public outcry became too hot and shows toned down their violence. In one *Lawman* episode, "The Showdown,"* a gunfight is treated in an antiviolent fashion. The camera focuses on only the heads and faces of the two combatants not on their bodies or their guns. One man is reluctant to kill, while the other man is plainly gun-crazed. Shots ring out. The camera avoids the dying agonies of the loser; instead it merely tilts down at his lifeless body for an instant to show who won. The fight is over. In the *Colt .45* episode entitled "The Devil's Godson," the outlaws murder two men in cold blood without any apparent motivation, while in another sequence they kick a drunk. This is neither "adult" nor is it justified.

A *Gunsmoke* episode, "Vengence" (1966), is an even more graphic example of this pornographic violence. The opening teaser of the episode is a sequence depicting the beating of two men by several outlaws. The violence of the episode is enhanced by the director's use of a moving, subjective camera which cuts from outlaw to victim and

---

*When watching reruns on our set it was sometimes impossible to get the exact date for a particular episode. On those shows where we were able to obtain dates, they are cited.

back again. The sequence begins with a shot of a man being beaten in the face with a rope, cutting alternately from the victim's face to the man beating him. Another shot shows a man being pushed away from an outlaw's horse with the camera focusing on a close-up shot from above of the man's head hitting a log. Then comes an even more repugnant sequence in which the outlaws drag one of the men behind their horses—the camera again dwelling on the faces of the victim and the outlaws. The concluding sequence manages to top even this with shots of the outlaws' horses trampling the older man who is trying to protect the younger one from the horses' hooves. The camera switches again and again from close-ups of the hooves striking the man's back to a tilt-up at the hooves coming down on the man. All these acts are enhanced by an equally graphic soundtrack of thumps and breaking bones.

As Fritz Lang pointed out in an interview on NET's *Film Odyssey* series, there is no need for this type of violence since it serves no purpose except to play to the viewer's basest instincts. Lang said that in his film *M* the violence of the child murderer is deliberately understated by allowing it to occur out of sight of the camera. This allows the viewer to use his own imagination to visualize the most horrible thing that can happen—enhancing the horror in a way that no graphic depiction of violence can. Several of the horse Westerns used variations of this technique, but apparently the adult Western considered it part of the childishness of the early Westerns—as unrealistic as trick horses and guns with an unlimited supply of bullets.

In the world of the adult Western, violence, then, becomes the synonym for adult. The heroes are allowed only an occasional kiss or two, but violence, well that's another story. In a 1949 pamphlet, Gershon Legman wrote, "There is *no* mundane substitute for sex except sadism."[4] And so it is with the TV Western. As we shall see, though, even the violence has a sexual dimension. As though finding one primal instinct blocked, the producers turned to emphasizing another until its dimensions encompass both instincts, in an asexual or homosexual orgy of violence. (Notice how little TV Western violence is linked with women.)

The role of violence in these adult Westerns is especially evident in their dominant image, the gun, a symbol which has been compared to the cigarettes which sponsored several of these shows. The man, who is the star of the adult Western, rarely smokes and unlike Roy Rogers and Guy Madison he never advertizes his sponsor's product, but on his hip he carries a long barrel, which when smoking helps convey the same image of masculine power as the cigarette held by the Marlboro man. In the world of *The Rifleman, Colt .45, Restless Gun* and *Yancy Derringer*, the gun becomes an important member of the cast and usurps the place that had been occupied by the horse. Trigger is replaced by the Buntline Special, Champ loses his title to the Derringer. In the adult Western the horse is merely something to get you where you are going. Some of the new stars, like Paladin, rent their horses at the livery stable or ride the stagecoach, and what's more, some of these stars even ride black horses.

But their guns, that's a different story. In contrast to the nondescript horses they ride or rent, many stars carry guns with very distinct characters. Like 1950's hot rods these guns are chopped, lengthened, embellished, super-customized and one-of-a-kind versions of the plain everyday ones used by everyone else. Wyatt Earp carries a gun called the Buntline Special, a long, sleek rail job with a sixteen inch barrel. The extra barrel length is especially handy for cracking the skulls of recalcitrant outlaws, something Earp does fairly often. As much a club as it is a lethal weapon, the Buntline keeps the kill ratio on *Earp* pretty low—which is to the show's credit. In contrast to the Buntline is the Derringer carried by its namesake (or is it vice versa) Yancy Derringer. Then there is the custom chopped shotgun carried in the holster of bounty hunter Josh Randall of *Wanted: Dead or Alive.* Randall's weapon combines the size and handling ease of a pistol with the firepower of a rifle. It's like putting a 400 hemi in a Model A. Randall's custom job, though, might have trouble if it tangled with the rifle carried by Lucas McCain of *The Rifleman.* McCain may carry the ultimate weapon in this battle of the gun, for his rifle has the uncanny ability to outfire anything but a modern machine gun—and even that might be a stand-off.

Although there are some stars who don't carry custom guns, even some of these stars feel the pressure of this arms race and adopt some pretty individualistic weapons of their own. Jim Bowie carries his famous knife, which looks huge on a twelve inch screen. In fact the lifesize model might not even fit on the screen. Dapper dresser Bat Masterson carries a fancy cane which he wields so expertly that it is a match for any gun. The weirdest weapon in this galaxy is the hat worn by Sundance in a show called *Hotel de Paree.* Sundance's hat contains a band of mirrors which he uses to blind his gunfighting opponents. Sundance against Lucas McCain wouldn't even be a fair fight on a sunny day. Of course, Sundance manages to make himself rather scarce on cloudy days and has a self-imposed sundown curfew, except when he's at the hotel run by two comely looking French girls who specialize in extra bright bar lighting.

The symbolic role of the gun is emphasized in the openings of several of these adult Westerns. In *Colt .45* a man is walking into a building when someone shouts "Colt!" The man turns and fires directly back at the camera, with each shot spelling out the letters of Colt .45 which dissolves into the stylized logo of the gun company. If one weren't a regular watcher of the show, he might think someone was shouting at the gun, not the man who is walking into the building—the man whose name is Colt. Here man and gun are most explicitly intertwined. The opening of *Have Gun, Will Travel* utilizes a similar gun motif. The first thing one sees is the white emblem of the knight chess piece, then this image clears slightly to reveal part of a holster. The camera zooms out for a waist level shot of a man in black, who draws the gun and cocks it while giving a little speech: "Quantity, Mr. Carrington, is never a worthy substitution for quality whether it is in the choice of a book, a play, a friend, or a gun." After the speech he places the gun back in his holster and the camera zooms back in on the chess emblem. Fittingly the chess emblem on his holster is also the emblem employed on the business cards Paladin passes around, cards which read "Have Gun, Will Travel." The horse has been reduced to a stylized decoration for the gun. It is interesting to note that in later episodes of *Have Gun*—those filmed in the sixties during the heat over TV violence— there is a change in the opening. In this sequence the show opens with a full shot of Paladin in silhouette, he draws, then the camera zooms in on the gun and chess piece emblem. In the early opening the gun and its role (the chess piece) are emphasized, and Paladin's face never even appears. In the later opening the man is emphasized, the gun de-emphasized. *Lawman's* opening also uses a gun, in this case a rifle, prominently. We see Marshal Troop from the waist up cocking the rifle. He tosses the rifle to his deputy, Johnny McKay, and the camera focuses on the rifle in a medium range shot, following it from Troop to McKay in a pan shot. McKay then takes the gun and aims it at some imaginary target. The rifle symbolically forms the bond between marshal and deputy, between older man and youth. What is passed is not a torch, but a gun, and the young deputy appears to know what to do with it; in fact he seems to enjoy playing with it. Several *Lawman* episodes carry this theme from the opening into the first sequence of the show. In these episodes McKay is shown cleaning the gun or ejecting shells from it (you mean it was loaded?) or fondling it, as though the opening sequence was being continued right into the episode.

Although these shows all emphasized guns there is some disagreement among them about the dimensions of this symbol. Many anti-gun control freaks ride around in cars with bumperstickers that say, "Guns don't kill people, Criminals Do." In this sense the gun is virtually an inanimate tool, following the desires of the man controlling it. Some TV Westerns tend to see it this way, although in others the line between tool and symbol becomes blurred. On *Lawman*, for example, Marshal Troop states that he does not believe in "deadlines"—making people turn in their guns when they come to town. Troop's philosophy is spelled out most explicitly in an episode entitled "The Showdown." Responding to Johnny McKay's suggestion that maybe Laramie needs a deadline, Troop says: "If men are going to fight they'll fight. Now you take away their guns, they'll think you're afraid of them." Clearly there is a link here between masculinity and guns, for Troop feels that men will regard him as weak if he takes their guns. He goes on to say, "These aren't riffraff. These are honest men, but you go telling them they can't be trusted and they get way out of hand." Again the issue has a masculine sexual dimension—you try to deprive them of what's theirs and they'll fight you. Troop ends his speech by saying that someday men won't have to wear guns; yet the speech suggests that guns and masculinity are so inextricably linked that it will be a long time coming. Another *Lawman* episode, "A Man On A Wire," carries this view of the gun in its final sequence. After Troop and Johnny McKay catch the baddie there is a shot of the baddie lying on the ground wounded with Troop and McKay standing over him guns in hand. The camera then moves in for a close-up of the guns as the final shot of the episode.

Unlike Troop, Wyatt Earp does believe in deadlines. In a 1957 episode "Old Jake" the camera focuses on a sign posted by Earp: "ATTENTION: Carrying of guns is forbidden by law, under penalty of 10 days in jail. Guns must be checked at bars and hotels." In episodes that confront this issue it is clearly the impotent man who fears having to turn in his gun. A gun is something a man hides behind, a cover for his lack of masculinity. Yet Earp carries a gun, the biggest pistol ever made—and it looms even larger when no one else carries a gun. Earp himself is willing to unbuckle his gun and fight "fairly." He doesn't appear hung up on it, but what about his TV fans? The connection between Earp's gun and his own strength is hard to ignore. Unlike Sampson, Earp is willing to part with the symbol of his potency, but not for too long.

A third attitude towards guns is found in *Colt .45*. Everything in this show from the themesong, to the opening, to the fact that man and gun have the same name, to the treatment of the gun in various episodes suggests that the gun assumes a character of its own—that it is a thing, not just a tool. "There was a *gun* that won the West." The opening confusion or fusion of man and gun. In an

episode entitled "The Pirate" an ex-Southern general remarks, "I've heard a great deal of this gun. History might
have been changed if we had had one of these." There is
the sense in the quote that he is talking about an animate
object, not a tool.

In all these examples—including even my language
"tool"— there is the compelling sense that the gun is a
symbol for masculine potency and strength. Phallic symbolism is important here, but only as a part of this larger
meaning. This sense of the gun as a symbol of masculine
potency and strength is broad enough to include other
weapons like Bat Masterson's cane and Sundance's hat.
Cane and hat are symbols of the strength and potency of
the hero in the same sense as the gun.

In line with this TV arms race it is interesting to note
that it occurs at the same time we are engaged in another
bigger and more dangerous arms race. Like John Foster
Dulles, rifleman, bounty hunter and U. S. marshal all
seem to be yearning for the biggest bang for the buck.
Western potency and national potency are all wrapped up
in weapons. Stanley Kubrick's beautiful image of Slim
Pickens riding the bomb to Armageddon in *Dr. Strange-
love* seems to sum up this connection of TV Westerns, guns
and the arms race of the 1950's.

Slim Pickens riding the bomb in the ultimate shoot-
out is paralleled by the dominant feature of the adult
Western, the gunfight. Gunfights were not that prominent in the early, horse Westerns, rather most of the hero-
villain conflicts in *The Lone Ranger* and the other early
shows were resolved by fist fights. In situations where
guns were used, the hero didn't shoot to kill. Not so in
the adult Western. Here the gunfight is the classic one of
fight to the death, where the teamwork of hero and gun,
unlike the earlier teamwork of hero and horse, operates

Bat Masterson "Stampede at Tent City" James Best (left) and Gene Barry.

Bat Masterson "The Desert Ship" Gene Barry and Karen Steele

with deadly intent. For James Arness and other stars of
the adult Western, the gunfight is *the* classic symbol of
the Western tradition. In one of the openings used by
Gunsmoke, hero and villain stand at opposite ends of the
street as the staccato beat of the opening theme marks
their footsteps. The camera is at waist level, gun level.
Two shots ring out, one closely followed by another.
The villain falls and the hero has again triumphed: for
once and for all. Here is a classic melodramatic confrontation: hero and villain, each dependent only on his skill
and his gun—and the equally classic melodramatic answer
—immediate, decisive, simple.

   In a perceptive article in *Television Quarterly*, John
Evans theorizes that the gunfight is modern man's "substitute in fantasy for the grand confrontation scene which
in real life is impossible."[5] Evans believes that the popularity of the adult Western and gunfight is due to its appeal to the alienated, anomic "organization man" of the
middle fifties. "Through his vicarious position in the
powerful and final act of the gunfight," says Evans, "the
factory worker or the organization man symbolically
shoots down all the individual officials and impersonal
forces that restrict, schedule, supervise, direct, frustrate
and control his daily existence."[6] Evans went on to note
that it was important that the villain be wounded rather
than killed, "in order that the hero (and the viewer) can
enjoy the effect on him of his total defeat and degrada-
tion."[7] While this may have been true of some of the
early adult Westerns, like *Wyatt Earp*, the kill ratio goes
up in later shows. Wounding the villain may degrade him,
but killing "rubs him out," "wipes him out" finally and
decisively. A wounded and degraded villain can take revenge, a dead one can't. There is a scene that constantly
occurs in many of these "wipe out" gunfights. In this

scene the hero outdraws the villain, wounding him, but the villain manages to find the strength to lift his gun and get off another shot—sometimes hitting the hero, sometimes missing, sometimes someone warns him just in time. The hero "finishes the job" with a well-placed shot. Occasionally the villain may even try a shot with a last dying gasp. The message is plain: The only good baddie is a dead baddie.

The truth in Evans' thesis applies not only to the middle-of-the-road, middle American organization man but also to the so-called right and left wing. Writing in the *National Review*, William F. Rickenbacker proclaims that if Wyatt Earp offers himself as a candidate, "sixty million of us Westerners will put him in office."[8] The appeal of the decisive and simple answers presented by the Western is too much for Rickenbacker to resist:

> *When Wyatt comes up with a difficult moral decision, nobody tells him, "Wait, Wyatt, there's two sides to this question. Maybe the guy suffered from a bad environment in his youth, maybe we should give him occupational therapy, maybe we should look to the values he has been taught in Cheyenne (or Denver) and try to Understand, Understand!" But "No," says Wyatt, "the dirty lowdown gunslinger is a dirty lowdown gunslinger and the hell with it!" This is the kind of law that might go a long way toward squelching the juvenile gunslingers in our modern cities.*[9]

Yet the right winger is not alone in his admiration for the Westerner. It seems to me that he is quite similar to the so-called "White Negro" described by so-called left winger and city dweller Norman Mailer. In fact Mailer even

describes his hero as "a frontiersman in the Wild West of
American night life."[10] Mailer states that "if the fate of
twentieth-century man is to live with death from adoles-
cence to premature senescence, why then the only life-
giving answer is to accept the terms of death, to live with
death as immediate danger, to divorce oneself from society,
to exist without roots, to set out on that uncharted
journey into the rebellious imperatives of the self."[11]
Mailer's "White Negro" has been called a proto-existen-
tialist, but he could have also been called Johnny Yuma,
the Rebel, or Paladin.

The appeal of the adult Western hero to organization
man, conservative and liberal, is further enhanced by the
position and image of the star. The star is never married,
and he has no family or relatives. But of most importance
he has no boss and is not part of some vast, impersonal
organization. As Evans puts it, the adult Western hero
"stands alone and independent, neither requiring the support of family members during times of crisis nor of having the responsibility of a family to restrict his freedom
and activity."[12]

Like his juvenile predecessor, the adult Western hero
is the epitome of the isolated, atomic individual. He may
be a wanderer, tied to neither town nor ranch, or like
Wyatt Earp or Matt Dillon he may be the town lawman,
but even these lawmen escape from town quite often, for
their jobs demand they pursue their quarry as far as necessary. Town itself is usually a wide open place, the
image of the mythic raw Western town where the only law
was the lawman. The adult Western hero still roams the
mythic "virgin land," that region of endless time and
space. He seems at once to be going nowhere and everywhere. Time-wise he is going nowhere, for to him time is
frozen at a moment that will last forever. Space-wise he

can go everywhere, for the mythic West he roams is a land
of endless possibility. If the early Western hero was a
juvenile—an eight-year-old kid—the adult Western hero is
a sort of virginal pre-adolescent. He is virginal because loss
of virginity implies a time scheme which is closed at both
ends. As a pre-adolescent he is forever in the stage of
being and becoming.

To label this an "adult" Western thus seems to be
rather strange, for Wyatt Earp and Matt Dillon are clearly
not adults. Leslie Fiedler might have been talking about
them when he described the American novelist as having
no history, no development, "Their themes belong to a
pre-adult world and the experience of growing old tends
to remain for them intractable."[13] For the so-called adult
Western as for the American novel, "everything goes except for the frank description of adult heterosexual love."[14]
If there is little doubt about what goes on upstairs at the
Longbranch, little doubt that Miss Kitty is selling "more
than Hershey Bars," there is a lot of doubt about who's
doing the buying. Certainly not the hero. Miss Kitty and
her counterpart, Lily, of *Lawman* may personify the good-
bad woman, but this is not enough to attract more than
friendship from the hero.

Though, in his essential innocence, he is similar to
the juvenile hero of the early TV Westerns, the adult Western hero plays a role that differs from the roles taken on
by the heroes of the early Western. The adult Western
hero has one job to the extent that hero role and job become one. The Lone Ranger, Cisco, Pancho, and others
had a role but they often took various jobs to carry out
that role. Sometimes these jobs and roles placed them on
the opposite side of the law, opposing a local sheriff or
mayor. In the adult Western the jobs and roles are always
on the right side of the law. The idea of Wyatt Earp or

Matt Dillon being called "the Robin Hood of the Old West" is preposterous. The adult Western hero is a lawman, a scout.[15] Some of them like The Rebel or The Texan, do roam from job to job, town to town, and sometimes they get in trouble with the law, but this is the exception. Several of the new heroes are bounty hunters, a role Roy Rogers would never stoop to playing. Worse yet one of these bounty hunters even passes out business cards. In the early Westerns the bounty hunter was an evil or at best, a neutral figure. The idea that someone should get paid for doing good deeds was an anathema to the Lone Ranger or the Cisco Kid.

The important thing for the adult heroes is the job, the role. Paladin charges a fee for his services, although he waives it for needy cases and only hires himself out to those on the right side of the law. With the lawman types, this emphasis on job takes precedence over everything else. Where Roy Rogers might let an innocent man, who has been unjustly accused, escape, not so with the adult lawman. He brings 'em in anyway. As Marshal Troop put it in a *Lawman* episode entitled "The Hunch," "I don't try 'em. I just catch 'em." And catch 'em he does.

This shift from role to job cannot be emphasized enough.[16] Roy Rogers and the Lone Ranger were above the law. They lived according to an abstract code of values. No matter what job the hero had, his personification of the values was what was important. Whether he was Jesse James, "Robin Hood," ranch foreman or lawman, the hero could always appeal to the values as a guide to conduct.

The adult Western hero also has values, but there is a subtle shift in both the values and the hero's relationship to them. In a *Have Gun, Will Travel* episode entitled "The Five Books of Owen Deaver" (1958) there is the

emphasis on a code of values. Deaver is a sheriff's son
who has been sent back East to read law. He returns to
the town of Three Winds to assume his father's job and
as a guide for law in his town brings along the five books
containing the municipal code of Philadelphia. Paladin
argues that to apply this code to a raw Western town like
Three Winds is absurd. For Paladin there is no written
law, "just a loose set of morals based mostly on Thou
Shalt Not." Then he goes on to outline these thou shalt
nots: "Thou shalt not kill a man unless he's armed and
facing you; thou shalt not steal a man's horse; thou shalt
not rob at gun point." All of which sound a good deal
like the code of the horse Westerns. But Deaver is not to
be put off. His reply to Paladin is "that's about as far as
it goes," and it is plain that he means that society needs
more than a few rules in an admittedly "loose set of
morals." Who is to decide what's loose? Who is to decide
whether acts like drunkenness or disturbing the peace are
crimes? Paladin answers, "It's mainly left up to the sheriff to decide what is a crime in any given area." Deaver is
quick to retort, "What if the sheriff gets up on the wrong
side of the bed one morning and everything's a crime?"
To Paladin the answer is simple, get another sheriff, but
what happens when the sheriff prevents you from replac-
ing him?

In the early Westerns we have spoken of the anarchistic implications embodied in the image of the hero as
representing the code of values no matter what his position
vis-a-vis society. Plainly the "Deaver" episode confronts
this dilemma head on. For Paladin and for the adult Western there is still a code, rather than the five books. In the
words of the *Colt .45* themesong, "there was a right,
there was a wrong," or the themesong of *Lawman*:

The lawman came with the sun
There was a job to be done

.   .   .   .

.   .   .   .

And as he silently rode
Where evil violently flowed

.   .   .   .

.   .   .   .

But the code is not personified by the hero, no matter
what his job. Notice that Paladin's answer to Deaver is,
"It's mainly left up to the sheriff," and when Deaver
raises the possibility of a bad sheriff, Paladin says get
a new one. The law and the code, then, are embodied in
the job of lawman. The code no longer is an abstract set
of values, but the code of the lawman. All good people
believe in the code, but it is up to the sheriff to enforce
it, not the Lone Ranger or "the Robin Hood of the Old
West." Notice the Lawman theme makes it plain that he
lives and dies "by the code of the lawman." The old
Gene Autry phrase, "where we sleep out every night,
where the only law is right" seems to be twisted to "where
the only right is law."
    The values are linked more to the hero's position in
society than to some abstract idea of "goodness." The
heroes of the adult Western do not wear white hats. Wyatt
Earp might be a gunfighter in an early Western and Paladin
dresses all in black, sometimes rides a black horse, and
wears a black moustache—a virtual carbon copy of many
villains of the early TV Western. If the adult Western
hero looks like the villain of the earlier shows, at least he
carries the fiat of the law wherever he goes. The good guy
values adhere not to some abstract good; not to the color
of ones hat, but to the job. Notice how many of these

shows are named after roles: *Lawman, The Deputy, Trackdown, Wanted: Dead or Alive*, while the early Westerns were named after people. (See Appendix) There is only one show that doesn't fit the pattern—*Cowboy G-Men*, but it belongs there for other reasons, including its use of the star-sidekick motif.

This idea of the importance of job and role suggest that for all his appeal to the organization man, the adult Western hero bears a great deal of similarity to the inhabitants of Park Forest and Levittown. Matt Dillon and Co. may not be organization men—they are free and they are capable of changing their situation decisively. Roy Rogers and Matt Dillon have this in common, but the disruptive, anarchistic possibilities which can be found in Rogers are not to be found in Dillon. It is as though there was a recognition of these anarchistic possibilities during the sober fifties—a period which came after a disruptive period in which a man, following some crazy code, sought to conquer the world and another man, following a code, sought to root communists out of the highest reaches of government.

Beyond the link between code and job, there is the recognition that there is an even closer link between the values of the adult Western hero and the organization man of the fifties. These values are the values of cautious conformism that one characteristically associates with the Eisenhower years. Wyatt Earp and Paladin may wear black, but they wear it impeccably. In fact Earp's whole costume is a banker's dream: black suit, black string tie, black hat and a shiny vest. Paladin may wear a moustache, but he keeps it neat and the rest of his face is clean shaven. Matt Dillon, unlike Roy Rogers, may take an occasional drink, but he never, never has more than one. The adult Western hero is the essence of sobriety and decorum. He dresses well, but not too well. He has a drink with the boys, but only one. Unlike the villain he is not pushy, never striving to reach the top, never stepping over anyone or anything that stands in his way. However he will not be pushed, either. He is, in short, a sort of super-organization man.

The villain, on the other hand, is everything the hero is not. As a character he is plainly a deviant. He is usually dirty and sloppy or else dresses too fancy. He tends to overdo. He always carries a joke too far and he is always after more than his share. A Cisco Kid invoking a moral code of what is good, even when it means fighting sheriffs, might well *be* a deviant in the adult Western. Certainly he dresses awfully funny and besides he never drinks.

It is appearance, especially, which gives the baddie away the moment he walks on camera. In a *Lawman* episode entitled "Red Ransom," Marshal Troop makes this clear. "Whiskey Jimmy. *Look at him.* (my italics) He's no good and he never will be." In another *Lawman* episode, "The Prodigal," (1959), an outlaw describes himself as a "big easy going slob." The baddie further betrays himself when he opens his mouth. The hero and the goodies usually talk in an accent I've heard described as "NBC Standard." That is, they enunciate clearly and impeccably. Marshal Troop of *Lawman* speaks in a sort of pseudo-Southern (or is it Western?—it's hard to tell) accent which tends to break down into NBC Standard now and then. Most of the other heroes speak NBC Standard. The villain, however, has problems when he speaks. He may have an accent, a thick one, he may have bad grammar or else he may speak too ornately.

Beneath this exterior the villain's behavior is pure cowardice. When faced with the hero or with a job, he

The Deputy "The Jason Harris Story" Air — October 8, 1960
Allen Case (left) and Henry Fonda

The Deputy "The Jason Harris Story" Air — October 8, 1960
Allen Case (left) and Henry Fonda

may have to work himself up to it. As Wyatt Earp puts it in the episode "The Gunfight at the O. K. Corral," (1960), "Men who pick a fight usually talk a lot, drink a lot to work themselves up to it."

Like the villains of the early Westerns, the adult Western villain is bad through and through, once and for all. Yet unlike the early Westerns where the possibility of redemption was emphasized the gun Westerns dispose of their baddies forever, killing them so they can't get off that last shot. With backshooters, say the gun Westerns, the only remedy is shoot to kill. Perhaps part of this contrast stems from the difference between the morality play baddie of the early Westerns and the baddie of the gun Westerns. The Lone Ranger's continual fight with Butch Cavendish seems an archetypal battle between good and evil, while Wyatt Earp vs. baddie X seems a battle between a good man and a bad man. Maybe if Earp had come along earlier, the Clantons might have achieved the status of Cavendish. In the Lone-Ranger-Cavendish fights to have killed Cavendish would have killed the reasons for the Ranger's existence, while in *Earp* a dead baddie is one less baddie. The Ranger *personifies* a code while Earp is merely the paid lackey of the establishment, and so the baddies must be of a similar stature.

But why kill the baddie? Like the horse Western's idea of redemption the idea that the only good baddie is a dead baddie is deeply rooted in our character. If certain New England Puritans like Charles Eliot believed heathens could be converted, quite a few also believed they ought to be exterminated. To some extent the shoot-to-kill mentality is a product of cultural fears—i.e., Mayor Daley's riot order—and perhaps in the gun Western the "better dead than red" mentality of that era. It also stems from a harsh view of man, for the gun Western seems to say men are either good or evil—it's their nature—and they're born that way and die that way. In a *Lawman* episode, "The Hunch," a character asks, "How can a man do something completely contrary to his nature?" He can't as the episode shows. The horse Western, on the other hand, seems to emphasize the possibility of redemption, for it is that possibility which makes the Ranger's conflicts with Cavendish so purposeful. An establishment and its defenders must be wary of any threat to its order and put it down decisively; a code and its defender need not be as brutal. (Although historically examples abound of just the opposite, perhaps the answer lies in the nature of the code.) What makes this Puritanism with a vengeance is the association of innate badness and innate goodness with external appearances. This was precisely the problem the Puritans encountered—the problem which Hawthorne was to make the theme of *The Scarlet Letter.* In that novel the seemingly innocent minister is in reality not quite innocent, while the seemingly guilty Hester is in reality not that guilty. The adult Western, however, seems not to have considered this possibility and like the Puritans goes blithely ahead, looking but not really seeing.

This neo-Puritanism is also evident in the role of the other characters in the adult Western. Plainly there is a dilemma here, as there was with Puritanism. If goodness is connected with job and appearance, what is left for those of us who do not have very good jobs, but yet who are not very evil, in other words the audience of the mass media. The Western resolves the dilemma and with a fittingly Protestant solution. When theologians had proposed the same basic problem to Luther and Calvin, they both came up with the concept of vocation. That is, each

man has a predestined job to perform and he must perform that job to the best of his ability. Ultimately we all
serve God no matter what our position, so there is as
much dignity in manual labor as there is in being a king.
The Western's solution is almost exactly the same as Luther
and Calvin's.

A *Lawman* episode entitled "The Prodigal" (1959)
deals directly with this problem. In this episode Timo
McQueen, a bartender, has received news that his son is
coming to visit. McQueen's problem is that his son thinks
he's a big landowner. Marshal Troop calms him down by
saying, "As long as you keep your hand out of the till
what's wrong with being a bartender?" McQueen's son
shows up. He's a young know-it-all kid, who quickly gets
into a fight with Johnny McKay, the deputy. It's good
kid against bad kid, one with James Dean haircut fighting
another with his juvenile delinquent haircut and his surly
manner, and of course good kid wins. Bad kid's problem
is that he doesn't want to be a bartender. "I'm gonna be
somebody. I'm gonna walk down the street and people'll
tip their hats to me. They'll say, 'He's got it made.' "
Troop is bothered by all this and gives the boy a lecture.
There's nothing wrong with his father or his job. "You
know what they say about him? They say there goes Timo
McQueen, he's tall as a tree when it comes to backin' down,
he's honest and godfearing, he never rolled a drunk or
mooched a dime in his life." Later on Lily, who manages
the saloon where McQueen works, says he's the best bartender she's ever had. "You know there's a lot more to
working behind that mahogany than meets the eye." In
the end father and son are reconciled, and as they walk
away arm in arm, Lily says of Mark, "You know he might
even have the makings of a good bartender."

Good people, then, don't aspire for higher positions,

they try to be the best at what they are doing. But what
happens if they lose their jobs due to some unforeseen
circumstance? Well, they just keep trying. They certainly
don't go on welfare, they "don't hold by no charity." In
a *Lawman* episode entitled "The Hunch" a boy's father
is in jail and he comes to Troop to find out why. After
hearing the explanation the boy remarks that he'll need a
lawyer. Lily says she and Troop will see to that. The boy
answers, "No, thanks just the same, but that'd be charity.
Pa wouldn't hold with charity." Troop and Lily both
agree that he probably wouldn't. So the boy asks for a
job in the saloon, cleaning up. That wouldn't be right
either because a saloon's no place for a boy. In fact Troop
gives him hell for even coming in the saloon to talk to him.
"There are some places a boy your age doesn't belong. If
I catch you inside these doors again you'll eat standing up
for a week." Luckily the boy finds another job.
     The situations of Timo McQueen and the boy in
"The Hunch" point to two problems for the organization
man of the fifties, problems which would become more
exasperating and open in the sixties and the Westerns of
that period. One problem is the whole question of the
dignity of work. The idea of vocation, the pride in being
a damn good bartender seems to be increasingly irrelevant
to the worker on an assembly line or the middle level
bureaucrat who passes papers from one office to another.
The problem is in the gun Westerns' belief that good people don't necessarily strive to accumulate wealth or accept
charity.
     This belief leads to an interesting paradox which can
be best summed up in the question of how *wealthy* good
people get their money. What motivation drives them to
accumulate more than others and then hold on to it when
others have less—when others may even be starving or in

need of charity? The answers to these questions gnaw at the very heart of wealthy 1970's America, for the paradox of these TV Westerns is the paradox of contemporary America, a society where the average man is richer than all but a few other men who ever walked the earth and yet a society where millions still live in squalid semi-starvation. It is with the property Westerns that we begin to see some answers to those questions. In all of them it is never really explained how and why Ben Cartwright and Co. accumulated the land for their huge ranches and the wealth to run them. The property seems to be a God-given gift and the motivation to acquire it and keep it is usually talked about in vague terms like the wish to conquer a savage land and hold on to it. Once the deed to the land is registered then the talk shifts to property rights and the dignity of work. Nowhere is there any allusion to the real cattle barons and robber barons who, as often as not, accumulated their fortunes illegally and immorally.

The attitude towards wealth and charity that is found in the gun Westerns becomes a full-fledged glorification of the big property owner in *Bonanza* and the other property Westerns. The lawman's defense of the organization man becomes a defense and glorification of the organization and its owners.

The rules around here are simple and they never change. This train started together, it stays together and it gets where it's going together. The only people we've left behind so far, we've buried.

—*Wagon Train*, "The Nancy Palmer Story" (1961)

CHAPTER IV

The Male Group and the Emerging Community: WAGON TRAIN and RAWHIDE

ALMOST AT THE SAME TIME THE GUN WESTERNS WERE REACHING their peak saturation point, two new Westerns, containing an entirely different format, made their appearance. These two Westerns were *Wagon Train*, which made its debut in 1958 and *Rawhide*, which aired its first episode in 1959. Both these Westerns emphasized community and the male group, as opposed to the individualistic emphasis of the gun Western. By the early sixties there was a series of Westerns whose titles all conveyed a similar emphasis: *Laramie, Iron Horse, Cimarron City, Laredo*. In the appendix I have chosen to list these as transition Westerns, since in theme they seem to be a transition from the gun Western to the property Westerns of the next chapter. Chronologically, of course, this is not exactly the case since *Bonanza*, the first and longest running property Western, made its debut at the same time as *Wagon Train* and *Rawhide*. Yet strictly speaking the property Western does not become popular until the early-middle sixties, while the brief run of some of the transitional shows occurs slightly before that time. As far as the TV Western goes there was a time in the early sixties when horse, gun, transition and property Westerns could all be found on the tube. *The Lone Ranger* lasted that long; several gun Westerns were

83

still around; *Wagon Train* lasted into the late sixties; and
Gunsmoke (which will be treated separately) is still on
the air but it will not be returning in the Fall 1975 schedule. *Bonanza* has been cancelled.

In an early episode entitled, "Incident at Alabaster
Plain" (1959), *Rawhide* made a direct frontal assault on
the gun Western and the gun mystique. The story deals
with the return home of the son of a wealthy landowner.
The son is a gunfighter and his profession comes in for
attack by the father, the *Rawhide* trail crew and the director of the episode. The gunfighter carries a fancy gun
with an ornate snake carved on its handle. It is the perfect symbol for the who's-got-more-firepower, who's-got-
the-neatest-gun syndrome of the adult Western. The snake-
handled gun might have had a featured role in an "adult"
Western, but here it is the tool of the villain. The phallic
suggestiveness of the symbol is quite obvious—but it goes
beyond this, suggesting also craftiness for evil purposes
and a blind desire to strike out and kill anything that acci-
dentally crosses its path. In the gun Westerns the horse
had become an ornament for Paladin's holster, now the
gun itself becomes the victim of a similar kind of image.
The gunfighter becomes an amoral "snake in the grass,"
killing as much for sport as for anything else. The big
unanswered question of the gun Western, "how could you
kill people?" is asked here and all the gunfighter can reply
is, "You gotta work at it, Papa. It takes practice." Killing
in a gunfight, then, is not something normal people do.
Even the abnormal have to work at it. It is not defended
with references to a code or the law or "I have to kill him
or he'll kill me." The gunfighter is abnormal and his ob-
session with his snake-handled gun is a beautiful bit of
characterization. No one else in the show carries a weird
looking gun; their guns are de-emphasized and they look

on somebody who would carry a gun and worship it as a real freak. The father, the big landowner, certainly doesn't like it, nor can he understand it. He states, "I'm a cattleman, not a fighting man," and the episode approves of his sentiments. Gil Favor and his trail crew can't stand this gun freak either. For them guns have a use, but they are not a way of life and certainly not something to worship. Ultimately even the gun freak himself agrees, saying, "Now there's something I respect, a businessman. You see there isn't much money in this anymore." (Looks at his gun.) The speech seems to have a double meaning, both as a comment on gunfighters and on the gun Westerns. The comment is prophetic for in a few years there wouldn't be much of a market for gunfighters or gun Westerns on television.

Unlike the gun Westerns which feature the isolated, free roaming individual, *Rawhide* features a free roaming community. The trail crew is a community outside communities, which is held together by a common purpose—getting the herd through—and a common set of rules. These rules exist outside the rules or codes of whatever territory or town the herd passes through. The rules of the herd, not these other rules, define what the crew can and cannot do.

The *Rawhide* community is not an ideal democratic community. First of all it is all male, like the steers they drive to market. Men and cows are linked by a job, the drive to market, and they are linked symbolically. One might see in this a variation of the Fiedler theme—both cows and men are sexless. The men are the Western version of a host of American all-male teams from athletics to the army. What Fiedler called "the camaraderie of the locker room," is replaced by the camaraderie of the long drive—of nights around the campfire and days spent keep-

ing the herd moving. Like the army and like a lot of so-
called teams, the herd has a rigid chain-of-command
headed by the trail boss, Gil Favor. Favor is the autocratic leader of the trail crew—he sets the rules on everything from drinking to who does what. He accepts total
responsibility for the fate of the herd and demands total
obedience to his decisions. All of this has a purpose, for
the first herd to the railhead can command the top prices,
which means a fat bonus for Favor and everyone in the
trail crew. The all-male community becomes a team,
which competes in a big game for high stakes against
other teams of herd crews. The best team is Number One
and year after year can command the top wages and contract the best herds. All of which puts an enormous responsibility on the trail boss.

In a 1962 episode entitled "Incident at Quer-
encias" this responsibility is severely tested. Favor
has allowed a friend, Lige, to mix his small herd in with
the trail herd. The episode revolves around the problem
posed to Favor's leadership role by having a friend on the
drive. The friend asks no favors, he just wants to be one
of the boys, but to the members of the trail crew, Lige's
mere presence threatens to disrupt the whole drive. His
cattle are ill-suited for driving—they don't mix with the
herd and are constantly threatening to return home, and
Lige isn't much better than his herd. He's a drunkard,
a braggart, and doesn't mix any better than his cows. At
the beginning Favor outlines to Lige the rules he must
follow: "and there's rules Lige . . . I expect them to be
obeyed . . . last thing, I give the orders." Wishbone, the
cook, tries to convince Favor to abandon Lige and his
herd, but Favor retorts, "You're paid to cook . . . when
I want your advice on the merits of cattle I'll ask you."
Later on Lige manages to get one of the trail crew drunk

on a bottle he has brought along—against the explicit
rules of the trail boss. Favor's discipline falls on the trail
hand, since he does not know of Lige's complicity in the
affair. Again the trail boss lays down his autocratic hand,
"When I say no drinking on a drive, that's what I mean."
In the end Lige redeems himself, but not before giving the
boss and crew a pretty rough time.

One of the last episodes before the death of Eric
Fleming, who played Favor, deals with the problem of
what happens to a trail boss whose decision cost him an
entire herd and the first place finish he was driving for.
The opening of the episode "The Lost Herd" (1964)
shows the trail crew arriving in town, herdless. They are
laughed at and jeered by the townspeople, like the team
whose bonehead play blew the big game. Dissension begins to grow among the team members and fights break
out between men who felt Favor's decision was right and
those who disagreed with it. The local merchants refuse
to extend credit to the trail crew and Favor has to pay
them minimal wages out of his own pocket. Meanwhile
the cattlemen's association is investigating the loss of the
herd, preparatory to setting up a new, even bigger herd
for a drive. The list of candidates narrows to three: Favor,
a rival trail boss, and Favor's ramrod Rowdy Yates. The
sporting nature of the drive is emphasized, "Every time
a cattleman ships he's gambling . . . more than anything
else he wants the best man driving his herd." The big
scene comes when Rowdy is interviewed on Favor's decision to take the lost herd through risky country. When
asked whether he thought the decision was right, Rowdy
answers, "I'm just his ramrod, I'm not supposed to judge
whether he was right or wrong." Favor gets the job.

The key factor in the decision is Favor's ability to
lead a team. A good trail boss attracts a good team, makes

them into a fine-tuned unit, and is able to keep the team
together through several seasons. What the cattlemen are
looking for is "a well-formed crew. Men who are used to
working together." Working together as a team means
that each man has a specific responsibility and a specific
place in the chain of command. A good team is one in
which the trail boss is able to command the best man for
each job. When Rowdy goes for his interview and gives
the answer he does, this implication is especially apparent.
His answer suggests both his devotion to Favor and his own
self-knowledge of his place in the team. Clearly Rowdy is
a good ramrod, probably the best, but he is not a trail boss.
Elsewhere in the episode Wishbone moans the loss of his
chuckwagon. Favor's decision may have lost the herd, but
the cook should have held onto the chuckwagon. "It's
the cook's responsibility. The wagon and the supplies are
his responsibility." The opening of the show further suggests this idea of teamwork. The camera first focuses on
the silhouette of a cow, then moves to statues of men roping cows, and finally to a statue of each member of the
trail crew doing his job. The camera zooms in on the face
of each—Favor, Yates, Wishbone and the others. In the
earlier episodes the opening wasn't as stylized. Instead it
showed shots of the herd and each man doing his job,
rather than the statues. These statues, which have the look
of athletic trophies, are the symbolic abstraction of the
entire meaning of the show.

In these episodes with Eric Fleming as Favor it is the
rigid tightly knit team that provides the main theme for
the show. The similarity of the statues with athletic trophies, then, fits right in. The trail crew is the team, Favor
the coach.

In professional sports today there seem to be two
kinds of coaches: one the Lombardi type who calls his

players "boys," institutes curfews and bedchecks and will not permit long hair, mod clothes, etc. The other type operates under the assumption that they're all in this together and are after the same thing. He treats his players as men, realizes they are individuals and allows them to be so as much as possible. "As much as possible"—now that's a tricky phrase and most opponents of the second coaching philosophy assert that it leads to dissension. Along with the two kinds of coaches, sportswriters also talk about two kinds of players: the team player and the individualist. The team player is always preferred above the individualist. The team player will do anything for the team, while the individualist is out for what he can get. There will always be individuals who, for whatever the reason, will sow dissension and cause a loss of team morale and sense of purpose.

Now in the Favor episodes it is plain that Favor is a Lombardi type coach and his trail crew are all team players. The trail boss is a father figure, with the drovers on his crew being his "boys." The coach runs the whole show, discipline is rigid and no dissension is permitted even though the dissenter might be a thirty-year-old man with as much knowledge of the game—or at least his position—as the coach. In the crew, the team, there is little room for individualists, deviants. Everybody is a team player. Everybody is also white, anglo-saxon and well scrubbed. In the episode about Lige it is obvious that Lige, like his cows, doesn't fit in. Lige may be obnoxious, but one wonders how another individualist, who wasn't the friend of the boss, would have been received.

With the death of Eric Fleming, Rowdy Yates assumes the role of trail boss and the emphasis of the show changes. As trail boss Rowdy is much more like the second kind of coach and the team is much more like a viable community. No doubt part of the change comes because it is Rowdy who assumes command. Although he was second in command, Rowdy was still a member of the team. In this situation the gap between Rowdy and Favor was much wider than between Rowdy and the rest of the "boys." As second in command Rowdy sometimes functioned as the spokesman for the crew. He was the one Favor went to when he wanted to know how the crew felt about a decision. He was also the one the crew went to when they wanted to let Favor know how they felt. Rowdy drank and fought with the boys. Favor was more stand-offish. So when Rowdy assumed command he couldn't very well become a Favor-type trail boss. It just wouldn't be credible.

The change in the trail crew is obvious in a 1965 episode entitled "Brush War at Buford." As a leader Rowdy is not the benevolent despot Favor was; rather, under Yates, decisions are made democratically. At one point in the episode a big meeting of the whole crew is held to make a decision. There is more conflict and more freedom among the drovers themselves. At one point one says, "The only reason I took to droving in the first place was I figured it was the only place left where a man could ride the way he wanted to." That speech could have never been viewed favorably under Favor, but here it becomes the credo of the whole crew.

The crew itself has changed, also. It is now more a melting-pot community than a team. The members of the crew come from a variety of backgrounds—there is even a black cowboy played by Raymond St. Jacques who gets billing as a regular at the opening of the show. As far as I know this is the only case in the entire run of a major TV Western that a black has achieved status as a regular cast member! The crew also has an ex-Yankee—fittingly

named Yank—and an ex-Confederate who engage in
friendly arguments over the merits of their old roles. The
trail crew is a microcosm of what we Americans like to
believe our society is. It is a melting pot where a variety
of individuals can live and work together, making all decisions democratically.

The herd as ideal community directly conflicts with
the old autocratic community in "Brush War at Buford."
The old community is represented by a big landowner
who is law unto himself. When Yates asks him whether
the law says he can do something, the landowner answers,
"That's right. The law around here does," then goes on to
explain that he is the law around there. The trail crew
eventually triumphs over this law, their victory being a
vindication of their own type of law and their own community.

Yates and the new trail crew represent a totally new
development in the Western. Favor, as autocratic coach,
owed a great deal to the lawman figures of the gun Western. Where Troop spoke of Laramie as "my town," Favor spoke of "his herd" and "his crew." Both had responsibility for a group of people and both ran things pretty
much as they saw fit. The difference is that in *Rawhide*
the group receives a bit more prominence than in the gun
Westerns. There is a move from individual to team, even
though the team is controlled by an individual. With Yates
it is the group, the community which becomes prominent.
The cowboy is no longer a free atomic individual, but the
member of a group. In some respects the Yates trail crew
evokes comparisons with the early horse Westerns. In
Yates' case it is the community with its own law and
morality which roams through the limitless space of the
West.

This theme of a community roaming the West is also

the main theme of *Wagon Train*, which once closed its episodes with the phrase "and it happened that way moving west." Like *Rawhide*, *Wagon Train* is run by a team, with the wagon master as absolute boss. Under him are a scout, the cook and an assistant. Yet the emphasis in *Wagon Train* is more on community than on the team idea of the *Rawhide* episodes with Favor. This sense of community is established from the beginning with the formation of the wagon train itself. Individuals and families contract with the wagon master and his crew to take them west. In this creation of the wagon train, they try to select the best crew—it's a Western election process with the best wagon master and crew continually getting the best contracts. In fact it's not unlike the old eighteenth-century contract theory of government which gave the people the right to contract with their rulers and break the contract if the ruler violated its terms. Eighteenth-century contract theorists argue over those terms and to what extent the people could break the contract, but in *Wagon Train* the terms are clear: the wagon master is the final authority and he has the final say in all matters relating to the welfare of the train. He has certain set rules—no gambling and no liquor and the people who contract to join the train must agree to abide by the rules if they wish to go west with him. They break the contract at their own risk.

There is some similarity between all these preliminary preparations and the preparations of *Rawhide*. In *Rawhide* a rancher contracts with the trail crew to move his cattle and accepts the authority of the trail boss in all decisions relating to the herd. On the surface *Wagon Train* merely substitutes people for cattle. The *Rawhide* crew moves cattle to the railhead, the *Wagon Train* crew moves people to California. All this similarity might seem more striking if *Wagon Train* concentrated on the wagon crew, ignoring the people on the train—treating them not unlike a herd. Then *Wagon Train* would seem much more a male-group, team-oriented show not unlike the Favor *Rawhide*'s. What makes *Wagon Train* more community-oriented and more like the Yates *Rawhide*'s is that even though the stars of the show are the wagon crew, the show focuses each week on a member of the train community— allowing the producers to make use of some high-powered guest stars. Where *Rawhide* episodes are about places on the trail and entitled "Incident at . . . " the *Wagon Train* episodes are about people and are entitled "The Link Chaney Story" or whoever happens to be the featured member of the train for that week.

A great many of these shows focus on conflicts—internal conflicts between members of the train, between members and the crew, and external conflicts against Indians, outlaws, natural forces. The Train's conflicts are not unlike the conflicts of Yates' *Rawhide*'s, except that where conflicts among members of the trail crew are usually sublimated into the great melting pot, the conflicts on *Wagon Train* are much more vicious. The contract is constantly threatened with dissolution, threatening the safety of the entire group.

One might see the *Wagon Train* crew itself as a microcosmic American government, with wagon master as President, the scout as Secretary of Defense and the cook and assistant as running various domestic departments. The wagon master is elected, serves a set term and is impossible to impeach except in the most difficult situations. Like presidents there has never been an impeached and ousted wagon master—they only die in office. Like their cabinet counterparts, the roles of the various secretaries are plainly advisory. The wagon master consults them and sometimes

Wagon Train with Ward Bond June 25, 1957

Wagon Train Ernest Borgnine (left), and Ward Bond

agrees and sometimes disagrees with them. Always the final decision belongs with the wagon master.

Perhaps of all the TV Westerns *Wagon Train* confronts most directly the basic political and philosophical problems of American society and the contract theory on which both are based. It raises questions about the individual's role in a community, about dissent, about the community's response to outside pressure, about how much authority the community should delegate to elected officials, about how much reliance should be put on experts, and about the relationship between the members of the "government." What *Wagon Train* does is take this microcosm of American society, this community and place it in a situation in which these conflicts are more crucial and more dangerous.

In all the episodes these conflicts are clearly resolved in favor of the community. As wagon master Seth Adams (Ward Bond) put it in a 1961 episode "The Nancy Palmer Story": "If all cooperate we'll make it all right." The *Wagon Train* community is founded on a mission—as wagon master Chris Hale (John McIntire) puts it, "to see that everyone on this wagon train gets safely to where they want to go." Like America the train has its Manifest Destiny, for West is where it wants to go. It is this mission that forms the bond of community among the people on the train. The point of Adams' remark is that they all do—or should—want to make it all right and they all want to make it to the same place, so they will cooperate. A lot of writing on social contract theory stresses this point, that a community must have a consensus on fundamentals or goals to keep that community from falling apart. In essence this consensus is what makes the community a community, at least in social contract theory. Sociologists and anthropologists no doubt would quarrel with this, since to them a community contains shared behavior patterns and mores that are more important than this consensus on fundamentals. What *Wagon Train* and America presuppose is that a community of diverse people can be formed on the basis of a consensus on fundamentals. This is the American dream and *Wagon Train*, the microcosm of America, is a microcosm of the American dream. In *Wagon Train* the dream triumphs.

The spirit of cooperation which supports this dream is always being attacked, but those who attack it on *Wagon Train* are clearly misguided. They are self-interested rather than community-interested. They place themselves and personal gain above the community and the welfare of the community. Although they may agree to the terms of the contract, they do not always understand the consequences of their actions. Some of these individuals state that they don't care if the train makes it to California as long as they themselves do. To the wagon crew this reasoning can lead only to disaster, for if all, or most, don't reach California nobody will. The community is plainly a protective device—a single wagon does not stand a chance, but a train does. Again this fits right into social contract theory, for social contract theorists like to assert that one of the primary reasons for the formation of the community and the contract was defensive. The nature of man in the state of nature was always the subject of controversy among social contract theorists. *Wagon Train* agrees with those who asserted that in the state of nature man is basically good, that bad men—men who threaten the community are the products of environmental causes rather than some innate evil. Even the Indians on *Wagon Train* are more in the noble savage stereotype than the "thieving, scalping redskin" of much of frontier literature. The misguided people who threaten the train, then, are capable of being converted, of being made to see the error of their reasoning, although this is not always the case.

In "The Nancy Palmer Story," Nancy and her husband join the train. They are rich people who have lost their money, and they resent the average people of the wagon train. Their bitterness is apparent when they speak of the people on the train and of their loss: "They're nobodies and their families are nobodies. How could they know what loss is. They never had anything to lose." In the early parts of the episode Nancy and her husband seem to be opposites. She is a favorite of all the children, everybody likes her, while her husband is a quick-tongued drinker. Nancy's relationship with the children allows her and her husband to assume the responsibility of watching over them while the people on the train go to town. It also gives them a chance to rob the train. They escape and are pursued by the wagon crew. Nancy's husband deserts her on the desert and tries to keep going. He dies, but she is rescued, gives back the money and everybody lives happily ever after. The moral is that Nancy was misguided in her attempt to steal the money and that this stemmed from her elitist upbringing. She thought she was above the people rather than one of them.

Another episode, "The Sam Pulaski Story," deals with a similar misguided individual in the classic East vs. West, city vs. country conflict. Pulaski is a small time Bowery crook. In the opening sequence he is shown in his Bowery haunts victimizing Coop, the scout, with the old "what are you doing with my wife" routine. Coop picks up a girl, who he assumes isn't married, but who is working for Pulaski; whereupon Pulaski busts in and tires to beat up Coop. Later he has Coop robbed. But pickings are getting slim on the Bowery—especially for small timers—

and Pulaski dreams of better territory. So off to California
he goes with his mother, sister, and gang on the wagon
train. Along the way the gang figures why not shake down
the train, which they try, only to get caught in the act. The
explanation for Pulaski's problem is that in the tough environment of the Bowery he had to turn to crime to support his mother and sister. He's just the opposite of Nancy
Palmer; he's never had enough. The East vs. West theme
is used to contrast the Bowery with the wagon train—the
ideal community with the community that is a community
in name only. In the Bowery law and order have broken
down; even cops are on the take. At one point one of
Pulaski's gang tires to pay off one of the wagon crew; after
all it's the thing to do. Not on the wagon train, though.
Pulaski's other problem with the train is that he does not
really agree on fundamentals, although he thinks he does.
When he tries to pay off the wagon crew it is plain that he
thinks the wagon community functions like the Bowery.
Only in the end does he realize his mistake, and like Nancy
Palmer he too is redeemed.

Although *Wagon Train* represents the American
Dream and does build its show around conflicts within
that dream, there are some serious cracks within its dream-
like facade.

One of these cracks is the nature of the community
itself. Unlike the *Rawhide* community which emphasizes
its melting pot aspects—even to the extent of including a
black in its cast—the *Wagon Train* community is lily white.
There are episodes with black guest stars, but these are the
exception. The nameless, faceless people who make up
the bulk of the train from week to week are all white. The
opening of the show, depicting the train moving west contains only white faces. *Wagon Train* is not really the ideal
community, it is the ideal WASP community.

Another problem deals with the community itself. In its episodes there is the suggestion that dissent is something that is perpetrated by misguided, deviant individuals. Nancy Palmer's problem is that she considers herself superior. In another sense that is Sam Pulaski's problem. Like American society *Wagon Train*'s community resolves the individual vs. society problem by appealing to the average. Those who consider themselves above average or different in some way are deviant and plainly a threat to the community. This has always been a heavy problem for Americans to resolve—as de Tocqueville aptly pointed out.

Wagon Train's solution is to ignore the problem. It assumes that everyone will want to be average—that only deviants want to be different. For all its stressing of individual members of the train, *Wagon Train is* a herd. It assumes people want to be part of a herd—that they will give up certain rights and certain aspects of their individuality in return for safety in numbers and conformity. This assumption is a radical departure from the basic theme of the horse Western, which found strength in the vision of a free individual living by his own moral code of right and wrong. For the Lone Ranger crossing the open frontier was something one did alone. The worst thing one could do was get in a position where he did not have control over his own destiny. Crossing the prairie alone was preferable to crossing it in a group, especially a group in which one delegated authority to a wagon master and his crew.

The final problem is an old one—the basic issue of human nature. *Wagon Train* rests on a benign theory of human nature, yet the events of the last thirty years suggest that this may be whistling in the dark. Traditionally the "man as evil" theory has been used by conservatives

as the basis for all kinds of strict governmental controls.
The Puritans were "man is evil" believers and set up a
society whereby those few who were good would have
absolute control over the community. Perhaps the burning problem of the second half of this century may be to
accept a "man as evil" philosophy without accepting the
strict government controls that go with it.

Both *Rawhide* and *Wagon Train* seem to grow out
of the gun Westerns and the 1950's and lead directly to
the property Westerns, the 1960's and Richard Nixon's
Manson speech. From the era of the lawman defending
the organization man, from the era of consensus history,
we move to programs glorifying the group and team
spirit while condemning dissenters, to programs which
glorify the big ranch and big ranchers or (as in *Gunsmoke*)
the town and its people. The lone cowboy with his code
must give way to law, then to the group and finally to the
settled town establishment.

In *Rawhide* and *Wagon Train* there is also a shift in
attitudes towards property and wealth that foreshadow
those of the property Westerns. In the gun Westerns the
man who is out to get more is looked down upon, in the
transition Westerns he becomes a threatening deviant like
Sam Pulaski and in the property Westerns this threat
shakes the very foundations of society.

The lawman, the organization man gives way to
shows named after the organization and to speeches that
ask "what can you do for your country." Seth Adams
and Gil Favor and John Kennedy ask not what you can
do for truth, justice and morality as did the Lone Ranger
or faith as did Harry Truman, but rather ask what can
you do for the trail crew, the wagon train, the organization, the country. True, Kennedy's Inaugrual did contain
rhetoric somewhat like Truman's, such as the famous sen-

tence about the torch being passed and the following
paragraph—"Let every nation know . . . that we shall
pay any price . . . oppose any foe to assure the survival
and the success of liberty." Yet for all this Kennedy
never spoke of a faith, a code like Truman. The emphasis one remembers, the phrase most associated with the
Kennedy speech is "ask not what your country can do
for you; ask what you can do for your country." The
group, the team, the country seems at once its own
justification and one doesn't ask *why* one should do
something for the group but *what* he should do for the
group. So when Jack Kennedy enlisted us in the Peace
Corps and sent the first of us off to what Hubert Humphrey would later call our "great adventure" in Vietnam,
many of us did not ask why we were going, we just went.
Those few souls who did ask why—and I must confess I
was not one of them—usually assumed that the why did
relate to truth, justice and morality. Some of us joined
the Peace Corps because it was what we could do for the
group and some of us joined because we believed that it
was to help poor persecuted people. There seemed little
difference at first, there seemed little difference in Jack
Kennedy's call and what Henry Fairlie called our "yearning for morality,"[1] there seemed little difference in Gil
Favor and Seth Adams' call and our yearning for morality. Yet as we were soon to see there was a difference
and those of us who followed the call for moral reasons
—who followed the *why*—would soon disagree with those
who followed the *what*. The generation raised on Roy
Rogers and the code would soon conflict with those
who glorified the group. Consensus history would become a yearning for consenses and finally emerge in
the bludgeon of a silent majority who despised dissent
as unAmerican. Jack Kennedy like Gil Favor, Rowdy

Yates, and Seth Adams seemed a knight on a white horse, leading us all through dangers to the promised land. Only too late did we realize the promised land was not what we thought it was—that the *what* we could do was more important than the *why*. Crusades—as so many have taught us—are dangerous things no matter who leads them. It happened that way, movin' West—west towards Vietnam.

Tales of Wells Fargo with Dale Robertson

The Chaparral is my kingdom and I'll make all the decisions for the best of everyone.

—John Cannon, The High Chaparral

When I first met you all, I couldn't believe it. The way you are, the way you care about each other. I guess I just wasn't used to it. You know the way I was always sayin' I wouldn't stay in the same spot very long. I was makin' out like I was gettin' ready to leave. I just never meant it, that's all.

—Candy, Bonanza, "To Die In Darkness" (1967)

The network may have cancelled a program but they can't cancel a way of life.

—Michael Landon

CHAPTER V

The Piece of Property:
Babbitt and Family Defend Law and Order

ON *WAGON TRAIN* THE COWBOY SOLD HIS HORSE, HUNG UP HIS gun, packed his gear, loaded it on a wagon and joined a group "heading west." He may have sacrificed some of his individuality, but he still maintained his mobility. The reasons for the decision varied from individual to individual. In some cases he temporarily sacrificed individuality in hopes of gaining it back at some future time and place. Maybe he was hoping to find once and for all a place where he could live without people moving in, settling down within hollering distance and disturbing his precious "elbow room." On the other hand maybe he had finally decided to settle down by himself on a small piece of homesteaded land and farm or raise cattle. As history and *Wagon Train* tell it a few did manage to find what they were looking for—whatever it was. *Wagon Train* may epitomize the American dream, but the real wagon train epit-

105

omized something else. Cooper was probably one of the first to see it. In *The Prairie* there is the realization that with the wagons must come the death of free roaming individualistic frontiersmen. As history tells it the wagon train was the beginning of the end for the cowboy, the scout, the mountain man, the individual. Yet the myth of the atomic individual roaming an endless virgin land has continued.

In 1959, with *Bonanza*, TV land began to catch up with history. As TV land tells it, what the free roaming cowboy did find was one hell of a big piece of property—big enough to keep the neighbors at a good distance—and settle down. He didn't settle down there alone, either. He settled down with his family and a few assorted ranch hands and founded a baronial estate which he named the Ponderosa, or *Lancer* or *The High Chaparral* or *The Big Valley*. One show gets named after a ranch foreman, *The Virginian*, but the error is corrected when the show becomes *The Men From Shiloh*.

It is with *Bonanza* in 1959 that we first meet what the producers of the show refer to as the fifth member of their cast—the symbol of this phase of the TV Western—the piece of property. The Ponderosa, the cattle kingdom of the Cartwright family, is given the place of importance formerly occupied by the horse and the gun. Reruns of *Bonanza* are even reissued and retitled *Ponderosa*. It is treated in the same fashion as the other symbols, even tending to take on anthropomorphic qualities. The prominence of the property symbol can be seen in the openings of these shows, all of which emphasize the connection between property and the stars who live on it. *Bonanza* begins with a map of the Ponderosa and Nevada, which burns away to reveal the Cartwright family riding across their land. Over time the opening has shifted emphasis

from the property to the domestic activities of the Cartwrights, showing them doing various ranch jobs, but the
map is still featured. *The Big Valley* has several scenic
shots of what obviously looks like a very, very big valley,
cutting to shots of the Barkley family. On *Lancer*, the
Lancer brand forms a matte on the land and the members
of the cast. It's as though men and land were all branded
Lancer. *The Virginian* uses a shot of all the members of
the cast riding together along some road that looks like it
might be on the Shiloh Ranch.

There is also an interesting conjunction between the
symbol and sponsor of *Bonanza*, for the sponsor is General Motors—the world's biggest piece of property. The
affinity of the sponsor with the piece of property is demonstrated by the Chevy commercial in which the Chevy
sign burns into the map of Nevada and the Ponderosa,
just as the Ponderosa burns into the map at the beginning
of the show. The Western hero has corralled his horse and
hung up his gun for a piece of property, which in General
Motors' world isn't a bad trade.

The piece of property is also a major figure in a host
of other Westerns which dominated the tube during the
late sixties. *The Virginian, Lancer, The Big Valley,* and
The High Chaparral all featured huge expanses of property on the same scale as the Ponderosa, and television
land, in its own queer way, has placed each of these huge
ranches in a different state. It is as if the producers so
believed in the reality of their creations that they had to
be sure to put only one Ponderosa in Nevada, *The Virginian* (Shiloh) in Wyoming, *The High Chaparral* in Arizona,
The Big Valley in California.

Besides their fixation with cattle barons, these shows
all emphasized groups as opposed to the individual. After
all, it takes several people to run an estate. Their use of

The Virginian (left to right) Roberta Shore, Clu Gulager, Doug McClure, Randy Boone, James Drury and Lee J. Cobb sitting

The Virginian "When You Say That, Smile!" (left to right)
Roberta Shore, Doug McClure, Lee J. Cobb, James Drury
and Anne Francis

The High Chaparral (left to right) Linda Cristal, Leif Erickson, Mark Slade and Cameron Mitchell

Bonanza (left to right) Dan Blocker, Pernell Roberts, Michael Landon, Lorne Greene

Bonanza "Clarissa" (left to right) Michael Landon, Loren Greene and Dan Blocker

Bonanza "The Bride" (left to right) Michael Landon, Lorne
Green, Dan Blocker, Suzanne Lloyd and Pernell Roberts

the group is not unlike that of the *Rawhide*s with Favor
as trail boss, for in almost all of these shows it is a male
group dominated by an autocratic leader—or maybe one
should say ruler. The only exception is *Big Valley* whose
ruler is a woman, Barbara Stanwyck. Several of the shows
—*The Virginian, Lancer, The High Chaparral*—have female
cast members who are either the daughters of the owner,
his wife (*Chaparral*), or in *Lancer* his ward. To paraphrase
the female star of *Lancer*, most of them seem added as
much to demonstrate the "normality" of the male stars as
for any obvious reason—especially since all most of them
do is sit around and look pretty. The father-figure implications of the autocrat-male group relationship are quite
prominent in *Bonanza, The High Chaparral,* and *Lancer,*
with their father-son motifs. The fact that the sons—or
in the case of *Chaparral*, the brothers—are in their twenties and thirties sometimes leads to absurd situations, with
thirty-year-old men bowing to the father and saying "yes
pa," "no pa." Pernell Roberts, who played Adam Cartwright on *Bonanza*, said that occasionally when an auto-
graph hunter would tell him that Adam was her favorite
character, he couldn't resist saying, "Thanks, but don't
you think there's something strange about the fact that
I'm 36 years old and still tag around after my father asking, 'What do we do now, Pa?' "[1] In the case of the
brother-brother relationship in *The High Chaparral* even
weirder things happen. The autocratic head of the Chaparral, "Big" John Cannon, has a brother named Buck who
is supposedly in his thirties but is treated as much like a
teenage son as a brother. In an episode entitled "No Bu-
gles, No Drums," this relationship leads a little girl to ask
the question, "Is John Cannon your daddy?" Buck's
answer defines his relationship with brother John, "Sometimes he's my daddy, but most of the time he's my big

brother.''

The Western hero may have settled down, but he
still is far, far from attaining adult sexual maturity.
Whereas in the horse Westerns he was a boy and in the
gun Westerns a pre-adolescent, here he at least acknowledges that women exist, although his acknowledgment
tends to be on an adolescent level. The sons of Ben Cartwright, John Cannon, Murdoch Lancer, and Co. go wenching—or at least go through the motions of it and once in
awhile fall head over heels for some virginal creature—like
a junior high school boy over a high school cheerleader,
or some movie star or the girl next door. The girls who
are on the receiving end of these adolescent crushes almost
always come to some horrible, unexpected end. It's as if
occasionally some beautiful young virgin is selected to be
sacrificed to preserve the male group and the good fortune
of that hallowed piece of property. As for the wenching,
it's all usually quite innocent: mostly looking and perhaps
a kiss—like some kid with his first *Playboy* or on the first
big date where he hopes to "make out." Only Manolito
of *Chaparral* makes a regular habit of wenching, but, of
course, Manolito's the old stereotype of the hot Latin, so
with him it's O.K. There are times when Pa, too, has his
affairs. After all sexually he's not an adolescent—those
kids had to come from somewhere. But while junior's just
beginning to "feel his oats," Pa's past his prime and so his
affairs are just as innocent. Of course the objects of Pa's
affairs end up the same place as junior's—the graveyard.
There is something quite striking about the fate of all
these female love objects. It seems to suggest that the
Western acknowledges the connection between sex and
death which has intrigued psychologists and formed the
grist for so much good and bad poetry. Perhaps it was
because of this TV land connection between love and

death that the hero of the horse Western avoided women
like the plague and saved his strength and shots for the
baddie. But why? After all it is the woman who ends up
in the grave. Is it some crazy justice that sacrifices women
and lets the men go free? The solution to this question
may lie in the fact that in these property Westerns it is the
hero who has the crush on the girl, rather than vice versa
as it was in the horse and gun Westerns. Here women
seem to exercise some irrational power over men, sending
them swooning like a scene from a bad story in a Hollywood fan magazine or an afternoon soap opera. In the
gun and horse Westerns the girl fell all over the hero, who
ignored her or tried to explain why she must not chase
him. In the end the girl may have stood with tears in her
eyes, watching the hero ride into the setting sun, but at
least she was alive and would soon get over her girlish
crush. In the property Westerns it is the hero who stands
with tears in his eyes, hat in his hand, head hanging as the
setting sun silhouettes him standing over his love's grave-
stone. Clearly a woman with this kind of irrational power
cannot be permitted to live. The woman of the gun Westerns was the girl or the good-bad girl; here she is the cas-
trating female. Like some Western version of a medieval
priest or knight of the grail, the hero's power is directly
related to his celibacy. To be a man, in the TV Western,
is not to be a man.

The virgin land of endless space also survives in mod-
ified form in the piece of property. The piece of property
may not be endless space, but it is as close as you can get.
If the Western hero had to settle down, it is best that he
settle down on as spacious and virgin a piece of land as
possible. Certainly the Ponderosa is so huge as to make
the notion of closed space seem absurd. The land, like
the hero, retains its virginity, for although the hero may

cut down a few trees, feed a few cattle and maybe do some mining, the land stays relatively untouched. In fact, one of the mysteries of these property Westerns is how the land barons manage to make a living. Perhaps like some of today's big landowners, they make it on government subsidies paid not to grow or raise anything.

Yet it is true that the virgin land myth has received quite a jolt from the property Westerns. The free roaming Lone Rangers who wandered over an endless space seeking wrongs to right have become cattle barons who control huge pieces of property. The space of the piece of property may be huge but it is closed space just the same and the magnitude of the change from infinite to damn big is tremendously important.

That the change is an uneasy one is suggested by the variety of devices used in the property Western to get the hero off that piece of property and once more roaming the open spaces. The land barons, their family and/or their ranch hands are sometimes called away on "business trips." Where once the cowboy's excuse for roaming—for being a lone ranger—was his duty to bring justice to the West, now the excuse of the patriarch of the Ponderosa is that he must bring more business to the piece of property. Then there is the annual round-up and cattle drive, where miraculously ten or fifteen ranch hands and thousands of cattle appear on a land which previously had been barren of all but the ranch house occupied by the stars. Another device is to focus on the various new settlers who are always moving into, and just as quickly out of, the area around the big cattle empires—sometimes causing problems for the owners of the property on the other side of that long, long barbed wire fence. These new settlers allow the cattle kings to solve the problems of peasants and reward their good deeds with water and grazing rights and perhaps if they're really good to give them some no longer needed piece of the estate. In the old Westerns a good man was rewarded with the knowledge that justice had triumphed and maybe a percentage of the payroll or the collective appreciation of the people he had saved. Now he gets rewarded with a piece of the Ponderosa. You too can own a piece of the rock—if you're good.

Of all the property Westerns it is *The Virginian* which appears most stretched by the limitations of its landed status. Perhaps this is because it does not have the family orientations of the other shows (two of the stars of *The Virginian* are ranch hands) which allow the other shows to resort to episodes and plots that make them seem at their worst, more like situation comedies than Westerns. *The Virginian* is in itself a strange creation, for although it makes much of its debt to the novel in its title, its star and its press releases, readers of the novel would scarcely recognize the show as having any connection at all with the book. The Virginian himself has settled down and become the foreman of a big ranch, Shiloh, while the baddie, Trampas (to whom the Virginian uttered the phrase "smile when you say that") has become a ranch hand and pal of the Virginian. The TV Trampas seems to be perpetually smiling, as he is played as a happy-go-lucky cowboy looking for fun and laughs. In order to get the Virginian—he still has that name, only it sounds funny when you hear him called that two or three times in an episode—and Trampas off the ranch and out into the open spaces, *The Virginian* makes a great deal of use of the flashback, more so than any Western I've seen, property or otherwise. It's as though the producers of this particular property Western were so unsure of their "package" that they are continually turning the clock back to the days of the gun Western, the days when their oddly named star was a gunfighter. *The Virginian* also has a "thing" for the old stage coach routine—put one or two members of the cast in a stagecoach with an assortment of characters and make like the old John Ford movie. Needless to say, it doesn't come off too well, especially when the show is shown in nightly reruns and you see this routine twice in five days. *The Virginian* appears to have TV Western schizophrenia, trying to be gun Western, property Western and an hour and a half movie all rolled into one. Things get a little better when the show becomes *The Men From Shiloh*—at least technically. Yet it is still unsure of itself. Where *The Virginian* was more about Shiloh than the Virginian, *The Men From Shiloh* is more about the men than Shiloh. Each episode features someone in the cast who is usually involved in a situation having nothing to do with Shiloh and rarely taking place on the ranch.

Lancer is not unlike *The Virginian* in that it too has a former outlaw-gunfighter as a member of the Lancer family. Johnny Madrid is now Johnny Lancer; the gunfighter has become a big estate owner, the kind of man he once fought, while the other son, Scott, is a New Englander who adds culture. All this enables the *Lancer* producers to send the two Lancer boys to opposite ends of the country. Paul Brinegar, who played Wishbone the cook on *Rawhide*, is now Jelly, a glorified hired hand. The Lancer family might be seen as an attempt to show in a family the same community one found on *Rawhide*, only here it is a father and his sons on a big piece of property, all stamped with a brand in the opening: the Lancer seal of approval. Where once the Western hero boasted that no one would put a brand on him, in the *Lancer* opening it happens literally as well as figuratively.

The High Chaparral emphasizes the fact that it is in a

primitive area—an area divided between the Mexican
Montoyas and the Cannons. What they don't control is
controlled by the Apaches, with whom Cannon has signed
an uneasy peace treaty. *Chaparral*, in fact, seems more
like a kingdom than any of the other shows. Cannon signs
treaties, enforces his own laws and even concludes an ar-
ranged marriage with Montoya's daughter, thus uniting
the two kingdoms like some European feudal alliance. Fittingly both Cannon and Montoya run their kingdoms like
feudal monarchs, commanding absolute obedience from
family as well as ranch hands. The primitive location of
the Chaparral at least allows for more plot development
that actually takes place on the piece of property. What's
more it allows the producers to include many Indian stories,
something lacking in the other Westerns.

The Big Valley is the conglomerate of the lot, for it
has a mine, grapes for wine, and an orchard of oranges,
as well as cattle. The conglomerate nature of the Barkley
holdings enable the producers to create episodes around
everything from the Molly Maguires and the Barkley mine,
to gypsies and the Barkley grapes, to a feud with a neigh-
boring rancher over the harvesting of the Barkley oranges.
In contrast to the Cannon house, which is an adobe and
wood structure with rustic furniture, the Barkley house
is a white pillared structure that looks like a Southern
mansion. In fact, in addition to its Victorian furnishings
and the best in wine, books, and china, the Barkley mansion comes complete with a uniformed black servant who
does everything except say yes, massa. As a family the
Barkleys are perhaps the most mature of all the cattle barons. The head of the operation, or at least its senior member, is Victoria Barkley, played by Barbara Stanwyck. While
Victoria Cannon (if you're wondering why so many female
property stars are named Victoria, as I did, what better

name for the female head of a cattle kingdom?) attends mostly to domestic chores, Victoria Barkley is more than a match for any man. At the opening of the show she is shown riding a horse in a way that would put may of TV's male cowboys to shame. The three male Barkleys, Heath, Nick, and Jarrod, attend to much of the day to day operation of the ranch, with family decisions being made democratically rather than autocratically, like the Cannons or the Cartwrights. Victoria Barkley also has a daughter named Audra, who like the *Lancer* ward and Judge Garth's daughter (*The Virginian*) spends most of her time smiling and looking pretty.

Bonanza, the longest running of the property shows, tries to put itself in direct contrast to the undercurrent of elitism that characterizes *The Big Valley*. The thing about the Cartwrights is that they're the middle class of the property owners. They're not *The Big Valley* nor are they *The High Chaparral*. The Cartwright house, like the Cannon's, is a large log structure that is furnished with sturdy wooden furniture. Only its interior suggests that its owners are a bit more refined than the Cannons, but not as aristocratic as the Barkleys. There are a few overstuffed chairs, a few Grant Woodish landscapes hanging on the wall, a big fireplace, a gunrack, and a few—but not too many— books, some probably from the Reader's Digest. Cartwright may offer his guests brandy, but he doesn't serve it in the delicate crystal of the Barkleys, maybe because he's afraid Hoss'll break it all. Besides he doesn't have a black servant to serve it; all he has is a Chinese cook. (It's funny the way these property Westerns have minority domestics, just like the folks in Grosse Pointe.) Of all the property owners it is the Cartwrights who seem to have the least visible means of support. Other than the Cartwright family, which seems to do everything but work, the only other regular worker on the ranch is cook-domestic Hop Sing. Not only are there no ranch hands, but there doesn't seem much else on the Ponderosa except a lot of open space.

Over the years *Bonanza* has undergone a great change in its basic orientation. In the earliest episodes everything is much more rustic and primitive. Virginia City is a raw frontier town with a number of drunken, brawling cowboys and the Ponderosa itself seems to have been just homesteaded. The log house is more rough-hewn and its interior does not contain the books, pictures and other assorted bric-a-brac of the later episodes. The relationships between the Cartwrights, their neighbors and the town of Virginia City are quite strained, sometimes breaking out into open conflict. In one early episode, "Enter Mark Twain" (1959), the Cartwrights are called the "fighting Cartwrights" and their general nature seems to be more pugnacious and less refined than it is today. "Mark Twain," for example, opens with a fight sequence between the Cartwright brothers, who are in the process of tearing up a bar. The attitude of the Cartwrights towards the Ponderosa is much more paranoid. The fighting Cartwrights seem to expend what energy they don't use in tearing up bars and each other, in patrolling the boundaries of the Ponderosa and chasing away the squatters, who seem to keep turning up. In the original episode of *Bonanza* the Cartwright family rides off at the end laughing, drinking and singing the words to the themesong of the show—"If anyone fights with one of us he's gotta fight with me."

In later episodes the connection between the town and the Cartwrights becomes much closer. The town itself has become larger, less rowdy. Where in the early episodes the marshal tells people to mind their own business,

it now seems everybody knows everybody and does mind
everybody's business. When the early marshal had a live
and let live attitude, allowing people—including the Cartwrights—to engage in fights, the later town is much straight-
er. The marshal is more impotent and the force of public
opinion seems stronger. Virginia City is characterized by
a booster attitude, pushing its rivalry with other towns
while its leading citizens throw balls and parties and run
off to San Francisco. The Cartwright ranch is not as emphasized—as the change in the openings shows—and the
family is not as paranoic about squatters. The log house
becomes more ornate; paintings and books are added. The
tie between town and the Cartwrights is now quite close,
in fact Ben is one of—if not *the* leading citizen of the town.
They are no longer the "fighting Cartwrights," but the
well-known, well-liked Cartwrights. Ben is the pre-eminent
joiner—going to meetings of some Chamber of Commerce
type group called the Nevada Club. Speaking of Ben Cartwright in a 1969 episode "Ride in the Sun," one outlaw
says, "He's also a joiner. Belongs to lodges. Never misses
a meeting." Where once the cowboy never set foot in a
town if he could avoid it, where once even the Cartwrights
had an uneasy relationship with a raw frontier town, now
they go to lodge meetings there. Virginia City has become
Main Street and the cowboy has become Babbitt.

This close tie with the town has been paralleled by
Bonanza's use of topical, "relevant" plots for many episodes. Conservation, long hairs, even elections come in
for treatment. An episode entitled "The Last Vote" deals
with a town election in Virginia City taking up the larger
issue of campaign managing and image creating which is
becoming the bane of today's elections. In the episode
Hoss and Joe undertake to manage the campaigns of two
good friends. In the course of this campaigning, slogan-

eering and false speech making, they manage to turn the town and the friends into two warring camps. All through the episode Ben keeps saying, "That's the American way." Townsman: "Nothing but eggin' folks on to tearing the town apart. . . ." Ben: "You're seeing healthy dissent in an election." Townsman: "I'm not." Ben: "Keeps our country strong. It's the American way." The implication is that hotly contested elections serve to divide the people and cause trouble because they threaten the great common consensus. The people are actually one, big happy community where dissent encourages divisiveness. It could be a speech by any of a host of politicians urging unity, etc. In this episode conservative conformity— which fits right into Ben's membership in the Nevada Club —is stressed. Yet in other episodes the show has treated some very controversial subjects in a controversial manner. An episode entitled "Pursued" (1966) deals with Mormon polygamy in a sympathetic fashion. Of course, the Mormons also own a big piece of property. However the mood of most of *Bonanza*'s "relevant" episodes seems to be more like that of "The Last Vote" than "Pursued."

Being landowners, upstanding citizens and members of the town's most important club, the Cartwrights, as well as the stars of the other property Westerns find the old isolated free-roaming individual an anachronism. After all he doesn't belong to any clubs, doesn't own any property; he doesn't even stay with any one job for very long. An anachronism—especially one who once was so important—can cause varied reactions from attempts at conversion—"settle down," to pity—"I feel sorry for you," to fear—"how can you trust a man with no roots?"

A *Bonanza* episode, "Yonder Man," deals with the return of one of these old individualists, an old friend of Ben's. Beaudry is dressed in buckskins, with a moustache

and unshaven face—he's been a trapper, a soldier, almost
everything. As Ben puts it he's "that yonder man looking
for the mountain over the next rise." That mountain, says
Beaudry, will have "wild running deer, a cold stream full
of trout, green grass so tender a man could eat." Beaudry
admits he's a "yonder man. When I move I might not be
coming back for some time." As he puts it, "Nobody
puts a brand on Beaudry. I got things to do and places to
see and I aim to be free and I got no need, for nobody."
But Beaudry and his kind know that they're a vanishing
breed. Beaudry talks about settling down, starting a ranch
not unlike the Ponderosa. "The world's squeezing down,"
he says. "Every man's entitled to at least one victory. You
had yours, you made it work." Ben answers, "Well, sweat
made it work, that and the need to settle down." Later
Beaudry meets an old friend who's now wearing a badge
and the friend asks, "Beau ain't you never gonna learn?
. . . Times change." He goes on to advise, "You better
make your peace, Beaudry, ain't no runnin' room left these
days." When Beaudry interjects that once, together, they
"tamed a few towns," Stryker answers, "Those were the
old times, the good times. Now all I got is a war bag full
of memories, and this here badge." Now all he's got is a
job. Beaudry, of course, can't change and rides off still
looking; an anachronism riding into a setting sun.

   Beaudry is portrayed here sympathetically. There is
no condescension or false pity for him. He is not asked to
become Babbitt and settle down, nor is he driven away by
a world he can no longer understand. In "Yonder Man"
there is no tension between the old individual and the new
settled group, but there is a reason for this. Notice that
when it comes down to it, Beaudry and Ben accept the
same values—that Beaudry concedes that Ben has made it
and he hasn't. Beaudry is more than a tragic figure—he is

not the man Ben is—for what the episode does is to show that the new property cowboy is better than the old individual. Beaudry may be a hell of a man, but Ben is even more so.

Beaudry, with his buckskins and his acceptance of Ben Cartwright's values is no threat, no problem for the owners of the piece of property. Not all individualists are like Beaudry and these do cause problems. What if the individualist wears a floppy hat with the brim down, a shirt open at the neck, and work pants? What if he doesn't want to be a joiner, but still wants to work his small piece of property right next to the big piece of property? An example of this kind of individualist is Justin in a *Virginian* episode entitled "The Nobility of Kings" (1965).

The opening of this episode is a classic confrontation involving the big ranch owners of the Cattlemen's Association with the struggling little rancher. The dispute is over branding mavericks and the cattlemen are not about to concede to the small man. Just a spot for the Lone Ranger to ride in in the nick of time to rescue the small rancher from the greedy cattlemen. Right? Wrong. In this case the cattlemen are the good guys. Only you wouldn't know it from the dialogue. Trampas, a co-star, "According to Stockman's Association rules . . . ." Justin, "I don't care what your association says." Tom Touchette, rancher, "Next time I might show him what happens to hot-eyed strangers who think they're bigger than the Association." Pretty tough talk, huh? Where's the Cisco Kid when we need him most? Later the Virginian himself explains to the poor rancher's wife about the stockmen. "Our Stockman's Association's got certain rules and regulations. A man brands a maverick before round up he could be blackballed. That means

he can't ship his beef out at the Association railhead at
Cheyenne; I wouldn't want to see that happen to your
husband." Sounds like a speech just made for Butch
Cavendish or Black Bart or some nefarious baddie. Here's
the big man threatening the little man with blackballing,
yet here it's the star of the show mouthing all these threats.
The tables have been completely turned, the cattlemen's
association is the good guys, and as for the poor landowner, well. . . . The poor landowner's a bit fuzzy in
the head, that's his problem. Should've known it by the
floppy hat he was wearing. As he says himself he's weak,
needs a bottle to build up his courage. As his wife describes him: "My husband likes to do things without anybody's help," so his wife falls for the Virginian. Actually
Justin's not a bad sort, he only wants to have a big ranch
of his own just like Shiloh. He just doesn't trust the cattlemen's association. Maybe he's seen too many Roy
Rogers movies. He's not a free roamer like Beaudry, for
he values land ownership above everything. "As long as
he owns his own spread," he says, "runs his own beef, he
can walk with the nobility of kings."

Those kings, the cattlemen, are basically good guys
who want to help Justin—as long as he joins the association and abides by its rules, so they invite Justin to one
of their meetings. Justin walks in the door to a jaycees
convention—young well-groomed men in coats and ties,
waiting to tap the keg. A shot of the cattlemen's hats all
hanging on pegs around a mirror says it all: We're all together and we're all the same. Mirror, mirror on the wall
. . . The Cisco Kid's sombrero would look out of place
here and what about the Lone Ranger? you can't see him
when he looks in the mirror. Is he one of us or isn't he—
his physical appearance tells the whole story.

Ultimately Justin gives in to the cattlemen, accepting

their help. The individual has become Babbitt. He joins—
on their terms and they accept him as one of the guys.
Maybe now he'll get rid of that floppy hat. Of course the
whole show never raises the question of what happens
when there's not enough land and the cattlemen's association controls what's left. Maybe the fate of the Lone
Ranger and Tonto is that they'll end up on welfare.

The Virginian's prejudice against individuals is especially strong against those whom he styles with the
epithet "drifter." Roy Rogers and the Sons of the Pioneers back in their movie days sang songs about "drift-
ing along with the tumbling tumbleweed." That was once
the image of the cowboy, but now a drifter is a vagrant,
because he has no roots, no ties, no loyalties except to
himself and that makes him potentially dangerous. As the
Virginian puts it, "He's a drifter, no sense of loyalty.
Can't depend on men like that." It used to be a man's
word was as good as, well. . . . Now it's who you know,
what you look like.

Murdoch Lancer, on the other hand, pities the old
individualist. When an old friend, to whom Murdoch once
offered a 50% share in the ranch, returns to find the Lancer
family now owns the ranch, he breaks the law. Murdoch's
analysis of the situation is "when a man's alone, when he's
got nothing, there's probably no one to have faith in him.
Maybe then he loses faith in himself."

The gunman—remember him?—another old individualist returns to haunt *The Big Valley* in two episodes,
"The Death Merchant" (1966) and "Image of Yesterday"
(1967). Both seem explicit attacks on the old legend of
the gunman for hire—even when he hires himself to the
forces of good (shades of Paladin). "Image of Yesterday,"
with its suggestive title, details how a group of professional
gunmen are hired to protect the ranchers and end up loot-

ing and destroying the community. Say the gunmen,
"We prefer to think of ourselves as protectors, just like
soldiers." Says Victoria Barkley, "It's not the same;
soldiers fight for what they believe in." The gunmen
don't believe in anything and so they can't be trusted.
Ultimately the Barkleys are able to evict them, with the
help of an ex-confederate—a soldier. In "The Death Merchant," the gunman is fittingly named Handy Ransom.
He uses an old shotgun filled with nails and hires himself
out for money after he has started a cattle war or sheep
war or, in the Barkley's case, an orchard war. What we
need, say the Barkleys, is not more gunmen but more soldiers. What we need says the Virginian is not more drifters but more members of the Cattlemen's Association.
What we need says Ben Cartwright is not more yonder
men, but more members of the Nevada Club.

   What we don't need, they all say, is more deviants—
and that's where the baddie comes in. The rugged individualist may be an anachronism, there may be times when
he can't be trusted, but usually he is not a baddie. The
baddie is a different sort. The baddie of the property
Western is almost identical to the baddie of the gun Westerns. He is still the deviant. You can spot him fairly
quickly—it may be his dress (too fancy or too messy), his
unshaven face or his bad grammar that gives him away.
Like the baddie of the gun Westerns he is an over-reacher.
If he is poor he wants to be rich. If he is rich he wants to
be richer. He's never content with what he has. In the
property Western all of this has obvious implications, because most of the time what the baddie is after is that
piece of property. In an abstract sense he is after power,
but power is almost always defined in monetary terms.
Power is a big bank account, a big piece of property.

   In its view of the baddie and his problem the property Westerns vacillate between the idea of evil as innate and the idea of evil as produced by one's background. In a *Virginian* episode, "Strangers at Sundown," the baddie is clearly innately evil. He even admits it himself: "There's a difference between them in there and us out here. . . . In there . . . is people. Not us. We walk and we talk; even look like people, but we ain't. I mean there's not a one of us wouldn't cut the other's throat and not think anything about it. And when you get to that, well, livin' and dyin' it just doesn't mean the same as it does to people." He concludes by saying, "What I'm saying is this. They're people and them in there they got a reason for living. And they're not about to get themselves killed for scum." In this view of the baddie, this self-analysis, the baddie is not only innately evil, he's subhuman and we all know it's easier to kill someone or send him to admittedly bad prisons when you believe he's subhuman. In the *Bonanza* episode, "To Die in Darkness" (1967) the baddie is plainly the victim of his environment. He has been sent to prison for a crime he didn't commit, in part because of Ben Cartwright's testimony. He returns a bitter man and traps Ben and Candy in a pit in an old mine—to show Ben what prison was really like. In the end Ben is rescued when the man admits what he has done. As for those baddies who are also poor and who covet the piece of property, they might also be seen as victims of their poverty—but the property Western doesn't always see it that way. In a *Bonanza* episode called "False Witness" (1967) someone says to Joe Cartwright, "Your father owns the biggest ranch in Nevada. I'll bet you never wanted anything you didn't have." Joe answers, "There are lots of people who wanted things they never had, but they didn't kill innocent people to get them."

The good men, the property Western seems to say,

stay in their station just like the good men in the gun
Western. There's nothing wrong with being a bartender,
said lawman Dan Troop, and a *Bonanza* episode, "The
Reluctant Rebel" (1965), echoes Troop's remarks in a
story about a pig farmer named Penn and his son, Billy.
Billy isn't too happy, especially when people call them
Pig Penns, so he joins a gang of young juvenile delin-
quents who terrorize the town. Basically, though, Billy
is a good boy—he just runs with the wrong bunch—and in
the end he joins his father in fighting off the gang. The
entire episode seems to echo Hank Penn's philosophy,
"Son, somebody's gotta raise pigs." Yes, somebody does
have to raise pigs, but pig farmers are not the stars of the
show, the big ranchowners are and they are portrayed as
paragons—kings as *The Virginian* would have it. In a
carry-over of the Puritan idea of the gun Western, the
man with the biggest piece of property is also the most
virtuous. Not a bad show to sponsor if you're G. M.

The good man, though, is even more than that. He
also dresses and behaves with decorum. A *Big Valley*
episode, "Pursuit" (1966), shows this aspect of the good
man most dramatically. In this episode Victoria Barkley
and Simon Carter, a shabbily dressed buffalo hunter who
drinks out of an everpresent bottle, track down an Indian
who has measles and is threatening to infect, and perhaps
wipe out an entire tribe. Carter isn't too keen on saving
them, figuring it's best to let the Indians kill each other.
He and Victoria quarrel over going after the Indian and
over the differences in their backgrounds. Carter doesn't
think much of himself, says that until he was ten he
thought his name was "no-account." Victoria asks if he
ever did anything to disprove it. "Why should I? and
don't tell me that stuff about for my self-respect. Because I don't believe none of that." Of course he really

does believe it, after all don't all good people? and he only needs to be convinced which, of course, he is. The final sequence of the episode shows him clean shaven, wearing a white hat (where have we heard that before?) and clean clothes. He makes a move to go into the bar and then stops and toasts Victoria with a canteen. The implication is that good people dress just like everyone else. People without self-respect don't wear white hats. At least in this sense the Lone Ranger might qualify for membership in the Nevada Club or the Cattlemen's Association. But maybe he ought to get rid of that mask and as for Tonto, well. . . .

The owners of the piece of property and the producers of these shows are not so secure about their status though; in fact in many episodes they are pretty worried about their piece of real estate. In that 1959 *Bonanza* episode "Enter Mark Twain," the Cartwrights spend half their time chasing people off their land. Says one squatter, "I'm just passing through." Says Joe, "Well, next time you go around, you hear?" That might be quite an order where the Ponderosa's involved. Later another squatter says it's "kind of hard to figure where your property ends and the world begins," since the Cartwrights own so much land. Joe answers, "Well if you have any trouble . . . we'll be happy to show you. . . . The next time you want to know where the rest of the world begins you might try asking." The Cartwrights apparently have the final say in such matter. This theme continues right up through recent shows. Although the Cartwrights' community status makes them less paranoid about squatters, in "Yonder Man," for example, Beaudry is ordered off the ranch by Joe Cartwright. The other property owners are not as perturbed as the Cartwrights, but still they plainly have moments of concern about their status. This

concern stems from a basic question: if we are not to
advocate cutting down the size of the Ponderosa, if we
are not to advocate land distribution, if we are not to
advocate taking over the property for ourselves and yet
we are convinced that we live in a land where, as Ben
Cartwright has said, it is possible for all of us to perhaps
own a Ponderosa, where, in fact, the motivation which
drove Ben Cartwright to acquire his piece of property is
treasured as a positive value—how are we to own our Pon-
derosas? Apparently the producers maintain that in fact
it can be done. Countless episodes show people making
it on a scrubby piece of land, although none of them make
it as big as Ben Cartwright and Co., and their success lasts
only one episode. In the infinite space of the mythic virgin land this problem does not exist, but what does one
do in a finite space where even advertisers and TV executives admit there is only room enough for one "Ponderosa" in each state? Well, at the moment Oregon, Idaho,
Washington, Utah and Montana are available. But where
are the Oregons and Washingtons in the automobile industry? The steel industry?

In the states already occupied by the big pieces of
property there has been a change in the value system of
the TV Western. The decline of the abstract value system
noted in the adult Western has now reached the point
where there really are no more abstract values. In the
place of values the property Western invokes a desire for
law 'n' order. The new heroes are constantly evoking "the
Law" but it is a strange law they invoke. Where in the
"adult" Western law and morality attached themselves to
roles, here the value of law 'n' order becomes linked with
property and institutions and law 'n' order becomes a
veiled defense of the status quo.

In the property Western the sheriff, the lawman who

was the key figure of the gun Western, returns to the
status he held in the early horse Western. The sheriff is
an impotent figure, unable to enforce the law in his own
town without the help of the property owners and the
townspeople. In a *Bonanza*, "The Night Virginia City
Died," a firebug terrorizes the town, so the lawman asks
Ben for help. "I been wearin' this badge for a lot of years
now and I can handle robberies and rustling and a lot of
other things, but . . . when it comes to a firebug I'm . . .
I'm just in trouble, Ben. I could use your help, Ben." Of
course he does. All this would seem normal except that
Roy has asked for Ben's help on a number of other occasions. On those occasions when Ben and the sheriff ride
together, they are usually shown side by side or with Ben
in front. Once in awhile the sheriff leads, but Ben is never
far behind. In "Amigo" there is a shot of Ben and the
sheriff, side by side, with the camera positioned so that
Ben is in a superior position. So property supports law
or is it vice versa?

The issue is complicated by the property Western's
own schizophrenia on the law 'n' order issue. In the
towns closest to and most involved with the property
owner, law 'n' order is stressed. What is law 'n' order?
What law 'n' order means for the property Western is that
the courts and the law must be upheld, no matter what.
There are no exceptions. This attitude is all wrapped up
in a phrase that continually crops up in the property Westerns—"He must go to trial. He's got to serve his time."
The sense of mercy that one found in the horse Westerns
is gone. Now, even if a man has done something to re-
deem himself, he has to go to trial. If he has committed
a crime—no matter how small—he must go to jail. (Shades
of George Jackson and ten years for a $67 robbery or the
Texas judge who sentenced a marijuana dealer to 20 years.)

The Cartwrights are not above bringing in friends when they have to. In "The Night Virginia City Died," Joe goes out to bring in a neighbor, "Bringin' the law here. I thought you were a friend of mine." Joe says he is, but what kind of friend would offer to go out and bring someone in before finding out his side of the story?

In the 1967 *Big Valley* episode, "Image of Yesterday," the tie between big ranchers and law is even more explicit. The ranchers have hired gunmen to protect them, since the sheriff is unable to. The gunmen terrorize the town and people complain, but one ranch owner tells the sheriff to lay off the gunmen. Ultimately the whole episode becomes a battle for power between the gunmen and the ranchers. The sheriff is impotent, he can do nothing without the ranchers because he has no power.

This is ultimately what the property Western sees as the basis for law—sheer power. Sheriffs are impotent, have no power without people like big landowners to back them up. This law becomes law 'n' order when it is coupled with the fact that the power is directly related to the big ranchers and/or the town. If the town is good—has good people—we know what it will look like: no deviants and no individuals, and as "The Last Vote" shows, no dissent. Just one big, happy family where everybody belongs to the cattlemen's association or the Nevada Club, and they elect the sheriff, who in turns depends on them for support. Thus law becomes synonymous with big ranchers and a homogeneous town.

This connection is especially obvious in *Bonanza* where Ben Cartwright plays the paternal old sage of not only the Ponderosa, but the town as well. He is the one everyone turns to for help and leadership in times of crisis —not the lawman, or the mayor (who's almost invisible) or some other city official, but the man with the big piece of

property. Ben Cartwright may have all the qualities of
the paternal old sage but he also owns that real estate.
The old sage and the autocratic landowner are the same
individual. In times of trouble he may even whip the
storekeepers into shape by threatening to boycott them
as he does in "The Return." Ben Cartwright takes care
of all the good little people who live around the Ponderosa, dependent on its water and food, but they are not
to covet his property. They are not to subvert law 'n'
order. It's paternalism with a capital "P."
      On the other programs ties with towns and with
society and its law are less cozy. In most of these shows
there is no law to speak of save the law of the cattlemen's
association. The landowners are a law unto themselves.
Significantly most of the good-bad conflicts on these
shows are resolved on sheer power, that power, of course,
going with the deed to the precious piece of property. On
High Chaparral the Cannons and Montoyas run the whole
territory and what they say goes. *The Men From Shiloh*
and other landowners end up settling their own conflicts, usually with a gun.
      This power aspect becomes especially obvious in
those episodes where the stars find themselves in strange
towns or on strange lands—controlled by baddies rather
than goodies. Again in these situations the sheriff is a
tool, but he is a tool for the baddie. Ultimately the two
powers must fight it out while the people watch huddled
in their houses or behind the pulled shades of storefronts
and hotel rooms. As Murdoch Lancer puts it, "We forget there's another world beyond the Lancer ranch. A
world of dog eat dog."
      So this is what the Western has come to. No longer
is there security in an abstract code, or even in the established roles of law enforcers or in a roaming community.

There is only security in a big piece of property, a kingdom unto itself, where those who wish can declare their
fealty to the lord of the manor and feel safe.

Looking at the changes which have brought the property Western to this point of view, we can see how they
grew out of the group orientation of the transition Westerns into Babbittry, community centeredness and the beliefs of Nixon's Manson speech. In the early property
Westerns the emphasis was on the security and unity of
the family group as idealized in the *Bonanza* theme song
—"If anyone fights with one of us, he's gonna have to
fight with me." The Cartwright family of these early
years was a group not unlike the *Wagon Train* team or
Rawhide trail crew—closely knit, fond of good times, lusty,
sometimes even drunken and brawling. By the time the
property Westerns came to dominate TV Western program-
ming, the emphasis had shifted from the family group to
the community and social conformity. The "fighting
Cartwrights" are now the decorous Cartwrights. The paranoia implicit in the security of the Wagon group and the
fighting family seems to have become full blown, extend-
ing out to the community at large and emphasizing the
security of conformity and reliance on the advice of the
town's "leading citizen." The connection between this,
the following chapter on *Gunsmoke* and Nixon's Manson
speech we leave for a later chapter.

Restless Gun "Revenge at Harness Creek" John Payne and Ken Tobey the Sheriff are the only ones identified.

Dodge is the only habit we got, ain't it Matthew?

                                        — Festus

Everybody's got a right to live in this town if they mind their own business and stay within the law.

                                        —Matt Dillon

CHAPTER VI

GUNSMOKE:
The Town and the Prairie

I MUST CONFESS THAT I AM A FAN OF *GUNSMOKE*, ALTHOUGH I wasn't when I began this study. It was only after watching the show for some time that I became convinced that it was worth watching. Now being a fan puts me in precisely the wrong position to comment on the worth of the show—since one of the charactertistics of a fan is an irrational attachment to the home team, even when the home team is bad. Some of my intellectual friends tell me that one of the reasons I'm a fan is because I expected the show to be so bad that even mediocrity seems good, or that I'd seen so many really bad shows that mediocrity seems good. The issue is complicated by the fact that in its long run on the tube, *Gunsmoke* has almost always been near the top of the ratings. There's a curious kind of elitism today which assumes a priori that anything which is popular can't be very good. I may be going out on a limb—because I'm no expert, I haven't had the lengthy exposure to TV or movies that helps make a good critic—but I would like to go on record as saying that from what I have seen, I think that the best of *Gunsmoke* can hold its own with all but the very best of television. Certainly it is heads above most network

139

series, which may not be saying much. I will go out even further—perhaps breaking the limb and falling on my face —by saying that I find some of the best *Gunsmoke* episodes every bit as satisfying as some of the so-called new wave Westerns of the late forties and early fifties. An episode, "My Father, My Son," with a powerful portrayal by Jack Elam, is as good a debunking of the gunfighter myth as *The Gunfighter*. Other episodes like "The Bullet" (1971), "Trafton" (1971), and "Nitro!" deserve to be ranked with all but the best Westerns—maybe not at the top, but certainly they deserve serious attention by those looking at Westerns and at television. They definitely deserve more than the neglect and/or contempt with which most so-called intellectuals have treated them.

Although the acting on *Gunsmoke* is almost always fairly good, I think what impresses me most about the show is its visual quality. Visually *Gunsmoke* is probably one of, if not the best, shows on television. I know of no other Western and very few other shows on television which emphasize visuals to the extent *Gunsmoke* does. By emphasizing visuals I do not mean the over-direction which currently seems to be the rage on television (and in the movies as well). John Ford's remark that a lot of young filmmakers today have found a new toy, the camera, might also be applied to television, which seems glutted with moving cameras, quick cutting, split screens, fast zooms, etc. Like Ford, the best of *Gunsmoke* utilizes an understated—or should I say unobtrusive—camera. The "teaser" sequences at the opening are classic examples of this technique, letting the picture statements carry all the meaning without over-emphasizing the fact that "Wow, I can shoot this whole scene without dialogue." The rest of the show follows a similar pattern. In most of the other Westerns the dialogue carries nine-tenths of the weight, which is one reason why so much of the last chapter contained quotations from the dialogue. In *Gunsmoke* the ratio between dialogue and visuals is about equal. The quality of the direction—especially in the last few years—has usually been high. The writing can also be quite good. It's amazing that in the length of time it has been on the tube, it has been able to come up with good scripts, year after year—especially without resorting to the "relevancy" devices of *Bonanza* and other shows or the flashbacks of *The Virginian.* They even manage to come up with scripts that allow the guest stars to be more than window-dressing, which is rare on other shows. Certainly they have avoided such banalities as using Wayne Newton as a singing farm boy.

The excellence of *Gunsmoke* can best be seen by analyzing particular episodes like one entitled "Nitro!" directed by Bernard McEveety.

McEveety appears to have a "thing" for portraying and classifying men in terms of natural objects. Philosophically he addresses himself to the question of tools and how a man thinks of them and his relationship to them. There are a number of episodes he has done in which cigars become symbolic objects that are linked to outlaws. In "Nitro!" a drunk's bottle and the nitro bottles are the same, and the protagonist's dilemma is whether he will become a "slave" to one of these two objects or assert his individuality and humanity. Some of McEveety's episodes even have titles like "The Bullet" and "Nitro!" while most of the other episodes on *Gunsmoke* are named after people.

The plot of "Nitro!" focuses on the efforts of a down-on-his-luck young man, George, and his attempts to earn enough money to marry his girlfriend, who works at the Longbranch. In the two-part episode George's job

choices boil down to four: he can work in Kitty's saloon,
washing dishes and cleaning up; he can work for a gang
of outlaws who specialize in using nitro to blow up safes
and need steady-handed men to make it for them; he can
invest money in the Kansas Petroleum Development Company run by a fast-talking character named Phineas Phifer
Pharnum; or he can follow in the footsteps of Louie, the
town drunk.

At the opening of the show George is put down by
Anne, the girl he wants to marry. She refuses to talk with
him while on duty hustling drinks, telling him that "time
is money" and money is something he doesn't have. Outside George meets Louie and together they go off to get
drunk. In one of the key scenes of the episode Louie
holds up a liquor bottle full of clear liquid saying, "Ya
got a crystal ball? There ya see a crystal ball. Ya see
yourself in thirty years." Full of liquor George staggers
back to the Longbranch where he ends up daring Matt
Dillon to kill him. The Nitro Gang, who had been sitting
in the saloon wondering how they were going to replace
the latest nitro maker who blew himself up, figure that
George is their next man. The following morning they
confront George in the saloon, where he is shown leaning over a tub scrubbing dishes, and offer him the job.
"You got a lotta nerve," says the leader, Steerman. "It
comes out of a bottle," says George. George makes a
few hundred dollars boiling TNT down into nitro and it
looks like—if he stays alive—he might make enough to
marry Anne and settle down. Enter Phifer Pharnum,
who convinces George to invest in the Kansas Petroleum
Development Co. Pharnum's scheme is not as wild as it
sounds, since he has a sample of oil from the site of a well,
and a guarantee that the scheme will make money if they
can come up with enough to cover a bank loan that will

get them started. In a long speech Pharnum, in his inimitable way, sells George on his scheme. "Pie in the sky says they, fortune says I. Do you realize what this is? (Holding up bottle of oil) This here's the future of our country. Dreamer says they, destiny says I. There's power in this. Power to move mountains." Destiny intervenes in the form of the Nitro Gang, which robs the bank that is holding the money for Pharnum. Once again George is destitute. Again he turns to the gang and at the end blows himself up.

The plot, which has several twists and turns to it including one incident in which George convinces Louie to make the nitro, moves quickly and the viewer is kept in suspense as to what George's final fate will be. McEveety heightens the suspense through the use of various natural objects, especially bottles, to continually keep the viewer in doubt. The bottle of liquor Louis holds up to the camera during his speech about a crystal ball, the bottle of oil Pharnum uses to punctuate his sales talk, and the bottles used to hold the nitro are all identical and all contain a neutral, clear liquid. In other places McEveety places hints to what will happen to George. When the Nitro Gang confronts him in the Longbranch, he is shown bending over a tub of sudsy water; this is a link to a subsequent scene in which he is shown bending over a similar tub covered with the sudsy white film of nitro. The Nitro Gang is also characterized through the use of natural objects. Steerman smokes a long, thin cigar: a device McEveety has used in other episodes to characterize outlaws. Bailey, who is the demolition expert, is constantly flipping a coin—a beautiful device which characterizes the gang and the heads or tails situation their use of nitro places them in.

Sound also plays an important role in "Nitro!" Like

the device of the bottles, McEveety uses the sound of
Bailey's whistling to enhance suspense. His whistling is
a nervous habit, and each time he is shown whistling,
something is blown up with nitro. In the opening sequence
the gang stands outside the shack where a man is making
nitro. Bailey is whistling. The shack blows up. Later
Bailey whistles as he lights the fuse which will blow up
the safe containing Pharnum's (and George's) money—and
blows up the plans of the Kansas Petroleum Development
Co. At the end, the Nitro Gang is in jail as Matt races to
stop George from making the nitro which is no longer
needed. Bailey is whistling and flipping his coin. An explosion is heard. George is dead.

The opening sequence of the episode contains in
brief all these devices. The camera focuses on Steerman
lighting a cigar, Bailey flipping his coin and whistling. The
men are agitated about something. Then there are quick
cuts to Dodge City showing George at the saloon with
Anne, Matt and Festus in the marshall's office, Doc in his
office. Festus pours Matt a cup of coffee, Anne is pour-
ing drinks in the bar, in the cabin the unseen man is pour-
ing nitro into bottles—although we don't know this. Then
the cabin is shown blowing up. Here in a nutshell is the
plot for the entire episode.

Episodes like "Nitro!" and perhaps our own fond-
ness for the show are part of why *Gunsmoke* has been
placed in a chapter by itself. In addition the show's long
run has taken it through changes that deserve to be discussed separately. These changes reflect the evolution of
the TV Western from gun to property-community Western. In *Gunsmoke* one can see these changes occurring in
a single show—which also makes a good reason to place
the show last.

This evolution can best be seen by the changes in the

opening sequence of the show. Those who remember the
earliest shows—and I wasn't able to obtain any of these—
say that the opening was a shot of Dillon walking on Boot
Hill talking about what happens to men who take up the
gun and go beyond the law. This opening changed into
the *Gunsmoke* opening which I remember—the classic shot
of Dillon drawing and firing to the staccato beat of the
background music. The earliest episode I was able to
analyze in any detail was made in 1962. In this opening
there is a hip shot closeup of Dillon's gun, then Dillon
slowly walks away from the camera revealing another man
standing out in the street. The town is an image of a young
frontier town, with its new white buildings and homes.
The street is short and at its end there is a church which
stands out quite prominently. As the two men draw the
camera cuts to a semi-front hip level shot that ends when
Dillon puts his gun back in his holster. The credits of the
show are shown over a line drawing of Dillon standing
with Boot Hill on his left, the town on his right, while
other credits at the end are shown against a shot of Dillon's gun hanging on a wall. In the episode itself the town
is quite small. The hills in the background seem to dominate the town. It seems to be a raw frontier town—there
are few people, few horses and wagons and many trees
and open spaces. My impression of the opening is that
this is the main and only street.

The 1964 openings I saw used the same gunfight
motif, except that there were some changes. Again the
camera begins with a hip shot of Dillon's gun and as he
walks away and the baddie walks out into the street, you
can see the town has grown. The street stretches out,
there are fewer houses and more shops. The town even
has street lights. When the camera cuts to Dillon firing,
the sign behind him says Dodge City Stage Depot. The

drawing of Boot Hill is used halfway through the show,
but the Boot Hill part seems to be receding into the distance. At the end credits are shown against a line drawing of a tree with the town in the background.

By 1966 the town has become quite large. The gunfight motif is still retained, but it is dwarfed by the town,
with its now gray and weather-beaten buildings. The
street is longer, it curves from the lower right to the upper
left of the frame and continues on out of the frame. Again
there is the by now classic shot of Dillon walking out from
the left, while an outlaw, who is not as distinct as in the
earlier openings, walks out from the right. The credits of
the stars that are shown after the opening teaser are shown
against a shot of a town that is bustling with activity: a
wagon pulls away from the camera while a buggy drives
toward it; a couple walks directly in front of the camera
while another couple crosses the frame diagonally.

The opening used during the 1972 season was first
used around 1968. The image of Marshall Dillon drawing
and firing—what James Arness called the classic symbol
of the Western tradition—is gone. The 1972 opening of
Gunsmoke reminds me of the ending of *Shane* where the
boy waves at the image of the cowboy fading in the distance, as though he were saying goodbye to a specter
which had never really existed except in his imagination.
The new *Gunsmoke* opens with Matt Dillon riding hard
across the prairie, going like hell for somewhere. This
image is quickly replaced by the picture of the main street
of Dodge City, bustling with activity. The town stretches
in the distance. There are no mountains or trees. When
the image of Marshall Dillon riding is suddenly replaced
by the image of Dodge City, you don't ask what happened
to him, why the sudden shift in images. Here fused in one
sequence is the old Boone myth of the Westerner as a har-

binger of civilization with a newer emerging image of
man in a community. The image of Dodge City doesn't
strike you as a specter; what strikes you is that the image
of Matt Dillon, like that of Shane, seems to be the specter. Only now we know where Matt and Shane were
riding, for the cowboy has settled down and joined a
community. No better picture of this change can be
found than the second part of the *Gunsmoke* opening—
the image of the bustling street of Dodge City. Against
this image are projected the faces of the old and new
stars of the show. Doc and Kitty and Matt are joined by
Festus, who had earlier replaced Chester as Matt's deputy,
and Newley, who owns a gunshop. The faces of the stars
are not just projected against the streets of Dodge, rather
they seem to emerge from them, as though the stars'
faces were enlargements of some of the faces of the many
people walking and riding down the main street. In *Gunsmoke* the old cowboy has become a member of a community. It is the image of the town that forms the dom-
inating backdrop for the faces of the stars, not the specter-
image of the open plains that preceded it.

What we have in the *Gunsmoke* openings is a visual
statement of the transition of the show from an "adult"
gun Western to something not unlike the community of
Wagon Train.[1] As a statement of *Gunsmoke* as a gun
Western the iconography of the 1962 opening and closing are essentially triangular compositions: the opening
with Dillon and the baddie on either side of the church
at the end of the street, and the ending with Boot Hill
and the town on either side of Dillon. The triangular aspect is further heightened by the fact that the church of
the opening and Dillon at the closing seem the apex of a
triangle whose other two corners represent opposing
forces: good vs. bad and life vs. death. In the opening

the church stands as a commentary on and an affirmation of the triumph of good. It's similar to those old
medieval paintings in which Christ is shown as a judge
holding a set of scales, weighing the souls of men on
Judgment Day. In the *Gunsmoke* opening the scale is
quite obviously weighted in favor of the lawman, for Dillon looms larger than the baddie. Dillon's looming figure
occupies the center position of the church in the closing
sequence—the parallel construction emphasizing the gun
Western's theme that goodness is related to the role of
the lawman. The figure of the lawman at the end seems
to be Dillon, but it is an abstraction as if Dillon were a
universal figure representing all lawmen and the drawing
were a universal statement of his role of standing between
the town and Boot Hill. The composition of the ending
is much more balanced, with town and Boot Hill seemingly equal. As the openings progress to the present opening the town becomes increasingly prominent and both
Boot Hill and the church disappear. In the 1964 opening
Dillon stands in front of the Dodge City Stage Depot,
representing the lawman who stands between the town
and the baddie. New people come to town on the stage—
perhaps the baddie himself has just arrived—and the marshal has the responsibility of protecting the town from
the threat that some of those new people from outside,
from beyond the town might represent. The church as a
symbol of the relationship between town, morality, and
marshal is gone. Now it is the stage depot which forms
the backdrop for his actions. By 1966 it is plain that the
town now dominates the theme of the gunfight. Dillon
seems to draw his power from the town as much as vice
versa. Where once he loomed as the avenging angel of the
church and the morality it represented, now he looms as
the avenging angel of the town. He must have done his job

well because in recent years the gunfight of the earlier
openings is gone. Dodge is now a peaceful city with
people going about their business. The members of the
cast are but faces in the crowd, members of a community,
which unlike the *Wagon Train* community is a settled
community. The wagon train appears to have reached
its destination and the cowboy-marshal has settled down.
Like the property Westerns *Gunsmoke* affirms that the
free-roaming, atomic individual is dead.

Actually on *Gunsmoke* the old individual isn't really
dead. He's alive, but not too well, living in the wide open
spaces beyond the town. Only, where once the wide open
spaces were symbolic of the unlimited freedom and innocence of the West and the Westerner, here that freedom
is very fragile. It's an image of the prairie that changes
the old optimistic conception of the freedom of
open spaces to a more negative vision. The freedom of
the open spaces creates a freedom to do evil as well as
good. It is a freedom which allows the evil in man to flow
unchecked, a freedom which gives as much comfort to
the outlaw as the lawman. Where once the cowboy was
leery of towns, afraid to place himself in a situation in
which a group of men using the law could impinge on
his freedom, now he is leery of the open spaces, afraid to
place himself in an environment that allows a man to do
anything he damn well pleases. Where once the cowboy
was paranoid about towns, now he is paranoid about the
prairie.

This attitude towards the open prairie often erupts
when members of the cast are talking about the past—a
time when all there was was open space; no towns, no
laws. In "9:12 To Dodge" Doc says, "You see this state
and most of the territories beyond, ten years ago were a
battle field and that violence loosed a lot of violent men

and we still have our share of incorrigibles." The memories of that recent past and the knowledge that "the
territories beyond" are still like that past, is not a com-
forting thought. It is fitting that Doc's speech should be
made from a train, for *Gunsmoke* has many episodes
involving trains—more than any other Western—and in
these episodes the train becomes a sort of town beyond
town. It is a symbol for the town against the open
spaces, an outpost of civilization that carries the values
of civilization from town to town. The whole train
theme reminds me of a similar symbolic impression I
had of Washington, D.C. where government officials, re-
porters and tourists moved from building to building in
hermetically sealed limousines, taxis and buses. Like the
train tracks connecting town to town in *Gunsmoke*, the
streets of Washington connected government office to
office to hotel to homes in the suburbs. It was especially
eerie to look out the windows of our motel across to the
lit-up Capitol Dome at night. The sidewalks were de-
serted except for one or two blacks, while the streets
were crowded with cars seemingly creeping from "town"
to "town."

    There is a characteristic visual quality to the open
spaces on *Gunsmoke* that reinforces Doc's view of them.
Unlike some Westerns, which feature scenic shots of
mountains and rushing streams, *Gunsmoke*'s landscapes
are the gently rolling hills and trees of the Kansas prairie.
The scenery is a monotonous, neutral ground on which
a man can blend in and hide forever or stand out like a
sore thumb. It can lull you to sleep and then rudely
awaken you with a storm or the crash of a bullet from
ambush. It is outlaw country, for the baddies on *Gunsmoke* almost always live in, strike from, and return to
the open spaces. Some of the baddies' names even evoke

the creatures who inhabit these open spaces: Gecko, Steerman, Jaekel. Conversely, in the horse Westerns it was the hero who lived in, struck from, and returned to the open spaces.

The only episode I have seen which has a scenic background is one entitled "The Lost" (1971), which is a well-executed *Gunsmoke* version of the wild child theme. Yet this episode, too, affirms the *Gunsmoke* theme of the open spaces. The plot revolves around the adventures of Kitty and a wild child who is called "the animal." Kitty's stagecoach has been wrecked, but she escapes serious injury and wanders through the open spaces trying to get back to the town. The tone of the episode is established from the beginning, with Kitty riding in the dust-choked stagecoach, where someone suggests, "Pull back the curtains, it'll keep out the dust." When Kitty finally comes upon "the animal" she is in a lush mountain setting, with pines and the prerequisite rushing stream. Since "the animal" cannot talk, but can only make noises, she cannot help Kitty find her way back to civilization. At one point Kitty gets mad at her and says, "You just go ahead and be a dog in the manger. I hope you'll be happy, real happy." Eventually she and Kitty make friends and Kitty is able to communicate to "the animal" what she wants. Significantly she draws a house and some people in the sand and says, "People . . . people like you and me." The wild child scratches out the drawing for the only people she has known are the people of the open spaces—people who call her "animal" and have put a bounty on her for stealing from them. As "the animal" and Kitty approach a house with some of these people, the scenery becomes bleaker, as though "the animal" lived in some fragile, innocent enclave in the midst of this openness. The people are able to outwit Kitty and capture "the animal," putting her in a cage. As they load the cage on a wagon to take "the animal" to town where they plan to make money exhibiting her as a freak, Matt rides up and rescues Kitty and her friend. Obviously though "the animal" may be innocent and edenic, her innocence makes her vulnerable to the people on the prairie and she cannot continue to live her fragile, wild existence. Yet because she is an "animal" she cannot yet live in town. As an "animal" she was pre-human, sub-human and lived in a place even beyond the lawless open spaces. As Kitty puts it, "She's lived like an animal and she's absolutely terrified of people." Kitty's solution is to let Bess, who has 17 kids, raise "the animal." At the end of the show the wild child is shown riding the merry-go-round with the other children. "The animal" has become human. She is cleaned-up, wears a nice dress, and is now a part of a community. "The lost" is now "the found."

A parallel episode to "The Lost," "Prairie Wolfer" (1964), is the first in which Ken Curtis appears as Festus. This early Festus is not like Deputy Festus, rather he is a wolfer, a loner who lives by himself on the prairie. He doesn't even live in a house or log cabin, but in a low dirt dugout something like the dens of the wolves he hunts. In stressing the wild, free nature of Wolfer Festus, he is portrayed as an expert trapper and hunter who lives as one with nature. He describes himself: "I don't hold with no roads. I get to fixin' to go somewhere, I just point my nose and go." A girl who is attracted to animals and to Festus says, "He's like the animals. He wouldn't be happy there [in town]. He's got to be out on the prairie, free." Life on the prairie isn't the naive, innocent thing the girl thinks it is, though. She's one of those people who think all animals are cute pets. When she sees a wolf in a trap and tells Festus to let it go, Fes-

tus isn't so naive. He knows life on the prairie is violent
and sometimes not very pretty. It's not what the nature
lovers think it is, for wolves can kill in ugly ways: "Have
you ever seen a little calf with his throat all tored open,
half beat up by wolves like him?" he says. "Or a little
antelope or a buffalo cow? As for chickens like you got
up at your house, why they kill them just for sport." In
the end Festus, like "the animal," gives himself up to civilization, saying he's "never going wolfing no more." The
human wolves that inhabit the open spaces turn him to
the town and Wolfer Festus turns his talents to being
Deputy Festus. Again the old individual settles down and
becomes part of the community.

Like Festus, the other rugged individuals who live in
the prairie outside the town must make their peace with
the community. In *Gunsmoke*, as in the property Western, these individuals are an anachronism—ghosts from
the violent past which Doc described. Some of them were
friends of Matt Dillon, but unlike Matt were unable to
adapt to the new way of life in the community. Some of
them even become menaces to the town, threatening its
established law with their own anarchistic codes.

Among these figures is Drago (1971), an old mountain man similar to Ben Cartwright's buckskinned "yonder man," Beaudry. Drago has settled down with a widow
and her child. They live unmarried, untied to the rules
and restrictions of the town. Like Festus and "the animal," the small eden that Drago has created for himself
is fragile. One day the violent forces that inhabit the
open land beyond the town strike unexpectedly and his
wife is murdered, the child lingers near death. The murderers turn out to be an outlaw gang Matt and Newley
have been following. Matt has to leave on business, so
Drago agrees to help Newley track down the killers. The

rest of the episode deals with the conflict between Drago's methods of vengeance and Newley's. With the aid of a cur dog named Hound, Drago tracks down and traps the outlaws—each time cleverly setting the trap so that he can kill the outlaw who killed the widow and beat the boy. Newley, on the other hand, insists on bringing them in so they can stand trial. The climax occurs in a desert town, the perfect setting for a confrontation between lawman, criminal, and the man with a code beyond the law. Drago wants to gut-shoot the outlaw who killed the widow, letting him die like the animal he is. Newley finally persuades the old mountain man that "it isn't worth it," especially if Drago must hang or go to jail for life, leaving the motherless boy without a family. Drago and Hound return to the boy. The cur dog, who once snapped at anyone who came near him, allows the boy to pet him and the mountain man, who didn't want to be tied down by anyone, walks off with his arm around the boy. Mountain man and dog are domesticated.

Besides the old mountain man other rugged individualists still haunt the prairies. Among these are two familiar figures: the big rancher and the gunfighter. The problem with these figures is that like Drago they too often think of themselves as being above the law, and like Drago, they are anachronisms. They came to the country when it was still a battle field, before there were laws and towns; they had to live by their own values and their wits. As the phrase goes, they had to take the law into their own hands—they were a law unto themselves. As Matt puts it, "These ranchers without fences, you know, they more or less have to go by the golden rule." He says that there is no law "against branding calves on your property. It just depends on how neighborly you want to be."

One of these old ranchers is Jonah Hutchinson,
another is Gentry. In "Jonah Hutchinson" (1964), Hutchinson returns to Dodge and to his old ranch after spending
time in prison for going beyond the law. Hutchinson is
now an old man, embittered by his experience, unable to
understand the changes that have occurred in the once
open territory. When he first came there was no one and
a man made his own laws. Now there are more men and
more laws. From the minute he walks into town Hutchinson's anachronism is stressed, as he dodges wagons and
people like he wasn't sure they existed and then must
grudgingly concede that they are there in a place that
once was just space. His dream is to rebuild his crumbl-
ing old stone ranch house and re-establish the Hutchinson
Kingdom. To most of the settlers, like Kitty, he has a
reputation as a ruthless man, although he doesn't look so
ruthless anymore. But Matt questions the term ruthless,
"You know in those days it was a question of might was
right. . . . The only way a man could hold his property
was if he had the most guns." For Matt Jonah's problem
"was he didn't realize the law had moved in for good."
He still doesn't. He teaches his grandsons to shoot, buys
dynamite and begins harassing the small ranches near his
own, trying to drive them out so he can buy their land.
Matt cautions him, but Huchinson will have none of it.
"What happens on Hutchinson land is my business."
Matt replies, "There might be a time when it's everyone's
business." It becomes everyone's business soon enough
and Matt, serving a warrant on Hutchinson, is forced to
shoot him. The old man dies in the ruins of his ranch
house, still trying to live a life that was only a crazy old
man's dream. Later in the Longbranch Hutchinson receives his epitaph. "He may not have been the wisest."
But he was the first man to come to the territory. "The

first man to see this country was worth selling. Put a marker one hundred miles from the sound of the nearest human voice." Hutchinson even receives a toast, "Good or bad I gotta drink to a man like that."

In "Gentry's Law," Matt faces another big rancher whose sons have lynched a man they thought was a squatter. Like Hutchinson, Gentry believes he is his own law and that any crime committed on his land is his to prosecute and judge. Gentry is also an anachronism. He says that when he first came there wasn't any law. "We had to establish our own law. Break Gentry's law, answer to Gentry. Likewise Gentry takes care of his own." The problem is that Gentry is "fighting for something that doesn't exist any more." Eventually Gentry must give in and turn his own sons over to the law. The problem with the Gentry sons is that they're "milksops," they've been over protected, pampered. The moral of the story is "a scrawny calf is better than a healthy one that's overprotected."

Some, but not all, of the gunfighters who appear on *Gunsmoke* are portrayed like Gentry and Hutchinson—as anachronisms who are no longer needed. At one time they were needed because there was no law or inadequate law. It allowed guilty men or bad men to go free and someone was needed who could stand up to these men on their own terms. One of these gunfighters, Nick Skouras, explains why he started killing other men. "I don't know. The first one needed killing. Wasn't just me, the whole town says so." Eventually he had to face the man or back down. "After that I don't know. Always seemed to be someone that needed killing. Somebody the law could not or would not touch." In "Blood Money," Skouras is shot in his gun hand by his own father, and becomes an easy target for other gunfighters. Although Matt Dillon doesn't like gunfighters in Dodge, because they're too much of a threat to the law and order of the town, he has a grudging respect for what the good ones had to do, but sees no need for it in a society ruled by law. Skouras' injury poses a dilemma, though. He can throw him out of town, making him an easy mark for rival guns or allow him to stay. When he decides to lock Skouras up for his own protection, Skouras resists and there is an understanding between marshal and gunfighter that such a man must stand by himself, injured or not. Skouras practices with his left hand, but he isn't that good, and he dies facing the baddies who have kidnapped his father and sister just so they can lure the injured gunfighter into an unfair fight.

The gunfighter in "My Father, My Son" (1966) also is an anachronism but unlike Skouras he realizes it. Like Gregory Peck in *The Gunfighter*, Jack Elam plays an old gunfighter who is weary of constantly having to face down punk kids and constantly having to look around for someone who'll shoot him in the back for revenge. Elam knows he's "gonna have trouble" as long as "you wear that gun," but he also knows that "if I don't wear the gun I'm dead." He's "gettin' tired," yet he has to keep the gun and stay alert because of the young punks and the people who always have a score to settle.

What "My Father, My Son" does is add an additional twist to this equation, for one of the punk kids who hunts down Elam in Dodge is his own son. This twist perhaps makes the episode seem a bit melodramatic, especially when the old gunfighter is ambushed by the Jeffords clan, who had lost one of its members to Elam, just as father and son have made their peace. Perhaps I am susceptible to this kind of melodrama, but I think that Elam's portrayal and the direction of the episode make it as interesting a debunking of the gunfighter myth as *The Gunfighter*. "My Father, My Son" may walk a thin line between drama and melodrama, but at least it seems to avoid the nostalgia which characterizes *The Gunfighter*. Besides, the ending of *The Gunfighter* seems every bit as melodramatic as this *Gunsmoke* episode.

The grudging respect Matt Dillon has for the gunfighter, the big rancher and the mountain man seems to revolve around two things: their roles in opening up the country and allowing the towns to develop and their adherence to their code. In "My Father, My Son" Elam the gunfighter goes to great lengths to avoid confrontation with the punk kids, because he knows they're no match for him. With the kids the gunfight is no longer a fair fight; it's murder even though the law might not see it that way. In "Drago" (1971) and "Gentry's Law" there is the feeling that it is a code or a feeling of decency which moves Drago and Gentry to eventually side with the law and turn in the baddies. The good individuals, then, are not unlike the old cowboys of the horse Westerns in their instinctive sense of right and wrong. Dillon respects their code, in part because he lives by a code as well as the law and in part because he once was an individual not unlike these individuals. What his old friends cannot understand is that the days of the old individual are dead and these trappers, ranchers and gunfighters must make their peace with the society of the town. The choice for an anachronism like Drago or Jonah Hutchinson—or for the Lone Ranger or the Cisco Kid—is to either become a member of the new community or die trying to preserve an outmoded way of life.

The baddie, on the other hand, has no code. He ambushes Elam and fights Nick Skouras when he can't use his gun hand. Unlike Drago and Gentry, some indi-

viduals do not see the light and turn to the life of out-
lawry, which is really the only way of life on the open
prairies. Kitty's friend, "the animal," may have lived for
awhile on the prairie, but she turns to civilization. The
real animals on the prairie are the baddies and they turn
away from civilization. Like the baddies in the gun and
property Westerns, *Gunsmoke*'s prairie villains are deviants. They dress sloppily, speak bad grammar or else
they're too neat, too proper. McEveety's touch of showing the baddies with cigars is a beautiful symbol for this
deviancy, because no one else in *Gunsmoke* smokes.*
The goodies may drink but they never smoke, and besides
the goodies always drink out of a glass. The baddie, well
. . . in one episode a group of especially obnoxious baddies are shown drinking out of a wooden bucket with a
dead mouse floating inside. That's the kind of people the
baddies are.

Coming from the open prairie beyond the town the
baddie is the epitome of the isolated anarchistic individual. Only this anarchy is full of negative connotation, for
the anarchistic individual is someone who can and will do
anything to anyone at anytime for any reason. He is not,
like the Lone Ranger, a defender of justice; rather he is a
subverter of it, because he threatens its very foundations.
Where Roy Rogers made movies as Jesse James, here the
Jesse James-type outlaw is only another outlaw. All the
old Jesse James legends, all the arguments in favor of
this "Robin Hood of the Old West" are advanced and
dismissed in a *Gunsmoke* episode, "The Raid" (1966).
The episode is about Jim Stark, but Stark is given all of
Jesse's history except his name. He's an ex-Confederate

*An exception is Doc's replacement, who is also a sophisticated
city dweller, but who becomes "one of the boys."

veteran, gives money to the poor, etc. In a sarcastic
speech Doc recites Stark's credentials, "He's a fine fella.
Good Samaritan and everything. Gives money to folks.
Poor Confederate veteran abused by Federal troops."
Then he drops his sarcasm and lays it all out in a monu-
mental put down of the whole Jesse James mystique,
"Five years now he's been getting away with murder and
robbery." Stark apparently believes the legends about
his robbing from the rich and giving to the poor, for
according to him, he never takes money from honest
working folk. "That money comes from banks and
trains and Northern millionaires who get rich on the blood
of innocent men." According to Stark he does the right
thing—he puts the money back where it belongs, in the
pockets of the people, or at least so he says. The problem
with Stark is that his Jesse James routine has unleashed a
lot of dangerous forces, like his own gang, which takes all
this pious talk as an excuse to loot and murder for their
own enjoyment. Also Stark is no saint. He gives money
to people, all right, but not very much, rather it's more
like crumbs for the poor or a way of bribing them into
silence, than it is an attempt to help them. Stark and his
gang are no match for Matt Dillon and Dodge, though, and
they get what's coming to them. Matt's epitaph for Stark
is a beautiful pricking of the inflated Jesse James legend,
"Why do the McConnells and the Starks think it's an easy
way to make a living?"
   Stark's real problem is the same problem as Drago's
and Gentry's—he just doesn't understand that the days of
raiding on the prairies are ending, that no longer can one
play at being "Robin Hood." If one is going to make it,
if one is cool he packs up and moves into town, because
town is where it's at. Where the horse Western found its
eden in a limitless virgin land, where the property Western

created its bit of eden on that huge ranch, *Gunsmoke*
creates its bit of eden in a small town. The town is where
virtue resides. It is a bastion against the forces of anarchy
and evil which threaten it from the prairie. If one were to
draw a symbolic representation of the town, he could find
ample precedent in those drawings of medieval walled
cities. As some medieval historians have commented, the
medieval town was a refuge for the middle class burgers
and lower class artisans from the deprivations of amoral
bandits and the amoral lords of manors, who were constantly threatening their existence. Unless one was very
strong and also very lucky, to live alone on the medieval
countryside meant one had to put himself under the protection of one of the lords or else leave himself wide open
to the robber bands who freely roamed the countryside.
The *Gunsmoke* town is a great deal like this.

Like the medieval town Dodge is a fairly exclusive
WASP haven. Except for a token black or Indian who
might put in a brief appearance as a guest star, there are
only whites in town. Dodge, if you're black, seems to be
a nice place to visit, but you wouldn't want to live there.
Since most of the deviants are baddies there aren't many
of them either. There is a token town drunk, though, who
has a blank check at the Longbranch—although not *too*
blank.

Dodge is not unlike Virginia City in its vision of
Main Street, small town America. However, even though
Dodge has a lot of the features of Virginia City, including
a Chamber of Commerce somewhat like the Nevada Club,
it doesn't appear to be run by an elite like that which runs
Virginia City. Rather, *Gunsmoke* seems to emphasize the
common, everyday people of the city instead of the country
club set of the Nevada Club. The town drunk is accorded
a featured role, as is Sam the bartender. Burke, the owner

of the freight depot, also appears quite regularly, and a
star, Newley O'Brien, is a shopkeeper—although the shop
he runs is, significantly, the gunshop. The ruling elite
types who appear so often in *Bonanza* just don't appear
in *Gunsmoke.* In fact *Gunsmoke*'s Dodge doesn't seem
to have a mayor, a newspaper, a city council. Even the
aforementioned Chamber of Commerce is never shown.

When Doc Adams' replacement comes to Dodge,
he remarks that one of the reasons he came was because
he was tired of a big city hospital and wanted to practice
"where your patients are your friends and your friends
are your patients." The town's clannishness leads to
some resistance to the new doctor, especially one who
wears a white linen suit and talks like a sophisticated city
dweller. Festus won't buy him a drink, and the people
won't come to his office. The new doctor has to prove
himself, which he does by curing Newley who has been
seriously injured by an explosion in his gunshop. Festus
buys the new Doc a drink, the town pitches in and re-
builds the gunshop, and everyone adjourns to the Longbranch for a round of beer and good natured joking. In
Bonanza Ben Cartwright begs the town to accept new
people, working mostly on the bankers, etc., and when
this doesn't work—as it didn't in one episode—he threatens
to boycott various businesses. Not in Dodge. Matt is
quick to accept the new doctor, but he cannot convince
Festus or the rest of the town, because the town must see
results, and judge the man for themselves. When the new
doctor operates on Newley, the townspeople stand around
watching and he must shoo them outside. When the operation is over he goes outside and talks to the skeptical
townspeople. After an emotional speech in which he admits he's a bit stand-offish, he asks for a match to light
his cigar, whereupon someone lights one, breaking the ice

between doctor and town. Together all go inside to wait for Newley's recovery because "his friends should be there at this time."

The values of these townspeople are like those of the good people of the gun and property Westerns—sobriety and decorum. One should work hard, have a drink with the gang now and then, but never be over-ambitious or drink more than a few. This message is central in an episode entitled "Cleavus" (1970). Cleavus is a friend of Festus who comes to Dodge. As Cleavus puts it, "I'm tired of being poor." He wants to be rich, have people look up to him—he wants to marry Kitty! The episode draws a contrast between Festus and Cleavus, for while Cleavus schemes and plans to make it big without hard work, Festus is shown as hard-working and satisfied with his position in life. "I got me two jobs. Deputyin' part of the time and takin' care of the stable the other time." He tells Cleavus he can "sleep in the stable if you don't mind." Festus doesn't mind, but Cleavus does. Like the gun and property Westerns *Gunsmoke* stresses that old Protestant idea of vocation—the virtue of staying in your place and working hard in it. Festus doesn't want to marry Kitty, and he doesn't want to be marshal, and although he wouldn't mind being rich, it's just not in the cards and he's not about to cheat to get it.

The decorum part of the equation forms part of the subject of a two-part episode entitled "Pike" (1970), which is concerned with Sally Fergus, the town eccentric. Sally is a ragged looking old woman with stringy hair and no teeth, who lives in a rundown shack outside of town, picking up junk to pay for her booze. She never takes a bath and wears a tattered old dress. When she rides into town in an old wagon pulled by a mule named "Worthless," and the children make fun of her, Festus is moved to lecture them: "All folks is different. Some are good, some are bad. Some are clean, some are middlin' dirty and some are just plain dirty." He tells them to look in the mirror the next time they decide to call someone names, "You might get some idea of what somebody might call you." The whole speech sounds good, but I venture to say that the people of Dodge could look in a mirror and see that they are clean and good and that the only name anybody could call them is "straight." Festus is the only "character" in Dodge, the only one who talks funny and dresses funny. He's their token weirdo. Sally Fergus shows up now and then as a token freak—she's middlin' dirty. Festus is at least clean, although he looks like he needs a shave. By the end of the episode Sally Fergus has been accepted by the townspeople. She's still the town eccentric, but now she at least has taken a bath, fixed her hair, and washed her clothes. What's more she has even bought a set of false teeth. She's no longer as irascible as she was, although she still continues to pick junk and take a snort now and then. She's not embarrassed to come into town, and the town's not embarrassed to have her come. A town eccentric is one thing, but a sloppy town eccentric—well . . . that's too much.

Festus is not really a weirdo—he's just different. But in keeping with the pattern of a lot of TV shows his difference is played for laughs. He and Doc are always having humorous arguments that revolve around Festus' grammar or his lack of knowledge. Festus has his aches and pains and he's always trying to get somebody to buy him a beer. He's what used to be called a "character." The wolfer has become the humorous deputy. It's as though if one is different he's either a "character" or a baddie, which doesn't leave much room for freaks to wander.

Yet neither decorum nor sobriety are enough to

keep the town from exploding, to keep people from killing one another or fighting or whatever. The town is constantly threatening to degenerate into the anarchism of the prairie and the sober townspeople seem helpless to prevent it. This fear of disruption stems from the town and *Gunsmoke*'s view of human nature as balanced precariously between good and evil. As Kitty observes, "I've been running a saloon for a lot of years and everybody's got some weakness." Or as Doc puts it in "The Mark of Cain" (1968), "In times of civil war the code of humanity disappears completely." In Doc's remark and in many of the *Gunsmoke* episodes there is the belief that given the right environment and/or the right circumstances almost any man can "turn bad." Perhaps this is why the town is so fearful of the anarchistic possibilities of the prairie and why it emphasizes sobriety, decorum and order at the expense of diversity. As Kitty sees it, "If there weren't a law there'd be an awful lot of us doing a lot of things and feeling pretty smug about it."

Notice that Kitty says "a law," not "laws" or "courts" or any of a host of other things. On *Gunsmoke* "a law" is Matt Dillon. "A law" is a lawman and without him Dodge City would become the prairie. The town has no security in law or laws; its security is in the lawman, for laws can be subverted, lawmen can't, or at least so says *Gunsmoke*.

In an episode, "The Wreckers" (1967), Matt is captured and held for ransom by a gang of outlaws. Doc and Kitty try to raise the money, even though they suspect the outlaws will kill Matt anyway. A heated meeting is held in the Longbranch as Doc tries to convince people to contribute money—even though they too know that it will be in vain. Doc describes what Matt has meant to the town:

Now there's not enough money in the entire
State of Kansas to pay another man to do what
Matt's done. Now we've built this town and
seen it grow because Matt gave us the security
of knowing that Tate Crocker and a hundred
others like him can't come in here and burn it
to the ground every time they think about it.

He goes on to cite the debts individual citizens owe Matt:
"Jim Taylor, how many times has he put up with your
viciousness every time you have an argument with your
wife?" etc. The money is raised, but it is Matt himself who
has to escape when Doc and the townspeople's fears are
realized.

We get a glimpse of just how much Matt does mean to
the town in an episode entitled, "Dead Man's Law" (1968).
Here we see why the people put their faith in "a law"
rather than laws. When Matt is shot and left for dead by
an outlaw, the town is left without "a law"—the citizens
are left to rule themselves. Festus and Newley, as deputies,
try to maintain law, but they are subverted by two men
who organize a cattleman's co-op and proceed to raise the
ugly specter of vigilante justice. "You and the rest of the
cattleman's association might see to form the spine of a
committee that would see to law enforcement in this town."
The town falls into chaos when Festus rides out to con-
firm whether Matt is dead or alive. The chaos is emphasized by a shoulder level medium range shot of a frightening scene of the townspeople engaged in a huge anarchic
brawl with each other. The town has become the prairie.
This chaos provides the perfect opening for the cattlemen to take over the town, which they do by convincing the townspeople to accept the appointment of a shotgun toting killer named Erickson as their acting marshal.
Doc cautions them to wait until Festus returns. "For

twelve years you've had law and order in Dodge City because one man enforced the law. Now that he's not here you're willing to give the town away to the first incompetent that comes along with a shotgun and is anxious to use it."

And that's just what they do. The ordinary people seem a weak and spineless herd in need of strong leaders. Erickson soon begins using his shotgun. In an effective violence sequence, the camera focuses on Newley's horrified face, as Erickson blasts an "escaping rustler" from pointblank range, then moves to a shot of the blasted timbers of the door. Later when Doc gives his speech about turning the town over to Erickson and his cronies, the blasted bulletin board that holds the wanted posters punctuates his speech, suggesting that Erickson's version of "a law" has blasted Dodge's law, leaving only a shattered reminder. Erickson's enforcement of the law is not only harsh with "escaping rustlers," it is harsh for the rest of the townspeople as well. When he throws two men whose quarrelling is notorious into jail, Doc objects, "Lathrop and Simmons have been quarrelling for years. You can't arrest a man for something like that." A few more similar acts of "enforcing the law" put Erickson in total control of the town. After Doc is beaten by one of the co-op men for objecting to Erickson's tactics he can only mutter in shock, "The whole town just set back and let them run the law in this town." Kitty, too, is harassed and one-time acting deputy Newley is powerless. When Festus finds Matt, who has been cared for by an Indian, he tells him about the town, "Folks just plain ole let it happen." Erickson and his men trail Festus and try to kill the two lawmen, but Matt triumphs and returns to the town to once again establish "a law."

The sense that what is needed is "a law," not laws,

is conveyed in several episodes where men subvert or try
to subvert "a law"—Matt Dillon. In "Jonah Hutchinson"
the old rancher bends the law to his own purposes, telling
his grandsons, "You want something and the law's a shade
on your side, you go ahead and take it." Why? Because
you "let the lawyers and their judges argue over it. They'll
go on arguing it until the day you die, but the thing you
want done, you done." In "Murdoch" a lawman who
once knew Matt bends the law in his search for revenge
against a gang of outlaws. Murdoch has an execution warrant entitling him to hang any members of the gang he can
catch. Matt asks, "Whatever happened to justice and due
process?" Murdoch answers, "What's the difference between a piece of paper if you hang a man!" Matt retorts
that if he doesn't know he doesn't deserve to wear his
badge. Besides how does he know which men to execute?
In "Lynott" another old friend of Matt's returns to Dodge
and like Murdoch he too causes chaos with the law. Matt
leaves Lynott in charge of town, while he goes on business.
Lynott is an old style lawman who "worked " the rough,
raw cow towns and helped turn them into towns like
Dodge, but the towns have changed and Lynott hasn't.
A bunch of old friends come to town, brawling, etc. Lynott lets them off. An old buffalo skinner knifes one of
the townspeople and Lynott gives him his knife and lets
him go. The wife of the man goes to Lynott's wife and
pleads with her to talk to her husband. She tries to convince the old lawman, "This is Dodge City. . . . People
trying to make something last and only laws will do it."
However, what Dodge needs is not laws, but lawmen. As
Matt puts it when Lynott asks him why he became a deputy, "The law. The law needs men to work it." As the
town puts it, "Lynott ain't marshalin' like we're used to."
　　The contrast between "a law" in Dodge and the law

/

in other towns also serves to suggest Matt's value to the
people he "marshals" for. In "Vengeance" (1966) a contrast is drawn between Dodge and Parkerville, which is
run by Parker and his stooge, Sheriff Sloan. Once Parkerville was as big as Dodge, but now it is a bunch of ram-
shackle old buildings, a town as outmoded as the kind of
law it signifies—a one man town. Matt remarks that
Parker "got himself in a whole lot of trouble by trying
to be his own law out there" and "that's something no
man does is make his own rules."

Yet the question arises as to whether that isn't exactly what Matt Dillon is doing. The town wants law, but
more importantly it wants "a law," a man who will be
flexible and yet not too flexible. The written laws on the
books are subject to various interpretations by various
individuals and various towns, so the town needs "a law"
like Matt Dillon, not like Lynott or Murdoch or Sheriff
Sloan. The people of Dodge City believe the limits and
enforcement of the law lie with a man, not with the people, for doesn't "Dead Man's Law" demonstrate that
the people themselves are impotent without their lawman? What makes their lawman so unique is that he
knows the people, understands them and is willing in
certain cases to bend the law for them. Where Matt
might break up a fight between two cowboys in one episode, he allows two brothers to fight in "The Money
Store" because one brother "needs it" and because he
knows neither of them will seriously hurt the other. To
some extent Matt Dillon's version of law 'n' order is a
little less strict than that of the property Westerns,
allowing for quirks of character and for extenuating circumstances. Basically, though, there is really little difference between Dillon's "law" and Ben Cartwright's.
The difference is one of style and degree rather than of

basic philosophy. Both are benevolent social dictator-
ships, stressing social conformity and depending on the
whim of one man or family to decide what is "right" and
what is "wrong." Both seem to grow out of a fear of "the
prairie" and find comfort in a conforming group. Both
view deviancy from this group as not only socially un-
acceptable, but in many cases a threat to the very security and order of society.

Like the property Westerns, *Gunsmoke* insists that
everyone "go to trial" and that every crime be punished,
but it does not insist on it to the absurd extent of *Bonanza.* All the episodes on *Gunsmoke* that involve sending
people to trial involve individuals who genuinely deserve
to go to jail, while many of those on the property shows
contain more questionable cases. There was one comic
episode on *Bonanza* in which two rather absurd Eastern-
ers, who had been reading too many dime novels, try to
become famous outlaws. They bumble through it in an
episode that seems to be a parody of the outlaw myth,
but still they have to go to trial, even though the Cartwrights sympathize with their position. Matt Dillon
doesn't lock his friends up, as Joe Cartwright did in "The
Night Virginia City Died," without talking to them first.

Yet for all this *Gunsmoke* is as frightening as the
property Westerns. You're okay, it seems to say, as long
as you're part of the town, but otherwise. . . . Where
once security lay in the open spaces and a moral code
and later in a piece of property, here it lies in "a law."
The Dodge City community is a lot like *Wagon Train* but
besides having the vices of that community—its emphasis
on conformity—Dodge's citizens seem afraid of freedom.
The TV Western which began on the prairie ends by negat-
ing the values of the prairie, and sleeping out every night
becomes something one does only at great peril.

Racial and nationality types shall not be shown on television in such a manner as to ridicule race or nationality.
                                                              —NAB Code

CHAPTER VII

Indians, Blacks, Mexicans, Women, Old People, Long Hairs and Other Assorted Deviants

IN THIS STUDY THERE HAS BEEN A GREAT DEAL OF TALK ABOUT change—especially cultural shifts in image and rhetoric. Yet through all this change there have been common elements that have not really changed. The strongest of these elements has been the cultural images we have had of "deviants"—especially minorities like Blacks and Indians. Through all the years of change in the TV Western these minorities have been portrayed in a similar and usually demeaning fashion. Truman's rhetoric may change to Kennedy's or Nixon's, but through it all Blacks, Indians and other groups continue getting the short end of the stick.

When my brother was reading the chapter on *Wagon Train* he noticed that I had said that the community of the train was not the ideal community, but the ideal WASP community. His reaction was, so what?—aren't all Westerns really WASP centered. I've never seen or heard of a Western movie, TV show or whatever that had a black star. A few movies have used Indians as stars, like *Broken Arrow* and *Cheyenne Autumn*, but even these are rarities, and besides, most of them use non-Indians in the starring roles. The same goes for Mexicans.

Then of course, there's the additional dimension that everyone has been pointing out these past few years, which

171

is that all movies and TV shows,—not only Westerns—
tend to be WASP centered. There are TV specials, books,
articles and college courses which all deal with America's
racism. Some of them are good, most of them are medi-
ocre—of the "yes we know we're racist, now that we've
admitted it, let's get back to business" variety.

When my brother and I talked about the WASP and
the Western, we both agreed that the airwaves were pretty
saturated with liberal WASPs writing confessional pieces
about the racist nature of much of American society.
What was once a skeleton in the closet has become a topic
for radical chic cocktail parties and barroom gossip. It's
common knowledge now and one's impulse is to say "so
what?" as you say "so what?" to the fact that someone
has just uncovered another Defense Department boon-
doggle or that Martha Mitchell has condemned some ef-
fete snob to be shot at sunrise.

There was a period when I did decide that it was
silly to pay attention to how TV Westerns portrayed
blacks and Indians because all one could say was: yes,
here's another racist episode; we all knew it would be that
way, so what? It seemed like beating a dead horse to
spend a whole chapter or even part of a chapter explicat-
ing the obvious. There were two things that changed my
mind. The first occurred during the mid 1960's when
many TV Westerns started having episodes which were
supposed to portray minorities sympathetically. These
episodes left me with a puzzled feeling. They seemed
racist but I couldn't put my finger on what was racist
about them. This led me to raise the whole question of
why something was racist and something else was not.
The easiest thing to do today is to fall into a kind of all-
Westerns-are-racist, all-TV-shows-are-racist pattern of
thinking—which is exactly what I had been doing. Be-

cause of the exposure the whole question of racism has received, it seems to me that we are falling into some new traps which are just as insidious as the old ones. Some of my liberal friends have adopted a knee-jerk attitude in which every time some black shouts "racist" they rise up and shout, "right on!" Now the black may be right, but when I try to find out why something is racist, why he's right, they can't explain it. They say something like, all blacks are oppressed or our society's racist to the core. On the other hand, there are those who say that though there may be a few bad apples in the barrel, our society as a whole is not racist. A lot of times they figure that when a black shouts "racist!" he's doing it to get on the tube or make the liberals feel guilty—mau-mauing the flak catchers as Tom Wolfe would have it. When you ask this group why the statement or whatever the black was objecting to wasn't racist, they usually say something like well, because it's not true that just because a man refuses to hire blacks or is against school busing he's a racist.

The problem with these new stereotypes and with my own is that they really don't get to the heart of the issue, which is really how we all can live in peace and avoid the sins of the past. Take television shows, or Westerns, for example. How can we avoid making racist television shows, shows which will not encourage racism but rather will discourage it? The only way to avoid repeating the sins of the past is to understand why the sins were committed. It doesn't do any good to keep going to confession week after week and say, "Yes, I've sinned," without knowing why we've sinned.

One obvious solution to the problem is to allow more minorities into television as producers, writers, directors and actors so that stereotypes can be stamped out. White people have proven incapable of portraying and under-

standing black people so why not let black people control
their own lives? As a professor of mine once put it as
long as whites control the definitions and the process of
definition for all groups, then they will continue to per-
petuate racial stereotypes. He who controls the definitions controls the society.

No one can argue with this or with the solution, but
I wonder whether to do *only* this doesn't let whites off
the hook. Like my liberal friends maybe we all ought to
just shout "right on!" every time a black shouts "racist!"
Being a rather feisty individual I resist this, if only because I don't like being put into a situation where someone else does *my* defining. As some blacks would say—
"You squawk pretty loud when the shoe's on your foot"
which is true. I also resist for another obvious reason,
which is what do we do when one black shouts "racist!"
and another says "bull" and then the first calls the
second an Uncle Tom? Ultimately there's no getting
around it, we whites have got to jump into the pit of the
hell we've created and try to climb our way out.

So, if only for my own satisfaction, I've got to do
this chapter. Doing it is not easy, either. Besides all the
traps I've already mentioned, there are a host of others.
In the Western they ultimately boil down to that one
nagging question, "What were or are those people really
like?" We're back at definitions again, running around in
circles and each time you go around you stop and wonder
if you aren't chasing your own shadow. We're understanding or trying to understand what it is about Westerns, about America, about Western civilization that makes
us continue to use certain stereotypes? Westerns, as I've
said, are only fables of our identity and we're presently
undergoing a hell of an identity crisis. In writing this
chapter I found myself reading Indian autobiographies,

black and chicano writing, white and minority essays on
American and Western racist patterns. I'd see an Apache
on *High Chaparral* and be moved to look up how Apaches
dressed, what their social and religious customs were and
what their attitudes towards the first white settlers were.

The more research I did and the more episodes I saw,
the more I became convinced that this racism is a part of a
much larger problem in the TV Western: the whole question of deviancy. It seemed to me that not only did the
pattern include blacks, Indians and Mexicans, it also included women, old people, long hairs, etc. All of these
people were deviants in the world of the Western and all
of them represented a threat to certain values and themes.
With each group the deviancy and the threat varied somewhat, but they still were part of this larger pattern.

With all these groups, as well as the others mentioned in the chapter title, the most obvious source of
deviancy is physical appearance and dress, for none of the
groups conform to the white, male, anglo-saxon, decorum-
conscious heroes of the TV Western. As with the baddie,
though, physical appearance is only half of the equation
which in its complete form reads: "baddies will be deviants." What the equation stresses is that anyone who
looks different from the established norm will also behave
differently than the established norm, perhaps to the extent that he will ultimately subvert the society which is
held together by those norms. Of course not all deviants
are baddies, although all baddies are deviants. A few
"characters" like Sally Fergus are token deviants who are
usually played for laughs. With those deviants who are
not humorously portrayed or aren't baddies, the equation
becomes more complex, especially in those shows or episodes that try to portray these deviants sympathetically.
Usually in these cases the classic maneuver is to deny that

deviancy exists, to assert, for instance, that blacks, as the
slang goes, are really oreo cookies—black on the outside
and white on the inside, plain folks *just* like you and me.
A variation of this approach is the so-called "super nigger"
strategy which asserts that blacks are not only like us,
some of them are even such paragons of oreo virtue that
they are even better than most of us. The problem with
all these approaches is that they are a denial of several
thousand years of history and culture. Moreover they
are insidiously racist in their insistence that what is still
the yardstick for judging these people is their conformity
to the norms of the white majority. In line with this there
was an article in *Rolling Stone* about Sly Stone, which
quoted one of Sly's managers or promoters as believing
that there were really two Sly Stones: one, Sylvester
Stewart (Sly's "real" name), was a good "boy" who
minded his manager, showed up for concerts and was
courteous at interviews. The other Sly Stone was an evil
bastard, who never showed at concerts, always argued
with his manager and treated the press with contempt.
With all these groups there are Sylvesters and Slys, those
who are what their white "managers" want them to be
and those who are something else. Now there is no point
in going into the Sylvesters, or the oreo cookies or the
"super niggers," because they are all just like us, or at
least what we like to think we are. They are like the members of the Nevada Club or the Cattlemen's Association
or the plain people of the towns, all of which we have
already described. The interesting figures are the Slys,
those individuals who don't follow their "managers,"
and what is interesting about them is not that they don't
represent the real people behind the labels anymore than
their antithesis, but that they represent a negative image
of ourselves. Above all we fear our deviants and in those

fears is an expression of those things we feel are the most vulnerable in our culture.

With the Indians of the TV Western this fear stems from a deep belief that Indians are so different that we cannot possibly understand them. The "good" Indian acts like a white man, with "rationality" and "decorum," while the "bad" Indian acts in some way that seems irrational or childish. As a character in *The High Chaparral* puts it, speaking of the "bad" Apaches who are threatening to attack, "There's no way to figure the way an Apache thinks." Behind this paranoia is the belief that Indians— at least TV Indians—are primitive people whose lack of sophistication and so-called civilized virtues makes them savages who are apt to commit the most heinous crimes or participate in the most irrational kind of actions.

This feeling is especially prominent when the TV Western attempts to deal with Indian religious leaders or prophets who oppose the white settlers as in an episode on *The Men From Shiloh*, "The Regimental Line," which deals with the Ghost Dance movement and a similar *Bonanza* episode, "A Sense of Duty." In the Ghost Dance episode the tone is set from the beginning when Colonel MacKenzie observes that the Ghost Dance seems like "the same kind of superstition" as one which had manifested itself "among the more primitive tribes of northern India." Colonel MacKenzie, who was a British soldier in India, makes an analogy not unlike that of his fellow European Christopher Columbus, who named the first native Americans he saw Indians because their physical appearance and culture were more "primitive" than the Europeans. Some five hundred years later a TV writer is still making the same mistake. A *High Chaparral* episode, showing Indians riding horses with blankets over what were obviously saddles, used Indian music—sitar music—as a back-

ground theme for the Indians, one of whom was plainly
wearing a gold wedding ring. As the episode portrays
them the Ghost Dancers are a bunch of renegade Indians
who go about wantonly butchering cattle ("Didn't even
butcher'm for eating") and scalping people. As TV land
would have it, the Ghost Dancers did a good deal of
raiding, but not too much dancing. How they got
their name seems to be a mystery to the TV writers,
even though the real Ghost Dancers were a pacifist
movement that did a good deal of dancing and no
raiding. In *The Men From Shiloh* the Ghost Dancers
are raiders because they carry an amulet which they
believe will make them immune to the white man's
bullets and enable them to drive the whites from their
land. The climactic scene comes when Colonel Mac-
Kenzie faces down the Ghost Dance leader by showing him a dead Indian who is also wearing a "magic"
amulet. The leader looks at MacKenzie, then at his
dead friend, then at the Ghost Dance amulet, like
some ignorant child trying to understand something
which is obvious to grown-ups. Suddenly his eyes
change expression and he rips off his own amulet,
throws it down on the ground, looks to the sky mumbling and then runs off.

As *The Men From Shiloh* portrays them, the Ghost
Dancers are similar to the historical Ghost Dancers in
name only. The historical Ghost Dancers didn't do any
raiding, had nothing to do with magical amulets that stop
the white man's bullets—in fact the only similarity is the
TV Ghost Dancers and historical Ghost Dancers did not
want to become pseudo-white hang-around-the-forts. The
question obviously arises as to why the TV episode should
so distort a historical Indian movement as to make it all
but unrecognizable, *except* for the name. One wonders

what the TV executives thought would be the reactions
of the living relatives of the Ghost Dancers to such a portrayal and only two answers seem plausible: either they
didn't even think about the Indians' reaction or they
thought that today's Indians would not mind this distortion of their history. Now, admittedly TV land has done
its share of distorting white history—but never to this
extent. It would be like taking Abraham Lincoln and
making him a midget from a big city who secretly was a
Southern spy with a big plantation.

The Men From Shiloh could perhaps plead ignorance
or some other failure, except that their distortion of the
Ghost Dance fits a pattern of distorting Indian religious
movements—a pattern which occures in the *Bonanza* episode "A Sense of Duty" (1967). The *Bonanza* doesn't
deal with Ghost Dancers, rather it takes a fictional Indian "holy man" named Wabuska and portrays him as a
fanatic who believes that bullets cannot hurt him, because
"fire, air, wind and water are the friends of Wabuska."
Of course Ben Cartwright exposes the farce of Wabuska's
claim by pointing a pistol at him and threatening to pull
the trigger—this occurs after Cartwright's militia detach-
ment and the Indians have lost a few men in trying to
escort Wabuska to jail for inciting the Indians. Why Cartwright didn't do this earlier is never explained.

The pattern that exists seems to revolve around
Ben's statement, "He's a man, a man like you and me."
Both *Bonanza* and *The Men From Shiloh* try to assert
that underneath Indians are just like whites. In order to
do this they have to demonstrate that something that
makes them Indians, their religion, is absurd; so they pick
the wildest and most distorted example they can think of,
stack the deck and invite everybody to a nice friendly
game of cards. Yet if they are so sure of themselves why

pick such a loaded deck—why not play fair? The answer
seems to lie in that phrase from *The High Chaparral*—you
can't "figure the way an Apache thinks." For over two
hundred years a heavily out-manned and out-gunned people held off the virtuous WASP advance, striking suddenly,
retreating and striking again. In the old Protestant mind
there could be only two ways of explaining this either
God or the Devil was on their side. To more recent Prot-
estants there could only be two explanations—either they
didn't play fair or they were so crazy that they were irrational. Either way you have it, you can't predict what
your enemy will do, because he isn't like "normal" fair-
playing Americans. The "didn't play fair" motif occurs
in the many examples of savage, scalping Indians in
movies and TV and in the topsy turvy situations in which
several hundred Indians with rifles lay siege to four or
five whites with pistols. In TV land it's the whites not
the Indians who are out-gunned and out-manned. The
Wabuska and Ghost Dance episodes seem to follow the
belief that Indians were primitive and irrational, as though
the only way you motivated Indians to futiley attack a
few whites was to convince the Indians that they were invincible. After all, as the Bob Dylan song goes, haven't
we whites always had God on our side?

Yet the problem goes deeper for it seems behind
this kind of self-righteousness lies the fear that God isn't
really on our side. Whites, when they haven't been mad
at or afraid of Indians, have always been puzzled by
them and all three attitudes seem to stem from a belief
that they know something we don't know—something
dark and mysterious about the natural world. From the
earliest writings we have through the man of the forest
of Cooper to today's fascination with native American
religions, whites have always both admired and feared

the Indians' knowledge of and attitude towards his environment. One of the best selling books in recent years among young people has been Carlos Castaneda's series on the Yaqui sorcerer Don Juan, all of which revolve around the immense and mysterious natural power possessed by the sorcerer. He looks at the world and "sees" it in a way we cannot. He can manipulate natural objects in seemingly magical ways. We whites with our positivistic world view, our science, our technology have always wondered deep inside whether the world was so orderly and whether all that seemed to be really was. The white man's contacts with the Indian occurred during the period of the rise of scientific positivism and it is perhaps no coincidence that our greatest persecutions of the Indian occurred during the late nineteenth century when many people thought science and positivism were about to plug the universe into one great natural plan. Yet even then there were doubters and the Indian and his way of life, his world view stood as an uncomfortable reminder of those doubts. Anthropologists would try to place him on some scale of primitivism as though he were a relic from another time period—but the time period was always that one that lurked in the back of white minds—of the middle ages and witchcraft and mystics.

Contributing to our feelings about the Indian have also been some rather obvious pangs of guilt.

The guilt comes not from the belief that particular whites like Colonel MacKenzie or Ben Cartwright are guilty of any of these sins, but that there are Indians who believe all whites are guilty, regardless of how virtuous we may think we are. Both Wabuska and the Ghost Dancers make it plain that they hate all white men, period, and that they're coming to scalp all of us. The good Indian, on the other hand, may dresss like an Indian, pound on the drums now and then, sing a few songs and smoke a peace pipe, but he judges his whites as individuals. This situation has the ring of a similar situation in the early days of the black power movement, when whites accused Stokely Carmichael of "reverse racism" for advocating black as opposed to some other kind of power. The black power movement as a whole, though, never subscribed to the dogma that all whites are a priori bad. The question does arise as to whether the TV Western's use of the good-bad Indian (or as we shall see, black) motif is racist. It is rather strange that the white world should see the bad Indian as a racist, that is, one who hates all whites. It's as though we were projecting our own sins upon those we have oppressed, perhaps out of guilt for this sin. The bad Indian is our own nightmare come back to haunt us. The good Indian is what we all think, or at least hope we are, since he judges whites as individuals, which means in our own minds most of us would probably pass muster. In its purest form the good-bad Indian motif is probably not racist, but in the context of the TV Western it is not pure. What makes the good-bad Indian motif or the TV Western racist is the fact that the standards the good Indian uses to judge his whites are white standards—i.e., the same deviancy vs. decorum scale—and that the Indians who are good Indians are not unlike good whites in their dress (which may be buckskins, beads and a warbonnet, but which is worn with decorum) and social status (notice how most good Indians wear warbonnets and ride fancy horses). All of this ignores Indian cultures, which have different standards of measuring good and bad individuals than ours, which have different standards of deviancy than ours. For example, some Indians might regard John Cannon as a bad individual because he purports to own a huge piece

of property with all its timber, water and game and that
he makes all the final decisions about how this property
is to be used autocratically. (Notice how TV land shows
the chiefs as exercising a similar autocratic political
power—which in actuality very few chiefs did.) Similarly
Indians would probably regard bounty-hunters Paladin
and Josh Randall as rather strange. In the TV land good-
bad Indian motif, however, none of these situations arise
since the good Indian uses the same standards as the show
and its stars which enables the stars to be fast friends
with the good Indians. The good Indian ultimately reinforces our own image of ourselves and our values enabling
us to have a clear conscience about them. We come to
see oppression of minorities as the acts of deviant individuals, both white and Indian, and never question the
role ideas about land use and manifest destiny played in
this oppression.

This theme of the good Indian is usually a dominant
one in those episodes which purport to treat Indians sympathetically. A 1968 *Bonanza*, "Burning Sky," dealt with
a white-Indian marriage by contrasting the attitudes of
prejudiced whites (who are "riff-raff," who don't shave,
dress sloppily, speak bad English—the head agitator even
owns a still) with those of good whites like the Cartwrights. The problem with this episode is that the Indian, her husband, and Ben Cartwright are all of the same
social strata. As Holt, the husband, puts it, "My wife's
father, grandfather, and great-grandfather were Sioux
chiefs and my great-grandfather served under George
Washington." What we have here is "a union of two established families," but the question is never faced about
what to do with those Indians who aren't chiefs. The
chiefs, their sons and duaghters (who in TV land were
wearing miniskirts before whites) are always the ones who

see the light first. Apparently good Indians are not unlike the good whites in that they are "quality people"
rather than "riff raff." Just to make sure we know they're
quality people, these chiefs and their offspring are played
by whites.

Using white actors isn't so easy to do with blacks,
though, since the old blackface routine has been out for
quite awhile. What the TV Western does with good and
bad blacks is to use the same physical deviancy routine it
uses with whites—after all don't the so-called "bad,"
"militant" blacks on the six o'clock news all wear afros,
dashikis and speak in ghetto dialect? In a *Gunsmoke* episode, "The Good Samaritan" (1967), the bad black has a
floppy hat and a leather ear—that's right, a leather ear—
which leads everybody to call him "old leather ear."
(Incidently, notice how many cripples are deviant baddies.) The episode deals with a conflict between the bad
black, who like the bad Indian doesn't like whites, and a
good black named Juba, who has a white beard which
makes him look like an illustration for *Uncle Tom's Cabin*
or Walt Disney's *Song of the South.* Juba's motto is
"just pray and believe and do," which he interprets as
meaning, "We're in the hands of the good Lord and when
it comes time for what we need, we'll have it." The militant, Cato, takes a more activist position, which gets him
into trouble. The militant black motif also appears in an
episode, "Crooked Corner," (1971) on *The Men From
Shiloh.* Here an over-dressed black in a fancy suit, bowler
hat, vest and tie, seeks to drive some German immigrants
away because "Heinies eat different, talk different, think
different."

The themes of both these episodes reflect the same
stereotypes as those dealing with Indians. Bad blacks
hate all whites, good ones don't. This is quite obvious in

an exchange between Cato and Juba where Cato says, re-
ferring to his ear, "They took it off," and Juba answers,
"Mr. Thomas Kingsley, not they." In the *Shiloh* episode
the black's problem is that he is as prejudiced as any
white. After all aren't they just like us, except, of course,
for the bad ones? Well, not exactly. The blacks in the
Gunsmoke episode speak a weird dialect that is a mixture
of nineteenth century pseudo-plantation black and twentieth century slang. Underneath, though, the good
blacks are just like the good whites, they aren't too pushy,
they stay in their place. After all we need bartenders and
pig farmers as well as big ranchers.

Of course, on TV there are no black ranchers, only
a few token cowboys, no black bartenders, and not even
one token pig farmer. The amazing thing about the portrayal of blacks in TV Westerns is that, even though historically blacks played an important role in opening the
West, they are never shown in episodes unless the episode
is for an obvious racial purpose—that is, to convey some
white's message about racial justice and equality. Indians
appear in quite a few Westerns, perhaps because they're
"the other side," while blacks don't, perhaps because
blacks helped us open the West. To show a black would
mean we would have to show someone who was equal or
superior to us—someone who could draw as fast as Wyatt
Earp, who could ride as well as Gene Autry, and who was
as big and strong as Matt Dillon. That, of course, would
offend some viewers and the last thing TV land wants to
do is offend. Someone might interject here that one
show, *Daniel Boone*, which is not a Western, did use blacks
as co-stars in almost an equal way. Perhaps, but notice
that Rosy Greer is made chief of an Indian tribe and
Gideon is a trapper who spends most of his time deep in
the woods. Also notice that although Boone respects

both men, he's still better than they are at woodcraft. Raymond St. Jacques of *Rawhide*, the only Western with a black co-star, is also a good cowboy but not as good as Rowdy Yates.

Unlike the good Indian, who is a chief or close to it, the good black is just folks. He's not "quality people," but is usually just a good, average, law-abiding citizen. Again this may come from a difference in the way whites view the two cultures. Indian culture is different and "primitive" so a good Indian has to be more than just a commoner, more than primitive. He has to be better than his people, and his people have to see him as better as if we needed to twist Indian culture to verify our own. Blacks, on the other hand, are different, but are a great deal more culturally like us than Indians, at least the stereotype seems to say so. While a good many whites still view Indians as wearing warbonnets, living in teepees and trading wampum, they view blacks as living and dressing like us. Ask someone to draw an Indian and he'll draw the whole warbonnet bit, but ask him to draw a black and he'll draw someone who looks white and then color it in. Even the term black or Negro refers to color while Indian is more cultural in meaning. The good black, then, can't be given a high station like the Indian.

Mexicans in the TV Westerns tend to be more in the pattern of Indians. *The High Chaparral* is most explicit in showing the Montoyas as a high class, noble family. Victoria was once courted by European royalty, but of course, she marries the WASP commoner, John Cannon. Then there are the priests. Notice how an inordinate number of good Mexicans are priests. Of course, there's always the ploy of showing that good Mexicans aren't really Mexicans but Spaniards. Once in awhile a Mexican peasant—and that's the term some episodes use—is por-

trayed as good, but it is interesting to note that these
good Mexicans live in, stay in, and are satisfied to stay
in Mexico. They're just happy, carefree peasants.

The Mexican baddie, on the other hand, is the classic
bandito figure—sombrero, moustache and cartridge belts
over the shoulders. Of all the TV Western baddies the
Mexican bandito is probably the most despicable—he's
dirtier, nastier, fouler than any other baddie. In a *Gunsmoke* episode, "The Jackals," (1968) a Mexican bandito
even picks his ears and uses the wax on his moustache.
No white baddie was ever shown doing anything like that
in any episode of any show.

Yet even though the good Mexicans are landowners,
or Spanish, or happy peasants, they too are sometimes
subject to the same racism as the bandito. Mexicans are
portrayed as being more emotional and more capable of
excess than whites. Manolito of *The High Chaparral* is a
hot blooded wencher and drinker—the old hot Latin
routine. Victoria erupts into tirades of shouting in Spanish or throws things and slams doors—the old "Latin spit-
fire" routine. Old Montoya is portrayed as being very
much like his son, Manolito. Mexicans are different,
whether good or bad, but as long as they stay on their
side of the border, they're okay. Blacks and Indians, on
the other hand, live here and present a more immediate
threat. The bandito does some of his raiding on this side
of the border, so he too is a threat.

Women, old people, and long hairs represent a different type of deviancy than blacks, Mexicans and Indians—
after all women are white. Yet their kind of deviancy
can also be a threat as insidious as the other three groups.

In a world where the heroes are celibate and avoid
any relationship with women, except an ogling look or
an occasional kiss, the position of women is unusual, to

say the least. Although our society purports to regard
marriage as the ideal man-woman relationship, the only
married people on the TV Western are the average, common people—and even in most Westerns there are really
very few married couples who appear as more than background figures. When marriage is shown the woman is
usually a submissive, kitchen-dwelling creature. In reality
we know that pioneer Western women often worked side
by side with their husbands in the fields, helped build
cabins, and tended the stock as well as attending to
household chores like cooking. Yet no married woman
on the TV Western is shown doing anything besides
cooking or "taking care of the kids." A few widows are
shown managing their own farms or ranches, but even
they are usually spoken of as needing men—not for sexual
or emotional reasons, but to "take care of" them and the
children.

Most of the women in the TV Westerns, though, are
not married and these usually fall into one of three stereotypes, which to some extent I've already discussed:
the good girl, the good-bad woman, and the bad woman.
The good girl is the girl of the horse Westerns who is virginal, virtuous and falls head over heels for the star. The
good girl is always submissive, except where her virginity
is concerned. She'll do anything for the hero and nothing
for anybody else. Like the celibate hero she de-empha-
sizes her sexuality, appearing to be some kind of asexual
symbol—what Eldridge Cleaver in *Soul On Ice* called the
ultrafeminine ideal—a woman to be looked at, set on a
pedestal, but never touched. In a *Men From Shiloh* episode entitled "Tate: Ramrod," (1970) a teenage girl falls
for Tate and puts on a low-cut dress to seduce him into
kissing her. Tate gives her a lecture instead, "No real
woman would have done that. . . . You want to be a

real woman, you act like one." Later the hot young
teenager appears in a long dress and shawl; she's now a
"real woman."

Unlike the good girl, the bad girl doesn't have to
worry whether she's a "real woman." In fact, she couldn't
care less. There are actually several types of bad girls,
ranging from the out and out slut to the scheming female
who uses men to get what she wants. The bad girl is no
ultrafeminine ideal; what she's got she flaunts. Where
the good girl is reserved or asexual, the bad girl is brazenly
sexual. For example, in a recent *Gunsmoke*, "Tara,"
(1971) Tara is a sexy brunette, who wears low-cut dresses
and seduces, sweet talks and lies to her husband, an outlaw, and Newley O'Brien, all to get her hands on $5,000
which her husband stole in a train robbery. The bad girl
may be a saloon girl in a revealing dress with a drink in
one hand, the hero in the other, while the good girl is a
schoolmarm in a granny dress, with a flower in one hand
and a lace handkerchief in the other.

Both good and bad girls are like good and bad Indians, mirror images in the minds of the dominant WASP
male majority. The good girl represents the old Protestant virtues of kinder, kuche, submissiveness, and an asex-
uality which comes natural to a tradition and a medium
(TV) which sees sex as something dirty that cannot be
discussed. The bad girl, of course, comes out of the same
tradition for she is a totally sexual being. She's the girl
that keeps the double standard going. Yet she's even
more than that, for like the bad black and deviant outlaw,
she uses her sexuality to advance herself in society, to
scheme and trick unwitting males into robbing banks or
whatever. Unlike the good girl, who is comfortable in the
kitchen, the bad girl wants to be somebody other than a
domestic drudge.

What the good-bad girl does is combine the best
virtues of both good girl and bad girl. The good-bad
girl is more independent and less submissive than the
good girl, yet is not as scheming as the bad girl. There
aren't too many good-bad girls in TV Westerns—in fact
it is difficult to think of one. Perhaps the only woman
who comes close is Kitty, of *Gunsmoke*. Aided by
Amanda Blake's portrayal, Kitty is the closest television
Westerns have come to a normal woman. Kitty has her
own career in running the Longbranch Saloon and she
runs it with an iron hand. She's not above beaning an
outlaw over the head or telling off some drunk who's
gotten obnoxious. Yet even Kitty must submit to male
domination in the figure of "big marshal" Matt Dillon.
Where Matt is reticent about his feelings for Kitty, it's
no secret what Kitty thinks of Matt. Once or twice she
has left town because she wanted Matt to quit marshal-
ing, yet always she's come back.

Other TV Westerns like *Annie Oakley* and episodes
like "Sam McTavish, M.D." on *Gunsmoke* have used
women in featured roles, but most of these women are
super-women, tomboys. Sam McTavish is a woman doctor who outfishes and outdoctors Doc. As Doc describes
her, "If I was a bettin' man I'd put my money on you to
outman any man I'd ever seen." Sam (note the name)
replies that that is a compliment, which prompts Doc
to add, "You're the only woman who'd recognize it."
Yet even Sam is submissive to Doc, for they fall in love.
Doc courts her saying, "Tomorrow you start doctorin'
. . . tonight you're a lady," as though the two are mutu-
ally exclusive. Annie Oakley like Sam McTavish is a
crack shot, who is shown shooting holes in a card while
standing on a galloping horse. Gene Autry's Flying A
Productions developed the Annie character during the

days of the early TV Western because they wanted to
produce a show for "distaff cowboys." Like Sam, Annie
can outman any man. Superwomen like Annie and Sam
fit into a pattern as old and compelling as the Amazons,
which is what they are. Unlike the Amazons Annie and
Sam are no threat to male society since ultimately they,
too, are different from males.

There's one final type of female stereotype which I
can only call "the meddling female." For some reason
the TV Western portrays all people who are interested in
social reform as "meddling females." If someone is interested in prison reform, or gun control or whatever, it is
almost always a woman and usually that woman is portrayed as a "flighty female" from the East who doesn't
understand the realities of the West. Needless to say
Women Libbers had the decks stacked against them from
the start, since they are either meddling women or bad
women. And as for male reformers, well there just aren't
any.

Women are fairly common in TV Westerns, at least
as window dressings as bar girls and farmers' wives, but
the amazing thing about old people in the TV Western is
that they're almost invisible. Everyone in television land
seems to be in their twenties or middle thirties, with a
few "oldsters " of forty appearing now and then. TV
land is youth land. Perhaps one of the reasons for *Bonanza*'s popularity lies in the fact that Ben Cartwright is
portrayed as being in his fifties, which makes him one of
the oldest stars on the tube, and that in Ben age becomes
a positive attribute suggesting visions of the wise old sage.

Other old people are not so lucky though. Many of
them are like the old man in a *Virginian* episode, "Old
Cowboy" (1965). "Gramps" is portrayed as an old man
who is still trying to live up to the tales he tells about

being one of the best ramrods in the days of the old
Chisholm Trail. Gramps tries to ride a bronc and rope
calves and ends up looking absurd. He's the old "second
childhood" stereotype—old people trying to relive or be
just like young people. All this is just another affirmation of the idea that young, male, and WASP is the thing
to be. Gramps is nothing like the old people I've seen
who have lived in wilderness or semi-wilderness areas.
Unlike Gramps these people are tough old guys who've
learned how to do a lot of work without the huffing and
puffing wasted motion of many young men. I can remember chopping wood with an old man who looked like he
was working half as hard as I was, but in the end he had
done just as much because he knew exactly where to
chop and with just the right amount of force. There was
no wasted motion in what he did, while there was quite a
bit in what I did. Gramps seems ready for an old people's
home, while the old man I chopped wood with probably
would have put me in one if I'd tried to keep up with him.

As opposed to the other deviants, old people really
aren't much of a threat, except when they decide to imitate the younger stars of the Western. Old people imi-
tating the action stunts of the younger stars would
counter TV's beautiful people images. To show old people
as heroes would detract from the young virginal heroes
of most Westerns and in turn the virgin land myth from
which they stem. The virgin land of the mythic West has
no room for old people, except in situations like *The
Prairie* where the aged Leatherstocking dies as his myth
is dying. The aged pioneer or cowboy suggests an aged
myth, an old gunfighter who's lost his speed.

As youth-centered as the Western and the myth are
you might expect young people to be fairly prominent in
TV Westerns, which they are. In most of these Westerns

the good-bad formula is plugged right into the culture's views of good-bad youth at the time. For instance the good youths of the fifties' Westerns were played like David and Ricky Nelson on the *Ozzie and Harriet* TV show. Some Westerns like *Lawman* seemed to make a play for hip viewers, featuring characters with hair combed in fancy styles—although not in DA's and shirts open down the front like Deputy Johnny McKay.

With the middle sixties and the advent of long-haired, media-labelled "hippies," the youth angle became a bit harder to play, especially when some of those long hairs were "our" sons and daughters. Some of the stars like Joe Cartwright let their hair grow a little. Even Matt Dillon's hair is a little longer although it is still fairly neat.

In one of its "relevant" episodes *Bonanza* decided to confront the so-called "youth movement" head-on and aired an episode entitled "The Weary Willies" about a group of long-haired civil war veterans who drop out (but don't tune in or turn on) looking for, well . . . something. Adopted son, Jamie, asks Ben about the Willies. To Jamie the Willies sound like "someone who doesn't know what he wants to be when he grows up," and Ben answers that it's "something like that." The Willies on *Bonanza* are drop-outs who build shelters, roam from town to town, trying to get by on as little as possible. Ben tells them they can stay on his land, if they'll work for it. Of course none of them do. There is a good Willie, though, Krulak, who is a silversmith and who makes Jamie a concho out of a silver dollar. Characteristically, Krulak is the neatest and shortest-haired Willie. Like the Indians and blacks, the Willies fall afoul of the town ruffians who beat one to death and burn their camp. That the deck is stacked against the Willies

as much as the other groups is brought out in a final
dialogue between Ben and a Willie who is walking through
the ruins of their camp. The Willie says he hopes people
will stop "being selfish and greedy and violent and suspicious," and Ben retorts, "and be like you?" When Willie
asks if that would be so bad, Ben says no, but goes on to
lecture him about withdrawing from the world telling him,
"Don't withdraw . . . become part of it. Make it better."
Rather than retort that he is making it better by not
owning a huge ranch or doing some violent, greedy, selfish
or suspicious act, the Willie says, "Why should I?" Ben's
answer: "It's the only world you've got."
    Yet in this only world it is plain deviants are not
wanted—so where are they to go?
    The Willies' episode makes it clear that they can no
longer go down the mythic road to the virgin land. The
Willies quote Walt Whitman on being free, sing folksongs,
and are characterized by a camera which always shows
them in nature—by a placid lake, lying on a hill with a
spear of grass in their mouths (visions of Walt and his
leaf). When the Willies are threatened by the townspeople, they do not, or cannot, or are not allowed to escape
to the virgin land; they are taken into "protective" custo-
dy" by the sheriff and Ben and "the good people." In a
torchlit scene the Willies and their possessions are loaded
into wagons to be driven off to jail or a detention camp.
Like *Gunsmoke*, *Bonanza* views the prairie with suspicion
and marches those who are identified with it off to jail.

PART THREE

Fables of Our Identity

195

The movie I selected, or, as a matter of fact my daughter Tricia selected it, was "Chisum" with John Wayne. It was a Western.

As I looked at that movie I said, "Well, it was a very good Western. John Wayne is a very fine actor and it had a fine supporting cast. But it was basically another Western, far better than average movies, better than average Westerns."

I wondered why it is that the Westerns survive year after year. A good Western will outdraw some of the other subjects. Perhaps one of the reasons, in addition to the excitement, the gun play and the rest, which is part of it but they can get that in other kinds of movies—one of the reasons is perhaps, and this may be a square observation, the good guys come out ahead in the Westerns, the bad guys lose.

In the end, as this movie particularly pointed out, even in the old West, the time before New Mexico was a state, there was a time when there was no law. But the law eventually came, and the law was important from the standpoint of not only prosecuting the guilty, but also seeing that those who were guilty had a proper trial.

As we look at the situation today, I think the main concern that I have is the attitudes that are created among many of our younger people and also perhaps older people as well, in which we tend to glorify and make heroes out of those who engage in criminal activities. This is not done intentionally by the press. It is not done intentionally by radio and television, I know. It is done perhaps because people want to read or see that kind of story.

—President Nixon
Denver, August 3, 1970

CHAPTER VIII

Nixon's Manson Speech and
Bob Dylan's JOHN WESLEY HARDING

PRESIDENT NIXON'S FAMOUS—OR INFAMOUS AS SOME WOULD have it—speech about the guilt of Charles Manson is a curious document and one which has not received the attention it has deserved. Placed in the context of the TV Western and recent film Westerns by Altman, Hellman and Peckinpah, Nixon's remarks on Westerns and on Manson become more than just a slip of the tongue, or as others would have it, a moment when the facade of the "new" Nixon was dropped and the "old" Nixon once again appeared. I am no great admirer of Richard Nixon, yet I see in his remarks an attempt to articulate his reactions to certain currents or trends in our culture, which can be seen quite clearly in an overview of the TV (and film) Western. In a large part Nixon and I are reacting to the same forces, although our political philosophies lead us to take different courses in response to these forces. We are also from two quite different political generations, and in the context of the TV Western this generation gap is unfortunately very, very real and very, very wide.

In a broad sense Nixon was merely articulating the so-called "law and order" philosophy which has become associated with his administration. He was reacting against the sensationalistic and sometimes glamorous picture which was being painted by many members of the press of a man who at the time stood accused of masterminding a series of brutal murders, just as he had in the past reacted to press stories which glamorized youthful demonstrators, especially at the 1968 Chicago Convention, bomb-throwing radicals like the Weathermen, and various dissident minority groups like the Black Panthers and the Young Lords. In the case of Manson, Nixon's remarks were quite justified—although he had no business commenting on the guilt or innocence of a man on trial for his life, especially when his remarks might have had the boomerang effect of allowing Manson's lawyers to move to dismiss the whole case on the grounds that the remarks make it impossible for their client to receive a fair trial. As for Nixon's remarks about student demonstrators as "bums" or his criticisms of the Panthers, enough has already been said by others.

Nixon's Manson speech and his other speeches on
law and order and the glorifying of criminals are part of a
larger phenomenon which Nixon and others speak of as
the erosion of law in our society. What he and others
usually mean by this is that no one in society has any respect for laws and their enforcers—not Manson, not demonstrators, not Weathermen, not Black Panthers, not the
hundreds of robbers, murderers and rapists who threaten
the citizens of big cities like Washington, D.C. and have
turned them into paranoid armed camps, with the white
middle class suspecting every black ghetto dweller of
criminal intent, the police equally paranoid about blacks—
especially with the increasing numbers of murdered
policemen—and blacks being paranoid about unjustified
police searches and unjustified white allegations about
the role of blacks as both criminal and victim in various
crimes. Almost a year after the Manson speech, Joseph
Alsop caught the spirit of this law and order thrust in a
July 19, 1971 column. I quote Alsop at length, because
his remarks seem to be a good articulation of the law and
order philosophy and because they have relevance to the
context of the TV Western:

> *Ten years ago, would many thousands of
> young people have invaded the national capital
> in order to "close down the government," com-
> mitting many illegal acts in that attempt? Twenty
> years ago?*
>
> *Ten years ago, would workers in essential
> public services—garbagemen, postal workers,
> police—knowingly break the law by going on
> strike? Twenty years ago?*
>
> *Ten years ago, would the editors of* The New
> York Times, *though advised by counsel that to
> do so might well be illegal, have published ver-*

*batim large numbers of secret government doc-
uments? Twenty years ago?*[1]

Characteristically Nixon and most law and order types
omit certain other crimes from their law and order inven-
tory. These are the white collar crimes.

Although at least politically the law and order philosophy has dominated the media, another current, perhaps
just as strong, was flowing underground where it had a
powerful influence on many who constitute the so-
called counter culture. As the Manson Speech was to the
law and order types, a seminal, but somewhat neglected,
document to this underground current was Bob Dylan's
1968 album, *John Wesley Harding.* Like Nixon, Dylan
goes to the Western for his metaphors, except that the
metaphor Dylan chose was John Wesley Harding, a Robin
Hoodish "outlaw" friend to the poor, who stood for right
and never hurt an honest man. One verse goes, "It was
down in Chaney County, a time they talk about, with his
lady by his side he took a stand, and soon the situation
there was all but straightened out, for he was always known
to lend a helping hand." Dylan's Harding is pursued by
the forces of law and order, but "no charge against him
could be proved." The most powerful song on the album
—one of the best Dylan has written and one of the best of
the decade—is "I Dreamed I Saw St. Augustine."

I dreamed I saw St. Augustine
alive as you or me
tearing through these quarters in the utmost misery
with a blanket underneath his arm and a coat of
  solid gold
searching for the very souls who already have been
  sold

The song triggers some very strong emotions in my head,

because we have already had far, far too many martyrs,— the Kennedys, massacred students, the civil rights leaders— everyone who seems to have stood out above the crowd because they believed in something, quite a few who believed but did not stand out, and a few who went on their way accordingly. "St. Augustine" is a credo for a generation and an epitaph for an era.

A third song on the album, "Dear Landlord," takes the themes of "St. Augustine" and the song "John Wesley Harding" and directs them explicitly at America. "Dear Landlord" is an attempt to state a philosophy and reach an understanding with a country that seems out of step with itself and with its people. The song begins with a plea, "please don't put a price on my soul;" moves into analysis, "I know you've suffered much but in this you are not so unique . . . and anyone can fill his life up with things he can see but he just cannot touch;" and ends with a firm commitment, "I'm not about to argue, I'm not about to move to no other place. . . . Each of us has his own special gift, and you know this was meant to be true, and if you don't underestimate me, I won't underestimate you."

As Dylan portrays him, John Wesley Harding (whose name is a corruption of the name of a historical Western gunman named John Wesley Hardin) is quite similar to the heroes of the horse Western. Like the Lone Ranger and the Cisco Kid, Harding is a two-gun cowboy who roams the West righting wrongs as a champion of the poor, but never hurts honest men. Like the Cisco Kid, Harding has troubles with the law, but he is too smart for them. Like both heroes he lives by a code rather than by strict adherence to the laws—which can be and are corrupted by those seeking material gains.

In contrast to Dylan, Nixon's law and order stance

is quite similar to the message of the property Westerns. Notice in the speech how he jumps from speaking of the classic melodramatic Western in the second paragraph— "The good guys come out ahead . . . the bad guys lose" —to speaking about the law, as though the good guys were always on the side of the law and the bad guys against it. And lest we mistake what he means by the law, the President adds a definition—"and the law was important from the standpoint of not only prosecuting the guilty, but also in seeing that those who were guilty had a proper trial." The point is hammered home by the reference to those who "glorify and make heroes out of those who engage in criminal activities" and specifically to Manson as an example. If one were to trace the course of Nixon's reasoning we find that it has the subtle implication of declaring that those who are prosecuted (who defy the law, since the law arrested them) are guilty— which is exactly what he said about Manson. Notice that all of this is not unlike the message of the property Westerns, especially in its definition of law as involving procedural guarantees, its emphasis on bringing everybody to trial, and its affirmation of the importance of law and order as opposed to a code of right and wrong. Unlike many politicians who wax long and laboriously on the Code of the West in speaking of Westerns or the frontier, Nixon makes no reference to the code or to morality— rather all his emphasis is on law. Finally it might be pointed out that *Chisum* is a property Western in which John Wayne portrays a big landowner.

Wayne's own portrayals seem to have followed the course of the TV Western: from playing free roaming cowboys who were the bane of the establishment to settling down on a big ranch and cloaking himself in the establishment. Wayne has gone from playing the Ringo Kid, through a middle period of movies like *Rio Bravo* in which he played a lawman, to playing the big rancher in *Mc-Lintock* and *Chisum*.

In John Wayne, in the Manson speech, and in *John Wesley Harding* we have parallels to the path followed by the TV Western. This path is not unlike that travelled by classical liberalism in the late nineteenth century, since both suffered through a decline of an abstract value system and an increase in the reliance on law as a law and order of procedural guarantees. Political historian John Hallowell points out that this leads to a belief that the only criterion of value for a law is its form, its technical efficiency, its mechanical certainty. The rights of men become not natural rights but legal rights, and these rights are but the state's concession to claims made by the individual. The result is either anarchy or tyranny:

> *For when belief in objective truth and abstract values is lost, when reason and conscience are given no place in social life, and when objective norms of right and wrong are dissolved, individuals can admit no control over their subjective desires. Or if the state is able to assert its power over the individual . . . the individual has no criteria for declaring the state wrong in oppressing him or unjustified in asserting tyrranical control over his thought and actions.*[2]

Michael Polanyi adds:

> *When the judge can no longer appeal to law and justice; when neither a witness, nor the newspapers, nor even a scientist reporting his experiments, can speak the truth as he knows it; when in public life, there is no moral principle commanding respect; when the revelations of reli-*

gion and art are denied any substance—then
there are no grounds on which any individual
may justly make a stand against the rulers of
the day. Such is the logic of totalitarianism.[3]

In the beginning, I suggested that it was impossible
to know whose values the TV Western represented, yet
the implications of the course travelled by the Western
from horse to gun to a piece of property make that question a naggingly important one. In Nixon's Manson speech
and in the Wayne movies there is the suggestion that the
values are shared by quite a few people who are neither
network executives or regular TV viewers. All of which
leads to the observation that there are some powerful
totalitarian forces at work—and one doesn't have to be a
paranoid to be able to look out and see them.

On the surface Dylan's *John Wesley Harding* seems
a negation of these forces, yet actually it is merely another
response to them. Faced with a decline in abstract values
John Wesley Harding calls for individuals who will stand
and affirm them, even at the risk of martyrdom, while
Nixon and the law and order types seek security in laws
which will prevent code-citing individualists from sub-
verting the established order. Inevitably this has produced individuals who purport to believe in a code and
deny that the law has any validity where it conflicts with
the code and others who believe in the law and deny the
validity of any code. Most of us are inevitably caught in
between and struggle to maintain our equilibrium. The
balance between anarchy and totalitarianism, between
code and laws which is inherent in the idea of open options seems to have been upset so that we now have only
conflict between opposite ends of the scale with little in
between—it's as though the scale threatens to break under

the weight of balancing something which perhaps cannot
be balanced, at least under the present conditions.

In a large part this conflict has become a generational
one. Nixon's generation has gone through several code-
wielding madmen, from Hitler and Stalin to Joe McCarthy,
while my generation is more disturbed about so-called
leaders who appear to have no code. When I talk with my
parents they seem worried that society could be under-
mined by individuals who deny law. To them and to Nixon,
Manson is but John Wesley Hardin in disguise, while to us
John Mitchell is like the baddies of the horse Westerns,
Southern strategy and all. In a curious way these two
views are actually not so far apart, as *Gunsmoke* demon-
strates, with its lawman who also lives by a code. Ultimately it is possible for an individual to put all his faith
in "a law" and let him make all the decisions about enforcement.

The situation, as Hallowell and Polanyi point out,
seems to generate an all or nothing conflict in which any
concession to law seems to weaken one's stand against the
state, and yet any concession to a code seems to weaken
the order without which no society can function. In
normal democratic societies there has always been this
conflict between the individual and the state—as theorists
have been pointing out since before *The Federalist
Papers.* In *Federalist #10* Madison tried to show how
the Constitution ingeniously guaranteed these individual
rights, and to some extent it has—with the notable exceptions of blacks, Indians, chicanos and other minority
groups. In fact the list of exceptions reads not unlike the
list of deviants in our last chapter. Besides these exceptions, it is pointed out by many political theorists, that
American democracy—in fact all democracies—tend to
"contract" during times of crisis leading to more emphasis

on law than on abstract morality. So we had the Palmer
raids and Japanese internment and today we have Vietnam coexisting with a massive push on the part of the
minority "exceptions" to gain equality.

Besides these political factors, which are common
to most democracies, in America, as de Tocqueville has
pointed out, the myth of individualism has always had
an influence on this conflict between individual morality
and the laws of the state. As was pointed out in an earlier
chapter, the strongest portrayal of this myth was the
Western. Central to the Western and to individualism
was the idea of open options—the idea that it was possible
for an individual to be free enough that he could choose
when, where and how he went and what he did. It never
mattered that in reality, options might be closed for the
workers at Homestead, or the girls at Lowell or the blacks
who struggled to make it on sharecropping plans that
made their lot every bit as difficult as it was under slavery.
What mattered was that people believed in the myth, and
they acted as though it were true.

The early TV Westerns, with their free roaming
individuals were pure expressions of this myth. With the
phase of the gun the myth begins to change and the open
options start to close. The gun heroes may have been
popular with 1950's organization men, but they were
themselves organization men whose position became
linked to a job. With *Rawhide* and *Wagon Train* the emphasis shifts decisively from the individual to the community or the group. Not only do the heroes of these
Westerns have jobs, but they share these jobs with several
individuals. In the property Westerns and *Gunsmoke*,
with their suspicion of drifters, mountain men, gunfighters
and other assorted individuals, the idea of open options is
all but dead. Whereas Roy Rogers and the Sons of the

Pioneers used to sing "Don't Fence Me In," the people of *Gunsmoke* seem to be singing "Please Fence Me In." The individual who once roamed the prairies with only his horse and sidekick as his companions, joins a group "moving west," and ultimately is so paranoid about the prairie that he seeks refuge in the towns and the big ranches he once despised. He is so afraid of himself that he is willing to give up his options and place them all under "a law" or trade them in on a share of some huge piece of property.

This theme parallels the depiction of closing options in the movies of Sam Peckinpah, Robert Altman, and Monte Hellman. In Hellman and in *Gunsmoke* the prairie evokes a paranoid feeling that is fed by incidents in which a chance meeting leads one to be hunted down by a posse or to participate in a hunt for a nameless killer who turns out to be one's twin brother. Once the idea of the prairie as a place where anything was possible presented a vision of a land of boundless opportunity enabling one to become something better than one was or thought he was, but now the idea of a land where everything is possible produces nightmares. "The animal" and Drago lived in what they thought was a pristine eden and the Weary Willies carried the dream of Walt Whitman to the West, but "the animal" was captured as a freak, Drago lost his eden in one terrifying raid, and the poems of Walt Whitman were burned by a mob, while the good people rounded up the Willies for "preventative detention." The naive socialism of Angel (in *The Wild Bunch*), which is not unlike that of the Willies, is dragged to death behind an automobile and even the Wild Bunch must yield to a newer brand of killer, who wears a uniform and runs his operation like an army. McCabe, who almost pulled off his own Horatio Alger myth, dies alone in the snow unaided by those he helped and loved, and the corporation inherits his town. Cable

Hogue is run over by an ancestor of a GM Chevy.

In Altman and Peckinpah there is the sense that the options never were open, or that those who acted as though they believed they were, were only opening the gates for a more rapacious individual who would close the doors forever on open options. The Wild Bunch is only a less organized, more spontaneous version of Mapache's army, Cable Hogue's waterhole monopoly leads him to become a money making businessman, and McCabe's town is only a miniature version of the mining company "company town" it was to become. In all of these movies there is the belief that, men being what they are, open options will allow only the strongest or the luckiest or the most violent or the most amoral to impose their wills on those who are less fortunate.

This seems to be the vision of the recent TV Westerns, especially *Gunsmoke*. Here the open options of the prairie become only licenses to steal and murder. As Festus pointed out in "Prairie Wolfer" the wolves of the prairie can make short work of the other innocent prairie dwellers "just for sport." Yet there is a contrast between the TV shows and the movies, for the shows do not extend their pessimism to cover all men nor do they link this pessimism with an indictment of America, past and present. The property Westerns and *Gunsmoke* purport to offer hope if the individual will drop his free roaming pretensions and become part of a group. He can choose whether to be a member of a herd (*Wagon Train*), the Nevada Club or Cattlemen's Association (*Bonanza* and *Virginian*), or become a townsman who puts his faith in "a law." These options are still open and are portrayed as virtues. While Peckinpah and Altman pessimistically present the idea of open options as creating the corporate state of twentieth century America, the TV Western

celebrates it. Jonah Hutchinson may have been a bastard, but he opened the way for Dodge City, its people
and its marshal. So one has a choice to either be more
violent, lucky or amoral than the next man or be killed
(which is the vision of Peckinpah's films *Straw Dogs* and
The Getaway) or to cash in his chips and back a group
or a man who will do his killing for him.

  To return to Nixon's Manson speech there is in it
a message not unlike that of the property Westerns or
Gunsmoke, for Nixon, too, seems to have a fear of the
prairie. Notice that the President contrasts "the time
before New Mexico was a state . . . a time when there
was no law," with the time when "the law eventually
came." The fear of the open options of the prairie is
wrapped up in the image of Manson, who gave many
"straights" a frightening example of what open options
could create. Like Drago and his edenic family, Sharon
Tate and her clique seemed immune from the hassles
faced by the rest of us—to some people this evoked
images of drugs, orgies, etc., yet still they seemed so
free—but unexpectedly, almost out of nowhere and
without reason, a band of crazed outlaws appeared and
in a nightmare shattered this eden. Crimes which were
once something that happened only to blacks in the
ghetto or poor whites in the city, became realities for
the once secure dwellers of suburbia. Anywhere, at any
time, who knows what crazy long hair might get an urge
to creep into the fenced compound late at night and dis-
patch whoever was asleep with some unspeakably horrible
murder. The only safety was in groups and in laws and
in more lawmen (and burglar alarms and guard dogs and
guns, guns, guns). In a small town or a group like the
cattlemen's association people knew each other and could
protect one person from harm. Now every deviant be-

comes suspect, for who knows whether the deviant of today might not become the Manson of tomorrow— especially if he took those horrible drugs. After all, didn't Manson say he took LSD and marijuana, and didn't his family? "Do you know what to expect from a trip on drugs?" said the football man and plainly the answer was no. In those areas where small towns and homogeneous groups do not exist this anti-deviant message and law become especially important. Law and legal definitions of right and wrong come to replace mores and other cultural norms, since in this environment there are many cultures and many norms. It is only a step from this precise legalism to reliance on laws to define who is good and who is bad, and from that to *A Clockwork Orange*, B. F. Skinner and the behavioral modification of deviants.

The other answer was to find a superman, or should I say a supermarshal, in whom one could put his faith—as Doc put it, "Matt gave us the security of knowing that Tate Crocker and a hundred others like him can't come in here and burn it to the ground every time they think about it." In many ways Dillon's theme is that of Howard Hawks' John Wayne movies, *Rio Bravo* and *Eldorado*— professionalism—Dillon, like Wayne, is the supreme professional. This theme is in turn a theme of much of our culture today—notice how the professional is the new TV hero: lawyers, doctors, policemen. There seems to be the feeling that only professionals can be really free, can be individuals. Yet there is also a more insidious theme— that professionals are people we should put our faith in. Even groups are sometimes powerless to prevent violence, in which case a strong man is needed. Philadelphia is a virtual armed camp where murder may strike without warning—I know, it happened to us—so elect supercop

Frank Rizzo mayor and all your troubles will be solved. America and the Western, both of which once put such stock in the individual human being, now either fear them or regard them as weak. No longer is there a faith in men. Dylan's "St. Augustine" looks for his martyrs among souls that "already had been sold" and the landlord is not about to go along with the deal "if you don't underestimate me, I won't underestimate you."

Ultimately the decline of abstract values and this closing of open options are interrelated, in fact it is difficult to see them separately. Open options can only be open if men believe that ideas like truth and justice have some validity and that other men can be convinced of this. Perhaps it all boils down to an essential question of human nature, whether we are willing to believe that a man, given a choice of doing right or wrong, will do right. *John Wesley Harding* ends with what seems like an innocent Country and Western song about a man and a woman spending the night together. Yet in the context of the album the song becomes more than that, "close your eyes, close the door, you don't have to worry anymore, I'll be your baby tonight." It's an affirmation that human beings can be human, if only for a night. Yet if one night. . . .

The 1971-1972 season of *Gunsmoke* suggested that the Western might change its orientation and that a climate of opinion was forming which could well make that one night more of a possibility than it has seemed at various times during the last decade.

The major change occurred in an episode, "No Tomorrow," in which for the first time in years Matt Dillon, the lawman, let a criminal, whom Matt believed to be innocent, go free even though he had been convicted by a judge and jury. The episode is all the more significant in that the man whose son actually committed the crime is a big landowner, who boasts "there's a man sitting in the governor's chair in Topeka, that I can count on as a very close friend." The climax of the episode occurs when Festus catches up with Justin, who has escaped from prison. The scene takes place on a wooded hill on— of all places—the prairie. Justin has gotten the drop on Festus, or at least his wife has, and Festus and the wife stand pointing guns at one another, neither one wanting to shoot. Finally the wife hands her gun to Festus, and after an interminable moment Festus walks away mumbling, leaning his shotgun against a tree as the camera shows him melting into the trees. A few minutes later Matt catches up and after asking Festus whether he caught Justin, the camera follows their eyes towards the prairie, where Justin and his wife are driving away in their wagon. Whereas once Kitty, Doc and Matt had toasted old Jonah Hutchinson, now Kitty calls for a toast "to the one that got away."

In one episode *Gunsmoke* seemed to once again affirm a faith in people, in individualism and the prairie. The town is still important, but now it is no longer the opposite of the prairie—nor is it paranoid about the prairie. The baddie in this episode is the establishment, the big rancher with friends in the capital, not the individualist. Once the town was paranoid about the prairie, now there seems to be a growing paranoia about bigger towns and big government.

Two other new episodes, "My Brother's Keeper" and "One For the Road," develop the theme of allowing individuals to decide their own destiny—to be individuals. "One For the Road" brings back Sally Fergus who rescues and then is courted by a rich businessman from "back East." Mr. Prince has taken to the bottle after his wife's death, and his daughter wants to put him in an institution, since his drinking is causing her embarrassment with her socialite friends. Mr. Prince asks her why he can't lead his own life, "You have your life to live, why won't you let me live mine?" and the episode seems to agree with him. The daughter's position raises the specter, which I talked about in a previous chapter, of having deviants declared insane. Mr. Prince's answer is, "I may be a drunk but I'm not insane," and again the episode agrees. After Sally saves him, Mr. Prince proposes to her, but she refuses saying, "We got different lives to lead." After all "you couldn't live in my shack and pick up bottles and stuff and I couldn't live no other way." In this episode Sally is allowed to go her own way and returns to her old toothless, scraggly-haired, sloppily dressed self. There is, the episode seems to say, room for diversity here.

Of course, it's not quite that cut and dried. When Sally fixes up Mr. Prince for his hearing with Judge Brooker, she emphasizes that he's "going to be stone sober and spit polished, and colored and dyed respectable." So still there is the intimation that respectable folks, sane folks, look respectable, at least if they're big businessmen. Then there's the role of Judge Brooker, which has been increasing in recent episodes. It is as though the town which once depended on "a law" is coming more and more to depend on "a judge." I'm not sure whether one is any safer than another, given Nixon's Supreme Court nominations. An example of the change from "a law" to "a judge," occurs in one of Matt's speeches in "One For the Road." The daughter has just given Matt a court order from a Philadelphia judge to lock up Mr. Prince, and Matt says he'll have to let Prince go (there's that theme again), at least for the time being, since "this is Kansas and all out of state warrants have to be approved by Judge Brooker." In earlier years the show probably wouldn't have shown such a situation, nor would Matt have relinquished his function to the judge.

"My Brother's Keeper" details another interesting change, this one concerning Indians. Although the episode still distorts Indian culture and religion, it does advance one major new theme, which is that people have a right to decide their own destiny. The episode deals with Festus' attempt to supposedly help an old Indian (hence the title) who wishes to go away and die by himself, which is, as Matt puts it, "an Indian custom." Kitty tries to side with Festus, but Matt and Doc argue with them. "This is an Indian custom that's hundreds of years old. Now you don't have any right to tell this man when or how to die," says Matt, and Doc adds later, "He's a grown man, an old man with dignity, now you can't treat him like a child." When Festus argues that he's only trying to help, Doc says, "I know, but you're taking away his manhood, his right to decide for himself what's best."

Like the Sally Fergus episode, this episode is not without its weak points. The Indian is spoken of as being Sioux, but nowhere could I find any mention of such an attitude towards death among the Sioux. The "old people going away to die" theme is one which occurs as a stereotype in Westerns, like the magic amulet bit, but what is interesting about the episode is that the old Indian is allowed to die in his own way—even if that isn't the way Sioux really die. Another problem with the episode is that the old Indian plays his role like a cigar-store Indian, with arms folded and eyes focused on the horizon. The episode tries to explain this by saying that the Indian believes he's already dead, but still the image is too close for comfort. Finally, there is one phrase uttered by Festus when he tries to defend what he is doing, "A horse or a mule or a dog can't tell you what he needs either, but he gets took care of, don't he?" Since Festus is the "racist" of the episode it might be excusable, yet no one in the episode challenges this quotation directly, with its analogy between the Indian and animals.

Yet for all this quarrelling over points, I do think this episode and the others point to a change in *Gunsmoke*'s thrust and perhaps a change in the climate of opinion as well. Even McEveety has gotten into the act with his cigar bit. In "The Predators," an ex-gunfighter named Cain is shown smoking a cigar, which led this regular McEveety viewer to assume he was a baddie. The whole episode evolved around whether Cain would "go bad" again and I naturally assumed he would, but he didn't.

It is too early to say whether the '71-'72 *Gunsmoke* was the beginning of a trend or a dead end. What we can say is that the alternative presented by the previous seasons is not a bright one. This nightmare becomes even more insidious when one thinks about the form of TV —thinks in McLuhanesque terms. Both McLuhan and the more obscure Harold Innis take the position that it is the form of the media—oral communications, print, "electrical" (radio, telegraph, television) which influences a society rather than the content. McLuhan emphasizes the effect of the various types of media on our sensory apparatus, while Innis belives that the media's most profound effects are on social organization and social consciousness.

As I've said before it is difficult for me to accept the media determinism of McLuhan.

However, this does not mean that McLuhan and Innis do not yield insights into the relationship between the form and content of television and contemporary society.

Both McLuhan and Innis' downgrading of content as opposed to form (leading to McLuhan's famous phrase "the
medium is the message") is in direct opposition to the
main thrust of this project. Yet as the New Critics
showed us only too well, form and content cannot be
split into separate categories. Keeping this in mind, I
think that one could probably take a sort of neo-Innis
position in which both form and content seem to be emphasizing the same values, influencing the creation of a
certain kind of human being or at least strengthening the
kinds of social beings that our society may well be creating. Following McLuhan one could also say that form
and content have an effect on how this human being experiences his world, i.e., on his senses.

To take Innis first, it seems clear by now that the
content of much of contemporary television, particularly
the Western, bolsters the totalitarian image of twentieth-century man. In turn it seems to me that the form
of television reinforces—or vice versa, whichever way
you'll have it—this image. Television is something which
most people watch in their own homes. As I alluded to
before in my image of all the people sitting at home
around their TV sets, this fact is destructive of a whole
social fabric and constructive in the creation of a new
type of human being. Human beings who once depended
on face to face oral contact to obtain their information
about the world, then came to depend on a combination
of oral and printed sources, have now become dependent
on television. In a sense the more one engages in the
sheer act of watching television, the more one is encouraged in his fear of "the prairie," and the more this fear is
encouraged, the more values like abstract morality and
individualism tend to suffer. Let us imagine someone
who watches TV six hours per day from the time he comes

home from work until bedtime. At work this person's social contacts and duties are fairly structured and when he gets home he encounters another familiar structure—not unlike the first (i.e., notice the TV Western's acceptance of roles and jobs and its use week after week of the same starring characters) which makes our tubie fairly comfortable. When this tubie leaves the comfort of job or tube for the larger society, i.e., "the prairie," he is apt to get very up tight—not unlike the *Gunsmoke* cast on the prairie.

In various cultures, of course, individuals who left the comfort of their cultural environment have always been up tight about moving into another culture or environment. Television culture is no exception. Most TV theorists, in fact, hold that rather than restrict our mobility, our paranoia about "the prairie" outside our TV culture has encouraged the destruction of such barriers, especially by producing shows that deal with other peoples or countries. McLuhan, for example, maintains that television is encouraging the breakdown of nationalism. Perhaps—the results are not all in yet, nor will they be for quite some time.

Yet I would assert that here is where McLuhan and Innis' emphasis on form as opposed to content becomes crucial. The content of most TV programs like the Western encourages rather than discourages the creation of a provincialism which is the most frightening in history since it involves such masses of people. This stereotyping, this provincialism which is the major feature of TV programing encourages people *not* to watch specials. Note how specials almost always draw low ratiangs. Furthermore, my own observation suggests that the people who watch these shows tend to be those who are most unprovincial, ie., who are widely read and travelled.

The TV viewer's fear of "the prairie" is encouraged by a content that reinforces his stay-at-home provincialism. In some cases, as I noticed when canvassing homes during the community action era of the anti-war movement, this leads to a lack of knowledge about those who live next door or even a block away. My image of Washington, D.C. and its relationship to *Gunsmoke* seems to have reached a point where one travels from home ("town") to work in a closed car ("train") across "the prairie" listening to a radio and then goes back home and tunes in his TV ("town"). The frightening aspect of this is when Mr. John Q. Tubie *has* to go out on the prairie, perhaps on vacation or whatever. How does he react to "new" people; people he hasn't seen before? The only way he can react is by using the resources at hand—i.e., the stereotypes he sees on the tube. When a long-haired kid comes to the front door he must be protesting something, so Mr. Tubie just won't answer it, even though the kid may only want to call a tow truck to start his stalled car. Need it be added that the TV stereotypes, as in the Western, are primarily visual and to some extent oral (patterns of speech) rather than intellectual—how something is said and by whom, rather than what they are saying, although there are "clue" words here too, as the TV Western shows.

What a neo-Innis position leads to, then, is the frightening thought that form and content together jive exactly with Fromm's twentieth century man.[4]

> *Our society needs men who cooperate smoothly*
> *in large groups; who want to consume more*
> *and more, and whose tastes are standardized*
> *and can be easily influenced and anticipated.*
> *It needs men who feel free and independent,*
> *who do not feel subject to any authority or prin-*

ciple or conscience, yet are willing to be com-
manded, to do what is expected, to fit into the
social machine without friction—men who can
be guided without force, led without leaders,
be prompted without any name except one: to
be on the move, to function, to go ahead. [5]

In *The Big Valley* quotation that forms the epigraph
for this study Barbara Stanwyck remarks that we've lost
sight of ourselves, but what is it we've lost—a myth, an
idea? And who is "we"? Myths and ideas are difficult
things to talk about in the face of alternatives like the
Cattleman's Association, "a law," and *Straw Dogs*, and
surely we do not lack self-appointed "we's" who are more
than glad to point out the way to lost souls. Yet it is
myths and ideas which do succor souls, and those who
stridently push people to speak out for what is right with
America—usually meaning themselves and their platforms
—as though they were selling a product, as though a man
could speak compellingly enough to move others if he
does not speak from deep inside himself, fail to recognize
this.

If for the TV Western individualism may be dead
or dying, there is perhaps a chance that someone will
return to the Western for a renewal of ourselves, and this
time he will not be so naive. When we parody the Western, we parody ourselves and parody can be healthy.
When we become critical of the Western myth we become
critical of ourselves, which can also be healthy. When we
lose faith in the myth, we lose faith in ourselves and that
is not so easy to recover. Whether Dylan's one night will
produce a nightmare reign of Nazi-like law and order,
whether we will awake alone and terrified after dream-
ing of St. Augustine is hard to say.

*As we look at Watergate in a longer perspective, we can see that its abuses
resulted from the assumption by those involved that their cause placed
them beyond the reach of those rules that apply to other persons and that
hold a free society together.*

*That attitude can never be tolerated in this country. However it did not
suddenly develop in 1972. It became fashionable in the 1960's, as individuals and groups increasingly asserted the right to take the law into their own
hands, insisting that their purposes repersented a higher morality. . . .*

The notion that the end justifies the means proved contagious. . . .

*If we learn the important lessons of Watergate, if we do what is necessary to
prevent such abuses in the future—on both sides—we can emerge from this
experience a better and stronger nation.*

Richard Nixon
August 16, 1973

*"Seek always peace. . . . We are all linked by our souls, and if one is
endangered so are all."*

*Between giving up and many bombs must lie many paths. Will shooting
guns and making bombs make you men and not dogs?*

A gun is not a tool for peace.

As far as possible without surrender, be on good terms with all.

Kung Fu

POSTSCRIPT: SENATOR BAKER'S QUESTION

DURING THE EARLIER PHASES OF THE WATERGATE HEARINGS,
before Dean, Haldeman, Ehrlichman, Mitchell and Co. had
testified, Senator Howard Baker asked a series of related
questions of witness Herbert Porter.

Baker: "Did you ever think of saying, 'I don't think this
is quite right, this is not the way it ought to be?' . . .
What caused you to abdicate your own conscience?"

Porter: "My loyalty to this man, Richard Nixon. . . ."

Baker: "The greatest disservice that a man could do to a
President of the United States would be to abdicate his

conscience."

After then this line of questioning became Senator Baker's forte (just as civil liberties became the thrust of Senator Ervin's questioning) and each time he asked the question of a witness it seemed to echo through my mind and ultimately through all America like some modern soothsayer's cry of distress, for Senator Baker seemed to be asking the question not only of Porter and the other Watergate witnesses but of us all. It is like similar questions that arose after the fall of Nazi Germany or the McCarthy period when more and more wise men came to see the aberrations of those times as not merely the aberrations of individual men, but as complex events in which sinner and sinned upon, executioner and victim became intertwined.

Evidently Senator Baker's question reached President Nixon and on August 16, 1973—a little more than three years after his Manson speech—he gave his answer. The theme of his speech parallels that of his Manson speech, the theme of the last chapter and ultimately of this whole book—the theme of law and order versus objective morality. It is this theme which lies at the root of Senator Baker's questioning and how we cope with it as a people in our myths and symbols as well as in our own everyday lives tells how healthy our republic is.

President Nixon's defense—for ultimately that is what it was—and the whole White House horrors of bugging, illegal entry, "plumbers" answerable only to the White House (which can only be likened to the KGB or the Gestapo), etc., is the worst fears of the last chapter brought to reality. It is paranoia over Weary Willies, Indians, Blacks, people who are different to the nth degree. It is reliance on a lawman (or a law 'n' order man) with a vengeance.

While Nixon's speech attempts to cloak the actions of the "plumbers" in a good vs. evil scenario that adopts some of the rhetoric of *John Wesley Harding* it is as plain as it was in the Manson speech that John Wesley Harding is the enemy and what the law 'n' order men were trying to preserve was not morality at all, but rather it was law 'n' order and what I can only call the Southern California way of life. Nixon, like the Nevada Club and the Cattleman's Association, has never had kind words for individualists of any kind, for to him as to the Nevada Club they're all deviants. Like Ben Cartwright in "The Weary Willies" he tries to blame them—the demonstrators, the anti-war groups, the hippies—for what happened at Watergate, just as Ben blames the Willies as much as the mob of townspeople for the destruction of their camp and the murder of one of their own. It's an insidious doctrine, but unfortunately it is one that runs through the TV Western and the rest of our society.

With their prairie paranoia and their fear of individualists and outsiders, *Gunsmoke* and the property Westerns of the sixties were evidence of this attitude. Coupled with this fear of outsiders and their dislike for deviants these Westerns blended law 'n' order with the attitude that tactics like back shooting, pistol whipping and head knocking were sometimes necessary to subdue those who crossed the law. "Preventive detention" of innocents like the Willies was sometimes required for "their own protection." Violence and violent tactics became as much the mark of the good guy as it was the bad guy.

This was a marked change from the early Westerns where the hero never shot to kill and always fought cleanly. Tactics and objective morality were two sides of the same coin for these early heroes. Like the early Christians and such groups as the Quakers, Hopalong Cassidy, Roy Rogers and the Lone Ranger believe that a good man, a moral man was one who used moral means to achieve his goals. If one was to fight the devil, fight evil, the worst thing he could do was to adopt the devil's methods—to get down in the pit and slug it out with the devil on his own terms. No matter what kind of dastardly thing the baddie tried to do to him, Roy never retaliated in kind.

With the gun Westerns of the middle fifties this attitude towards tactics and morality underwent a great change. *Gunsmoke*, the "adult" Western, touted the fact that its hero was a "real" man and like "real" men he sometimes shot people in the back or clubbed them into submission. Certainly there are all too many "real" men, who act this way, but as has been pointed out, violence is no synonym for "real" or for "adult." Perhaps in this era of "real" men and anti-heroes we have become contemptuous even to the point of disbelief about moral men. Morality and moral heroes have become camp, but if Roy Rogers' morality is camp where does that leave Martin Luther King? What it leaves us with is the attitude that everyone is immoral, that there are no absolutes, and hence opens the door wide to the totalitarianism and fascism that Hallowell and Polanyi warned about.

When this became coupled with the law 'n' order values of the property Westerns, an attitude was created that fostered the crime bills and tactics of the Nixon administration. Ultimately as John Ehrlichman stated, when the FBI wouldn't cooperate then you formed your own police force of plumbers to enforce the law the way you wanted it enforced. For all their talk about the nobility of the police and the FBI, the attitude of the Nixon Administration towards these established agencies of law enforcement was actually no different than that of the property Westerns, which featured weak sheriffs who

224 The Horse, The Gun and The Piece of Property

had to be prodded into action. The Nixon administration, which regularly accused "liberals" of attacking the police force, actually had no more confidence in it than those they accused of coddling criminals. The law in both the property Westerns and in the Nixon administration became a tool to be used and not a concept.

The Nixon administration, unlike the early Western heroes, believed that tactics and morality could be separated. It is plain that Nixon believed that one could use illegal and perhaps immoral means to reach what he believed to be a moral end. Nixon and his administration appear to have been confused as to the meanings of morality, legality, tactics and goals. Most of the demonstrations of the sixties were legal and moral. A few were moral, but illegal—that is a man may have broken the law by burning his draft card, but he harmed no one in doing it. Sit-ins may have disrupted a few people's lunches, but they did no harm to those who could not eat, for they could eat elsewhere. The peace and civil rights movements, though, are not blameless—not by a long shot. They did stray from the tactics of Thoreau and Martin Luther King and when they strayed, they did incalcuable harm. However, as Sam Ervin has pointed out this was no defense for Watergate and the White House horrors—"Murder and larceny have been occuring for thousands of years, but that doesn't make murder meritorious nor larceny legal." Watergate and associated horrors were illegal and were immoral. Perhaps, as one commentator has suggested, this was a natural occurrence in an administration of lawyers and ad men, for many of them believe the law and the media are but means to an end.

That such an administration lacked morality should not be a surprise, but it would be a mistake to say, as one columnist has, that they were nihilistic. Like the property

Westerns the Nixon administration did have a set of values
which they used their tactics to defend. Chief among
these values was property. Next was conformity. Beyond these values was a picture of what society should be,
which for the Nixon administration consisted of what I
call the Southern California way of life—short hair, a
house in the suburbs with a well manicured lawn, two car
garage, a wife in the PTA, two kids—the Loud family or
what Kevin Phillips in the June, 1973 *Harpers* calls "conservative chic." In the property Westerns we have these
same values translated into the 19th century of Virginia
City, Shiloh Ranch or the Big Valley.

The property Westerns, like some of the Nixon administration officials, are no longer with us. The last of
them, *Bonanza*, was cancelled last season. In fact there
was a decline in TV Westerns in general. Only three Westerns remained on the tube during the 72-73 season: one
old one, *Gunsmoke*, and two new ones, *Hec Ramsey* and
Kung Fu. The death of the property Westerns ends their
reign on the tube, suggesting that we are entering a new
period. The 72-73 Westerns provide contradictory answers
as to what this new period will be. Their answers to Senator Baker's question are not unlike the responses of many
of the Watergate witnesses—confusing.

Gunsmoke's opening episode, "The River," was a brilliant two-parter with beautiful photography, Jack Elam
at his roguish best, and Slim Pickens playing the baddie.
In "The River" two children take a raft down a river to
light out for the territories and become river pirates.
Along the way they meet Matt Dillon, a river rogue played
by Elam and escape the baddies led by Slim Pickens. At
the end Dillon takes the two kids to live with a straight-
laced aunt who could double for Tom Sawyer's Aunt
Polly. The children are washed, clothed in city duds and

herded to church and school. As Dillon is leaving the town the aunt runs up and asks where her charges are. On the ground Dillon finds their new clothes and from the river come the farewells of the children who have gone off to join Joe Snagg. Dillon lets them go.

This seemed to follow the trend of the '71-'72 season, but as the new season wore on *Gunsmoke* began to look more like the old show, presenting standard episodes of goodies versus baddies. The old prairie paranoia returned with full force in an episode where a bunch of half-white, half-Indian, dirty Dog Soldiers beat and molest Kitty, dumping her in the main street of Dodge, then shoot her in front of the terrified townspeople. Matt, of course, goes out and brings them in.

Prairie paranoia was a theme in a made-for-TV movie, "Bounty Man," that was aired during that season. In "Bounty Man" a callous, cold-blooded bounty hunter relentlessly tracks down outlaws. In one scene he brings in a man and the sheriff asks where his partner is. Bounty man Kinkaid replies that he shot him, remarking that there wasn't any reward on him. Later there are references made to Kinkaid's bringing men in dead not alive. At the climax of the episode we learn the bounty man's story and his justification for this killing. Kinkaid and his wife lived on a farm, happily enjoying their Eden. Then a friend who was a judge asked him to take a young robber to work on the farm as probation. As Kinkaid puts it, robber Paxton was "silver tongued" and easily swayed judge, jury, in fact the whole town. One day Kinkaid goes to town and returns to find out Paxton swayed more than just his neighbors, for he persuaded Kinkaid's wife to go with him. Kinkaid tracks them down relentlessly. Finally he finds his wife working as a bargirl in the cheap saloon where Paxton dropped her. She hears that her husband has arrived and

commits suicide rather than face him. Kinkaid vows to
kill Paxton. So he becomes a bounty man, killing lots of
other men, but not Paxton. A girl finally forces him to
give up the chase, but the movie does not seem to regard
his revenge, his extra-legal activities, his murders as repre-
hensible. Rather it seems to say that courts sometimes err,
that lawmen can't catch all the criminals, so maybe in such
a situation a man is justified in strapping on a gun and doing a little chasing himself.

One of two new Westerns was *Hec Ramsey,* starring
Richard Boone. As Boone portrays him Ramsey is a somewhat eccentric old gunman who has become a sheriff's
deputy in a turn-of-the-century Western town. Ramsey's
gimmick is that he has given up the gun and the old methods of fighting crime for newer, scientific, twentieth-century methods. Ramsey is more detective than cowboy,
and his new methods of fighting outlaws give the open options idea an interesting twist. In a way Ramsey is like
Bucky Fuller, who sees the salvation of planet Earth in
the wise use of technology. In one episode Ramsey is
tracking down a rustler/murderer, whose activities threaten
to cause an Indian war and perhaps disrupt the plans for
a railroad. The railroad company sends out two Eastern
dudes who threaten repercussions in Washington and continually are knocking the hicks in the dirty Western town.
At one point they ask Ramsey what he sees in such a
place and he replies clean air, pure water and green grass.

Like Fuller, Ramsey can see no dichotomy between
twentieth-century technology and nineteenth-century
pastoralism. He seeks a world where both can live together, for one without the other is impossible. Without
technology society crumbles, no longer able to combat
crime and disease, while without green grass and clean air,
men become greedy and self-interested.

This theme interestingly enough cropped up recently
in a speech Hubert Humphrey gave to the Rural Development Association of Minnesota. In the speech Humphrey
began by extolling the virtues of rural life, but noted that
these virtues are fast disappearing as young people move
away to the cities where there are better job opportunities.
What rural America needs, said Humphrey, is for rural
America to bring industry to the country. Then there
would be jobs and money to keep the young people "down
on the farm" and keep rural America strong. Nowhere did
he mention or even seem aware of the fact that it might
also bring with it the problems of the city—crime and pol-
lution and kill the clean air and green grass.

What Humphrey, Hec Ramsey and Fuller all seem
to want is an Eden of green grass and clean air and yet also
the benefits of technology. To paraphrase Leo Marx they
want a machine in their garden. The machine will keep
them happy, healthy and employed so they can enjoy the
garden.

If Hec Ramsey seems to be straddling the fence in
his attitude towards the machine and the garden, his attitude towards law and order is straightforward. Ramsey's
methods include all the standard law enforcement techniques of the sixties Westerns—pistol whipping, dirty
fighting, and, if need be, shooting to kill. In one episode
Ramsey quits his deputy's job in disgust at his boss's attitude towards civil liberties. The boss berates Ramsey for
his brutality and urges him to use a little more restraint
in collaring suspects. By the end of the episode the town
is in an uproar and the head lawman has to beg Ramsey
to return and use his old methods of keeping order.

Keeping order isn't even a consideration on *Kung Fu*,
the second new Western and one of the better TV Westerns in a long time. *Kung Fu* is in many ways a return to the

early heroes of the horse Westerns. It's hero is Caine, a
Chinese-American who has been raised in a Kung Fu
monastery in China. He has come to America to search
for his long-lost brother and flee from the bounty which
has been placed on his head in China for killing a member
of the royal family. In the monastery Caine learned the
Taoist philosophy of Kung Fu—a spiritual order that
teaches physical prowess as well as morality. By now, of
course, everyone associates Kung Fu with its karate-like
method of self-defense, but as anyone who is really into
Kung Fu can tell you, it is a spiritual discipline as well as
a way of fighting. Caine does not carry a gun—in fact he
refuses to use one, he does not drink, he is not a lawman
or a big property owner. Like the early heroes, he roams
through the West looking for his brother, righting wrongs
along the way. When forced to he will use his tremendous
skill at Kung Fu fighting, but most of the time will suffer
insults, drinks thrown in his face, and even an occassional
roughing up without retaliating. In an episode, "The Soul
of a Warrior," he is insulted, hog-tied and dragged, but
never raises a hand. In "Alethea" he is thrown a gun to
shoot to break up a hold-up attempt but refuses to fire.

   Like Roy Rogers, Caine is a silent type with unknown
power who roams through the endless space of the West.
Yet there are departures from the Roy Rogers hero mold.
Caine is even more decidedly non-violent. He doesn't carry
a gun or use a weapon of any sort. His weapon is his body.
Unlike later Western heroes he does not believe in killing.
He never kills or uses instruments of killing. He believes
killing is wrong and would rather die than kill. In *Kung
Fu* the all-or-nothing confrontation that has been so char-
acteristic of the TV Western never comes off—at least not
in the life and death context that we have come to expect
from Westerns. Rather for Caine "there are many paths

between giving up and making bombs." Characteristically in the climax of the show Caine usually triumphs or solves the problem of the episode with cunning.

Caine is also quite different in deportment than the average Western hero. He has no fancy costume, but rather dresses in sloppy clothes with a slouch hat and walks from town to town. (Notice how the horse has all but disappeared.) He is anti-property, believing that what a man is inside is more important than what he appears to be outside. This of course makes the commercials on the show sometimes seem almost ludicrous. In fact, I can't think of a show where commercials do not seem out of place. All the crazy characters who inhabit that weird world of TV commercials—the world of hairtonic hawkers and dream-world drummers—seem absurd.

If Caine is similar to any kind of hero it is to Don Juan, the hero of Carlos Casteneda's now best selling series of books about his encounters with a Yaqui Indian sorcerer. Like Don Juan, Caine seems to possess some inner power that makes him able to overcome obstacles in an almost magical way. In one episode Caine is sentenced to hard labor in a gold mine. When he is caught in the middle of a fight and forced to use Kung Fu fighting, he is sentenced to the hot-house—a small metal building that is unbearably hot in the day and freezing cold at night. No one has ever walked out of that house alive, but Caine not only walks out, he is able to spiritually "heal" another man who was sentenced with him and the two walk out together.

Both Caine's and Don Juan's power is enhanced by a fearlessness that baffles. For both men the key to their fearlessness seems to be their lack of fear of death. As Caine puts it, "there is no death." For Don Juan becoming a warrior means living with the reality of your own death every minute. You learn to walk with death at your side and look over your shoulder for it, says Don Juan.

Don Juan and Caine also have an unbelievable knowledge of plants and their healing powers. It is never quite explained how Caine knows this, being raised in China with its different plants, but nevertheless the power is there.

In fact, Caine doesn't even seem to believe in doctors. Doctors, lawyers, law men—all the authority figures of modern culture—the heroes of all the TV shows—seem to be irrelevant to him. In fact several of the episodes seem to deliberately force confrontations between Caine and these figures. In one episode he takes on a big landowner whose slogan is "there ain't no other law but property, private property" and bests him by walking through a pit of rattlesnakes. In another he takes on an ex-army colonel who was taught "guns keep the peace" and bests him. In a third he outwits the army's greatest tracker. In another he takes on a law and order sheriff who believes in busting heads and back shooting and shames the law man in front of the town council by revealing that the sheriff had one of his deputies with a rifle hidden on a rooftop to give him an edge in a gunfight.

Caine's power, then, is real, but the Kung Fu fighting leaves one with an uneasiness about the show. One wonders whether the spiritual nature of *Kung Fu* is important to the producers and audience of the show. Slow motion shots of Kung Fu fighting and its violence detract from the peaceful message of Caine. There also does not seem to be any consistency in his use of his self-defense techniques. One minute he will allow men to push him around and another he retaliates. Certainly the recent spate of B movies dealing with Kung Fu suggests that what infatuates most Americans is the fighting and not the spiritual message.

Kung Fu also all but ignores women. They hardly

appear at all on the show. Caine like other TV cowboys seems to be sexless.

Finally there is the question of racism. It is difficult to raise in a show with a Chinese hero, given our current fascination with things Chinese, but it is hard to avoid. The actor cast in the starring role is Anglo, not Chinese. The scripts seem to go out of their way to show people calling him names, abusing him all because, as one town bully puts it, he's a "slanty man." Caine triumphs over these figures, but the insults still linger in the air. An episode with Chief Dan George as a dying old Indian had a beautiful twist of an ending. (After winning his battle to be buried in the town, the old chief tells them he would rather be buried away from a place with so much hate.) Yet even this episode was unreal. The old Indian avoided confrontations and the townspeople by and large were portrayed sympathetically. A town which supposedly hated Indians was suddenly agreeing to have one buried there. No one tries to kill or even rough up the Indian; only a few bullies harass him by dumping flour over his head (to make him white) and break his glasses. Through all this the Indian sits impassively until Caine arrives to Kung Fu the baddies into submission.

In spite of the feeling of uneasiness the show leaves me with, its answer to Senator Baker's question is most intriguing. Unlike Nixon, the Weathermen, the Panthers, the property and gun Westerns, *Kung Fu* believes that tactics and a higher morality are related. It was John Mitchell who said, "Watch what we do and not what we say," and I think this as well as anything explains the relationship between tactics and morality.

There is a strange juxtaposition between the timespan of the TV Western, Richard Nixon's rise and fall from power, and my own growing up and loss of innocence. The

path travelled by the TV Western has been the same path
travelled by Nixon and through it all my generation has
grown up—perhaps all too quickly. For me the beginning
of the Fall came in 1963 with the death of a President,
followed by many deaths—the deaths of people I knew
in Nam, the murder of my mother-in-law, and the deaths
of leaders whose names were household words and troops
whose names were lost all too soon. Through all this Senator Baker's question rings incessantly—not like a clear
bell but with the thud of the cracked Liberty Bell. There
is a time for each individual, for each nation when it must
face that crisis which is the loss of its innocence and hopefully learn that there may be as much dignity and truth
in the thud of the cracked bell as in the tinsel tinny ring
of more shiny bells. Yet if we are to attain that knowledge
we must see that in the loss of innocence each one of us
was a cause as well as an effect: we must see that sin involves not only the sinner but the sinned upon.

Kung Fu is hopefully the beginning of this new
awakening, but like all of us it can easily backslide. In
that show the relationship between violence and morality
which is so much a part of the TV Western and of American culture still exists in a tenuous relationship. It is
instructive to note that the hero of Kung Fu is named
Caine and Cain, not Abel, is the father of us all. We bear
his mark just as the bell bears its crack: to ignore it is
hypocritical. This is why St. Augustine not John Wesley
Harding should serve as the anthem of our generation.
Let us hope it is not an epitaph for a nation.

NOTES

CHAPTER I

[1] London, 1969, p. 12.
[2] *American West*, I (Spring, 1964), pp. 28-35 and 77-79.
[3] *The American Adam, The Machine in the Garden, The Eternal Adam and the New World Garden.*
[4] Kitses, p. 25.
[5] In W. R. Robinson, ed., *Man and the Movies*, (Baltimore, 1969).

CHAPTER II

[1] *Cisco Kid* episodes were untitled, so it is difficult to refer to specific ones.
[2] Quoted in Michael Parkinson and Clyde Jeavons, *A Pictorial History of Westerns* (London, 1972), p. 205.
[3] *Virgin Land* (New York, 1950), p. 61.
[4] *Rolling Stone*, January 4, 1973, p. 22.
[5] c.f. Michael Parkinson and Clyde Jeavons, *A Pictorial History of Westerns* (London, 1972), and William K. Everson, *A Pictorial History of the Western Film* (Secaucus, N. J., 1969).

CHAPTER III

[1] George Eels, "TV Western Craze: How Long Will It Last?" *Look*, 22 (June 24, 1958), p. 70.
[2] "High in the Saddle," Anon., *Time*, 64 (March 4, 1957), p. 65.
[3] John Reddy, "TV Westerns: The Shots Heard Round the World," *Reader's Digest*, 74 (January, 1959), p. 136.
[4] Joseph Morgenstern, "The New Violence," *Newsweek*, February 14, 1972, p. 67.
[5] "Modern Man and Cowboy," *Television Quarterly*, I (May, 1962), p. 36.
[6] Evans, p. 36.

[7] Evans, p. 36.

[8] "60,000,000 Westerners Can't Be Wrong," *National Review*, 13 (October 23, 1962), p. 325.

[9] Rickenbacker, p. 322.

[10] "The White Negro," *Advertisements For Myself* (New York, 1959), p. 305.

[11] Mailer, p. 304.

[12] Evans, p. 34.

[13] *An End To Innocence* (Boston, 1955), p. 193.

[14] Fiedler, p. 144.

[15] T. J. Ross, "The TV Western: Debasement of a Tradition," in Alan Casty, ed., *Mass Media and Mass Man* (New York, 1968), sees the heroes of *Lawman* and *Colt .45* as "super-cops" who debase the earlier Western tradition.

[16] Again Ross makes this point. (see previous note)

CHAPTER IV

[1] Henry Fairlie, "Camelot Revisited," *Harpers*, January 1973, p. 68. Fairlie quotes John Steinbeck's letter to Adlai Stevenson in which he gives his impressions of the America he saw in *Travels With Charlie*. He found "a creeping, all pervading, nerve gas of immorality," accompanied by "a nervous restlessness, a thirst, a yearning for something unknown—perhaps morality."

CHAPTER V

[1] John Poppy, "The Worldwide Lure of *Bonanza*," *Look* 28 (December 1, 1964), p. 85.

CHAPTER VI

[1] It is, of course, possible to see these changes as the result of other factors such as the sponsor's desire to change the opening, a change in the set, the producers wish to add more members to the cast and hence enlarge the town, etc. Possibly any or all of these reasons are valid, but placed in the context of the TV Western

one can see them as part of something more than mere technical change.

CHAPTER VIII

[1] *Newsweek*, July 19, 1971, p. 84.

[2] Thomas P. Neill, *The Rise and Decline of Liberalism* (Milwaukee, 1953), p. 234.

[3] Neill, p. 243.

[4] Eugene Glynn, M. C., "Television and the American Character—A Psychiatrist Looks at Television," in Alan Casty, ed., *Mass Media and Mass Man*, makes a similar observation.

[5] Erich Fromm, *American Scholar*, Winter 1956, pp. 30-31.

[6] Edith Efron, author of *The New Twisters*, has advocated this approach.

Notes on Resources

SINCE TELEVISION RESEARCH IS A RELATIVELY NEW AREA FULL
of all kinds of anticipated and unanticipated hassles, I
thought it might help future researchers to add a small
note on resources and methodology.

As many other TV analysts have pointed out,
one of the basic problems is analysis technique—how does
one watch TV and what do you look for? From the beginning I felt forced into making a decision on whether to
do a great deal of theoretical reading or to concentrate on
viewing the episodes themselves. Originally I had planned
on doing no theory, but the inadequacies of watching and
not really knowing what to watch for led me into a study
of theory. There was a time when all this examination of
theory threatened to bog me down in irrelevant studies of
McLuhan and others. By that time I had read enough
that it seemed senseless to continue further and I returned
to viewing episodes. If I were to undertake a study of TV
again, I think I would begin by reading some film theory
and then a few basic books on television. I have included
in the bibliography those books that were most directly
helpful to me. These books contain some bibliographical
material which those who wish to get into the problem
deeper might find helpful. However, it seemed pointless
to clutter or pad the bibliography with sources that for
me were useless. Beyond theory the best thing you can
do is to continue asking questions of the media and ex-
pose yourself to it as much as possible. Ultimately if I
had to make a choice I would say that several hours spent
in alert, critical watching are worth ten books. Besides,
readers of books on film will find that much of the material makes reference to specific films—which is, of course,
meaningless if you haven't seen the film.

Hopefully schools will begin teaching film and TV analysis, but until they do most of us are in the dark. All I can say here is, follow your intuitions; do what seems right to you.

The method that I finally settled on for watching "live" TV (i.e., not on a tape or film playback machine) involved using a cassette tape recorder to get the dialogue. This allowed me to concentrate on visuals—which is hard to do if your are writing down dialogue at the same time. After the show was over I would immediately play back the tape, writing down pertinent dialogue and using the tape to refresh my memory of visuals. The method is fairly cheap—I bought a one dollar cassette that has been used hundreds of times—and is much more infallible than using your own ears. It also helps to watch with someone, who is also "into" what you're doing. My wife was able to see many, many things that I missed viewing episodes, and watching together enabled us to teach each other.

When I was in my McLuhan phase I spent some time wondering about things like how close should I sit to the set and how long should I watch. Having gotten into TV analysis from film I found myself creeping closer to the set and then catching myself a foot from the set, I would slowly creep back. I wondered whether even one *Bonanza* a day was too many. After watching for two years the only show I could watch without psyching myself up for it was *Gunsmoke*. This leads to the unanswerable question I raised in the Preface: how many shows can you watch in a "sample" before you become worthless as a critical viewer or go stark raving mad. All I can say again is do what seems right for you.

Resources for TV tape and film are quite limited. Stations were reluctant to allow me to view film on my own, which actually I don't blame them for since they do

not own the rights to most of their material, but rent it.
Yet still it seems to me that someone could work out a
method of working with local stations so you could do
research here. Perhaps if the local stations were more
public. . . .

The only place I know of where TV film is available
for scholarly study is the Library of Congress. The Library's collection of TV material is fairly sparse, since
they have little funding and try to use what funds and
space they have to preserve film. The staff was unbelievably helpful. I'm sure that when we walked in the door—
blue jeans and long hair—and announced that we wanted
to look at TV Westerns, they weren't sure what to make
of us. Yet they spent patient hours explaining their cata-
loging system, the use of the machines, untangling messed
up film, and even splicing one break we made (luckily it
was in a commercial) without complaining or even looking
like they were about to complain. Librarian Patrick Sheehan and staff members Joe Balian and Michael Godwin
helped and treated us like any of the "name" scholars.
I would advise those who wish to use the Library for film
or TV to write the Motion Picture Section, The Library of
Congress, Washington, D.C. 20540 before making a visit,
telling them what your project is and what you might wish
to view. The staff seems more than willing to discuss problems you anticipate—although they'll probably hang me
for saying it.

Other than the Library the only way to watch old
shows is reruns. This is easier on the East Coast, where
there are more stations. On a cable set-up in Jersey we
pulled in New York, Philadelphia, Wilmington, and Baltimore—which helped some. Probably the only answer to
the research problem is the networks themselves. The
local stations and networks seem unbelievably paranoid

about people investigating and researching them. Hopefully we won't have any networks someday and maybe then this resource problem, along with other more serious problems, will no longer be a problem.

Appendix:
A Partial List of Westerns

Horse

Roy Rogers
Gene Autry
The Lone Ranger
Wild Bill Hickok
Kit Carson
· The Cisco Kid
Hopalong Cassidy
Range Rider
Annie Oakley
Cowboy G-Men

Gun

Lawman
The Rebel
The Deputy
Trackdown
Colt .45
Branded
The Texan
Bronco
Restless Gun
Wanted: Dead or Alive
Broken Arrow
Cheyenne
Sugarfoot
Maverick
The Rifleman
Jim Bowie
Johnny Ringo
Yancy Derringer
Tombstone Territory
Black Saddle
Frontier Doctor
Judge Roy Beane
The Tall Man
The Life and Legend of
    Wyatt Earp
Sheriff of Cochise County
Have Gun, Will Travel
Stories of the Century

Tales of the Texas Rangers
Tales of Wells Fargo
Hotel de Paree
Bat Masterson
Tate
Wrangler

Transition

Rawhide
Wagon Train
Iron Horse
Laredo
Overland Trail
Stagecoach West

Property

Bonanza
Lancer
The Big Valley
The Virginian
    (The Men From Shiloh)
The High Chaparall
Empire

Others

The Outlaws
Cimarron Strip
Gunsmoke
Shenandoah
Alias Smith and Jones
The Westerner
Wichita Town
Zane Grey Theater
Death Valley Days
Wide Country
Laramie

BIBLIOGRAPHY

TV Western

Autry, Gene. "Producing A Western," *Television Magazine*, October, 1952, 25-26.

"Big Ego, Big Talent." Anon., *Saturday Evening Post*, 234 (December 31, 1961), 98-101.

"Conquest of the West." Anon., *Newsweek*, 55 (March 14, 1960), 60.

Cort, David. "Arms and the Man," *Nation*, 188 (May 23, 1954), 475-477.

"Dum-Tiddle-Dum." Anon., *Newsweek*, 59 (April 23, 1962), 94.

Eels, George. "TV Western Craze: How Long Will It Last?" *Look*, 22 (June 27, 1958), 66-71.

Emery, F. E. "Psychological Effects of the Western Film: A Study in Television Viewing," *Human Relations*, VII (August, 1959), 195-233.

Evans, John W. "Modern Man and the Cowboy," *Television Quarterly*, I (May, 1962), 31-41.

Golden, Joseph. "TV's Womanless Hero," *Television Quarterly*, II (Winter, 1963), 13-19.

Goldstein, Bernice and Robert Perrucci. "The TV Western and the Modern American Spirit," *Southwestern Social Science Quarterly*, 43 (March, 1963), 357-367.

Goodman, Walter. "Bang Bang! You're Dead," *New Republic*, 131 (November 1, 1954), 12-14.

"Happy Larceny," Anon., *Newsweek*, 53 (January 14, 1959), 52.

Hargrove, Marion. "This Is A Television Cowboy?" *Life*, 46 (January 19, 1959), 75-76.

"Have Guns, Will Teach." Anon., *Newsweek*, 51 (January 27, 1958), 64-65.

"High In The Saddle." Anon., *Time*, 64 (March 4, 1957), 65.

"Just Wild About Westerns." Anon., *Newsweek*, 50 (July 22, 1957), 51-54.

Kirkley, Donald Howe, Jr. *A Descriptive Study of the Network Television Western During the Seasons 1955-56–1962-63*, Ohio University Ph.D. Thesis, 1967, Speech-Theatre.

Lardner, John. "Decline and Possible Fall," *New Yorker*, 35 (February 28, 1959), 97-100.

———. "The Hybrid West," New Yorker, 33 (January 18, 1968), 86-89.

Miller, Alexander. "The 'Western'—A Theological Note," *Christian Century* LXXIV (November 27, 1957), 1409-1410.

Nussbaum, Martin. "Sociological Symbolism of the 'Adult Western'," *Social Forces*, 39 (Fall, 1960), 25-29.

Percy, Walker. "Decline of the Western," *Commonweal*, 68 (May 18, 1958), 181-183.

Poppy, John. "The Worldwide Lure of 'Bonanza'," *Look*, 28 (December 1, 1964), 80-90.

Reddy, John. "TV Westerns: The Shots Heard Round the World," *Reader's Digest*, 74 (January, 1959), 134-136.

Rickenbacker, William F. "60,000,000 Westerners Can't Be Wrong," *National Review*, 13 (October 23, 1962), 322-325.

Robinson, Hubbell. "How to Get a Hit—and Keep It," *Television Quarterly*, II (Fall, 1963), 30-35.

Sharnik, John. "Cowpokes on the Couch," *House and Garden*, 112 (September, 1957), 32-33.

Shayon, Robert Lewis. "The New Broncs Cheer," *Saturday Review*, 45 (October 20, 1962), 57-60.

Teeple, David Shea. "TV Westerns Tell a Story," *American Mercury*, 86 (April, 1958), 115-117.

"Togetherness on the Range." Anon., *Saturday Review*,

41 (October 4, 1958), 28.

Topping, M. C., Jr. "The Cultural Orientation of Certain 'Western' Characters on Television," *Journal of Broadcasting*, IX:4 (Fall, 1965), 291-301.

Trombley, William. "Another Western: Who Needs It," *Saturday Evening Post*, 235 (September 29, 1962), 85-89.

Walker, Stanley. "Let the Indian Be the Hero," *New York Times Magazine*, April 24, 1960, 50-55.

"Westerns: The Six Gun Galahad." Anon., *Time*, 73 (March 30, 1959), 52-60.

". . . Will Travel." Anon., *Newsweek*, 59 (January 22, 1962), 51.

Television

Chester, Giraud, Garnet Garrison, and Edgar E. Willis. *Television and Radio*, New York, 1963.

Goodman, Walter. "Mass Media: The Generation of the Lie," *American Review*, III:2, 71-76.

Johnson, Nicholas. *How To Talk Back To Your Television Set*, New York, 1970.

Lewis, Colby. *The TV Director/Interpreter*, New York, 1968.

McLuhan, Marshall. *Understanding Media: The Extensions of Man*, New York, 1964.

Millerson, Gerald. *The Technique of Television Production*, New York, 1968.

Rosenthal, Raymond, ed. *McLuhan: Pro and Con*, Baltimore, 1968.

Popular Culture, Film and The Western

Bluestone, George, "The Changing Cowboy: From Dime Novel to Dollar Film," *Western Humanities Review*,

XIV (Summer, 1960), 331-337.

Bogdanovich, Peter. *John Ford*, Berkeley, 1968.

Casty, Alan, ed. *Mass Media and Mass Man*, New York, 1968.

Cawelti, John G. "Cowboys, Indians and Outlaws," *American West*, I (Spring, 1964), 28-35, 77-79.

———. "Prolegomena to the Western," *Western American Literature*, IV (Winter, 1970), 259-271.

———. "The Gunfighter and Society," *American West*, V (Spring, 1968), 30-35, 76-77.

———. *The Six Gun Mystique*, Bowling Green, 1972.

Dessain, Kenneth. "Once in the Saddle: The Memory and Romance of the Trail Driving Cowboy," *Journal of Popular Culture*, IV (Fall, 1970), 464-496.

Etulain, Richard W. "Literary Historians and the Western," *Journal of Popular Culture*, IV (Fall, 1970), 518-526.

Fenin, G. N. and W. K. Everson. "The European Western," *Film Culture*, 20 (1959), 59-72.

Folsom, James K. " 'Western' Themes and Western Films," *Western American Literature*, II (Fall, 1967), 195-203.

Hall, Stuart and Paddy Whannel. *The Popular Arts*, Boston, 1964.

Homans, Peter. "Puritanism Revisited: An Analysis of the Contemporary Screen Image Western," *Studies in Public Communication*, III (Summer, 1961), 73-84.

Houghton, Donald E. "Two Heroes in One: Reflections Upon the Popularity of the Virginian," *Journal of Popular Culture*, IV (Fall, 1970), 497-506.

Huss, Roy and Norman Silverstein. *The Film Experience*, New York, 1968.

Jacobs, Lewis, ed. *The Movies as Medium*, New York, 1970.

Jones, Daryl E. "Blood 'n Thunder: Virgins, Villains

and Violence in the Dime Novel Western," *Journal of Popular Culture*, IV (Fall, 1970), 507-517.

Knight, Arthur. *The Liveliest Art*, New York, 1957.

Kracauer, Siegfried. *From Caligari to Hitler*, Princeton, 1970.

Kitses, Jim. *Horizons West*, Bloomington, 1969.

Noel, Mary. *Villains Galore*, New York, 1954.

Robinson, W. R., ed. *Man and the Movies*, Baltimore, 1969.

Rosenberg, Bernard and David Manning White, eds. *Mass Culture*, New York, 1957.

———. *Mass Culture Revisited*, New York, 1971.

Schein, Harry. "The Olympian Cowboy," *American Scholar*, XXIV (Summer, 1955), 309-320.

Sisk, John P. "The Western Hero," *Commonweal*, 66 (July 12, 1952), 367-369.

Warshow, Robert. *The Immediate Experience*, Garden City, 1962.

White, David Manning, ed. *Pop Culture in America*, Chicago, 1970.

Willett, Ralph. "The American Western: Myth and Anti-Myth," *Journal of Popular Culture*, IV (Fall, 1970), 455-463.

Wollen, Peter. *Signs and Meaning in the Cinema*, Bloomington, 1969.